The Elson Readers—Book Eight

A Teacher's Guide

Catherine Andrews

B.A. English Education, National Board Certified, Teacher of English, International Baccalaureate/Bartow High School

Mary Jane Newcomer

B.A. English Education, Teacher of English, Frostproof Middle-Senior High School, Frostproof, Florida

Lost Classics Book Company

Lake Wales, Florida

Publisher's Note

Recognizing the need to return to more traditional principles in education, Lost Classics Book Company is republishing forgotten late 19th and early 20th century literature and textbooks to aid parents in the education of their children.

This guide is designed to accompany *The Elson Readers—Book Eight,* which was reprinted from the 1921 copyright edition. This guide contains all the original questions and exercises from the reader along with suggested answers. It also includes new "Extended Activities" that reinforce and enhance the original study sections.

We have included the same glossary and pronunciation guide of more than 1746 terms at the end of the book that is included in the reader, and which has been updated with pronunciation notation currently in use.

The Elson Readers—Book Eight, which this volume is meant to accompany, has been assigned a reading level of 1120L. More information concerning this reading level assessment may be attained by visiting www.lexile.com.

ISBN 978-1-890623-32-6
Designed to Accompany
The Elson Readers—Book Eight
ISBN 978-1-890623-22-7
Part of
The Elson Readers
Nine Volumes: *Primer* through *Book Eight*
ISBN 978-1-890623-23-4

On the Cover:
Titania, Queen of the Fairies, Costume design for "A Midsummer Night's Dream" produced by Robert Courtneidge at the Princes Theatre, Manchester by C. Wilhelm (1858-1925)
Victoria & Albert Museum, London, UK/Bridgeman Art Library

Table of Contents

A Note about This Guide

Teachers and students alike may notice a difference in punctuation, capitalization, and spelling between the prose and poetry sections in the reader. Rules concerning these matters have changed since the original reader's publication, and we have decided that in the prose sections it would be in the best interest of the student to update these items so they will learn these rules as practiced today. However, the stories remain completely unabridged. We have exercised constraint, and typical changes consist of, for example: commas used in place of semicolons when appropriate, lowercase treatment of words not personified, or hyphenated spelling of words being contracted to modern spellings. We have, however, followed the traditional editorial practice of not changing these items in works of poetry, leaving these matters to the prerogative of the poet.

Language is always changing, and when the student notices these changes it is often a good place to start a discussion on topics such as: personification, comma usage, "up" or "down" style of capitalization, etc.

We have used *The Chicago Manual of Style,* 14th Edition, published by the University of Chicago, as our primary reference for these changes.

The reader was originally published just after World War One and many discussion questions refer to this great event. These questions can often be used to start discussions on that war and conflicts that occured after it. See the "Appendix" for a brief description of World War One.

Finally, we have provided references to Internet sites that may be useful for some of the exercises. These sites are the property of their creators, not Lost Classics Book Company, and we take no responsibility for their content. Considering the very changeable nature of the Internet, these sites may or may not exist by the time of printing and should only be considered a starting point for research.

The Elson Readers—Book Eight
A Teacher's Guide

How to Use This Book

This *Teacher's Guide* was developed to provide teachers with a guideline for appropriate, grade-level, student responses to the questions found in the "Notes and Questions" sections of the reader. Some extended activities have been added to those discussion questions in this manual and may be used at the teacher's discretion to reinforce comprehension and appreciation of the work in question. Unfamiliar vocabulary terms have also been added at the end of each discussion guide in the *Teacher's Guide* to encourage students to broaden their use of language.

Teachers may wish to have students begin with "Part One" and read the book in order, or they may pick and choose the works that fit their classroom goals. The parts are not sequential; however, skills introduced in one part may be reinforced in later parts allowing students to practice and master the various literary skills as outlined in the objectives found at the beginning of each part in the *Teacher's Guide*.

These questions and activities were designed to give the students a greater understanding of the world around them and a deeper appreciation for the contributions of those who have helped to build that world. In addition, students will receive instruction in the qualities so essential to their development as future productive citizens in the world they will inherit.

Prediction—It is important that students are able to make predictions about a text based on evidence from the story as well as from prior knowledge. Many of the selections in *Book Eight* are lengthy and are divided into sections. Have students discuss at the end of each section, based on what they have read and what they already know, what they think is going to occur next. Also at the end of each section, have students discuss whether their predictions were correct. It may be helpful to have students write their predictions and explanations in a reading journal.

Words in Context—Most of the selections in *Book Eight* have a list of glossary terms. Before students define the term from the glossary, have them identify the word in context and "guess" what they think the word means. Have students create their own definition of the word before they use the glossary. Students tend to be better able to apply and use the word if they can put the definition in their own words. It is also suggested that the students use the terms in their own sentences. Make sure when students do use the word that they are using it correctly. Have students look for context clues. These may be: 1. antonyms 2. synonyms 3. appositives.

Instructional Aids—Additional aids have been provided for instructing and evaluating students' progress in the "Appendix."

Part I: The World of Nature

In This Section—

Objectives—

By completing "Part I," the following objectives will be met.

1. The student will use effective reading strategies to construct meaning and identify the purpose of a text including:
    a. using illustrations
    b. defining unfamiliar words
    c. scanning for details
    d. retelling and summarizing
2. The student will determine the main idea or essential message and identify relevant supporting details and facts of a text.
3. The student will read and organize facts from the text and other sources to make a report, outline, and perform an authentic task.
4. The student will prepare for writing by focusing on the topic and organizing supporting details in a logical sequence.
5. The student will draft and revise writing.
6. The student will produce final documents that have been edited for correct spelling, punctuation, and grammar.
7. The student will write for a variety of audiences and purposes.
8. The student will write in a variety of genres including narrative and poetic.
9. The student will use reference materials (dictionaries, encyclopedias, maps, charts, and the Internet).
10. The student will use speaking strategies effectively such as eye contact, gestures, and visuals that engage the audience through poetry recitation.
11. The student will identify the development of plot and how conflicts are resolved in a story.
12. The student will identify and understand similarities and differences among the characters, settings, and events presented in various texts.
13. The student will identify the author's purpose and point of view.
14. The student will identify and use literary terminology such as alliteration and simile.
15. The student will respond critically to fiction, nonfiction, and poetry.
16. The student will respond to a text by explaining how the motives of the characters or events compare with those in his or her own life.
17. The student will use context clues to understand words and ideas.
18. The student will predict events that may occur in the text and explain the reasoning behind the prediction.
19. The student will understand the qualities necessary for people to become good citizens and apply those qualities to his or her personal life.
20. The student will understand the qualities necessary to develop good character and apply those qualities to his or her personal life.

THE WORLD OF NATURE

ANIMALS

COALY-BAY, THE OUTLAW HORSE, P. 29

1. **Which one of the four owners that Coaly-Bay had at different times made the best bargain? Which one seemed to get the worst of it? Which one made short work of his ownership? Did any of them show a sympathy with Coaly-Bay's spirit?**

Coaly-Bay's four owners were as follows: the owner who trained him to ride and sold him to a ranchman for $25, though he was worth $50; the ranchman who traded Coaly-Bay to the gardener to pay for Coaly-Bay's destructive raids on the neighbor's garden; the gardener who sold Coaly-Bay for bait to bear hunters for $5.00; and the hunters who finally decided to shoot him, though he escaped and returned to the wild plains. Students may have varying answers based on their perspectives of the various owners. Have students answer each of the questions, using clues from the passage to support their choices.

2. **Arabian horses are noted for graceful form, speed, intelligence, and spirit; can you tell why those who saw Coaly-Bay thought he must be of Arabian blood?**

Seton makes several references to Coaly-Bay's form, power, and free spirit, aspects of horses with Arabian blood. Encourage students to identify passages that support the writer's premise. Possible passages may include: "He grew up strong of limb, restless of spirit, and rebellious at any thought of restraint." "So each month the colt became more set on living free, and more cunning in the means he took to win his way." "It seemed to me the spirit of an eagle or a wolf it was that dwelt behind those full, bright eyes that ordered all his wayward life." "He was their kind, he was of the wild, free blood that man had never tamed."

3. **How does the leading guide's remark about Coaly-Bay's lameness show that it was a skillful imitation?**

The leading guide noted "That thar limp is no fake. He's got some deep-seated trouble." Doubtless the leading guide had some experience with the ways of horse, but even he was duped by Coaly-Bay's pretended lameness.

4. **Notice the beauty of the author's description of Coaly-Bay's joining his kindred. With this in mind, prepare to**

read aloud the last three paragraphs of the story; which sentences do you like particularly well?

Answers will vary.

5. **Compare the information on the sign with that given by the gardener to the hunters after the bargain was settled; how do you account for the difference?**

The sign advertised Coaly-Bay as a "First-class horse, sound and gentle." After the gardener received payment for Coaly-Bay and was asked why the horse was so cheap, he replied that Coaly-Bay was "dead lame when he's going your way and sound as a dollar going on his own; no fence in the country can hold him; he's a dangerous outlaw. He's wickeder nor old Nick." The gardener had received his payment so felt free to tell the truth about Coaly-Bay.

6. **How do you explain your sympathy for the horse in spite of his viciousness?**

Answers will vary. Students should identify the author's descriptions that elicit their admiration for Coaly-Bay.

7. **In the "Introduction" on pages 27 and 28 you read that some selections present the facts of nature as "interpreted through the imagination of the poets," while others show "what men of scientific training have observed"; to which of these kinds does this story belong?**

This story suggests "the imagination of the poets" in the ways the writer portrays the thoughts and actions of Coaly-Bay. His fierce, free spirit is imagined rather than taken from scientific facts of nature.

8. **On page 27 you read that "animals have personalities like human beings"; how does the story of Coaly-Bay prove the truth of this statement?**

Coaly-Bay is given human characteristics of thought, action, and desire that help the reader to identify with his personality.

9. **Find in the glossary the meaning of: foal, careering, vestige, bucking, hobbling, superb, limpid, caracoled, harry.**
10. **Pronounce: Arab, corral, indomitable, Salmon, subtly.**

Questions for Testing Silent Reading

The Willful Beauty

1. **Where is the scene of this story laid?**

The story takes place in Idaho's Bitterroot Mountains.

2. **How did Coaly-Bay get his name?**

"His coat was bright bay; his legs, mane, and tail were glossy black—coal black and bright bay—so they named him Coaly-Bay." His name sounded like "Kolibey," an Arab title of nobility.

3. **Tell about his nature.**

Coaly-Bay "grew up strong of limb, restless of spirit, and rebellious at any thought of restraint." He preferred the wild outdoors to the warm comfort of a stall. He was both clever and cruel and showed both traits when he was cornered.

4. **What is a "quit-the-bunch" horse?**
A "quit-the-bunch" horse is "a horse of such independent mind that he will go his own way the moment he does not like the way of the herd."

5. **Tell of the horse trainer's experience trying to break Coaly-Bay for riding.**
Though Coaly-Bay was tricky and vicious, the owner was skillful and powerful and mastered Coaly-Bay's "wild plunging, bucking, rearing, and rolling." When Coaly-Bay's behavior resulted in "lashings and spurrings," he pretended to reform.

6. **What was the horse's trick?**
Every time Coaly-Bay was saddled, he went lame. Upon being turned out to pasture he would be fine.

7. **For how much did the owner sell him?**
The owner sold him for $25.00, though he was worth $50.00.

8. **How did the new owner feel about the sale?**
The new owner initially "felt he had a bargain, but after being ridden half a mile, Coaly-Bay went lame." When the owner tried to examine the leg, Coaly-Bay broke away and returned to his former master. The new owner retrieved him and, "being neither gentle nor sweet, applied spur without mercy," and the meanness disappeared.

9. **What happened in the neighbor's vegetable garden?**
The night Coaly-Bay was purchased, horses raided the neighbor's garden. The gardener accused the ranchman's horses, but the ranchman was certain his horses could not have jumped the six-foot fence that surrounded the garden. However, the raids continued, so the ranchman invited the gardener to join him at night and watch to prove that his horses were not to blame. As the moon shone, they watched Coaly-Bay jump the fence and raid the garden. When the men approached him, he leaped the fence and disappeared into the horse herd.

10. **Why was Coaly-Bay called an "outlaw" horse?**
He was "an incurably vicious horse." He would not be saddled, he became lame when required to work, and would not stay inside any fence.

11. **How did the gardener come into possession of the horse?**
The ranchman traded Coaly-Bay to the gardener in payment for the vegetables Coaly-Bay had devoured.

12. **How did the gardener advertise?**

He hung a sign on his gate: "FOR SALE First-class horse, sound and gentle, $10.00."

The Bear Bait

1. **Who composed the band of hunters?**
   "There were three mountaineers, two men from the city, and the writer of this story."
2. **What did they do when they saw the sign?**
   "So, seeing the sign, the hunters called to the gardener: 'Haven't you got a cheaper horse?'"
3. **What was the bait used for bear hunting?**
   The bait was usually "some worthless horse or cow" which the hunters would drive to the mountains to use for bait.
4. **How much did the hunters pay for Coaly-Bay?**
   They paid $5.00 for Coaly-Bay.
5. **What was the gardener's explanation of the low price?**
   "Mighty simple. He can't be rode. He's dead lame when he's going your way and sound as a dollar going his own; no fence in the country can hold him; he's a dangerous outlaw."
6. **Describe Coaly-Bay as he was driven along with the pack horses.**
   He limped along, trying once or twice to turn back, but the hunters kept him in check. He appeared to be seriously injured and refused to allow any hunters on his back.
7. **Tell of his attempt to escape.**
   One day the horses became mired down in a bog. Seeing his chance to escape, Coaly-Bay "wheeled in a moment and turned himself from a limping, towheaded, sorry, bad-eyed creature into a high-spirited horse." Without a trace of lameness, he headed for his home a hundred miles distant.
8. **How was he outwitted?**
   The hunter took a short cut through the trails and headed him off.
9. **How did he vent his rage?**
   He soon took up his limp and his evil expression and was driven back to camp where he kicked in the ribs of a pack horse.

His Destined End

1. **What did the hunters resolve to do?**
   The hunters resolved to "end his dangerous pranks and make him useful for once," so they drove him to a glade where bears were hiding. There the hunters planned to shoot him as bait and wait for the bears to come after him.
2. **How did Ernest Thompson Seton feel when Coaly-Bay was driven away for bear bait?**
   "A thrill of pity came over me as I saw that beautiful untamable creature going away with his imitation limp."

3. **How did the horse look as he faced his tormentors?**
"He swung and faced his tormentors, his noble head erect, his nostrils flaring; a picture of horse beauty—yes, of horse perfection."
4. **What happened when the rifle cracked?**
"The great horse wheeled and dashed away...at his famous best."
5. **In what direction did Coaly-Bay flee?**
He fled, "not for his eastern home, but down the unknown western trail, away and away."
6. **Tell about his flight.**
"Down that trail with an inborn certainty he went, and on through the pines, then leaped a great bog, and splashed an hour later through the limpid Clearwater, and on, responsive to some unknown guide that subtly called him from the farther west. And so he went till the dwindling pines gave place to scrubby cedars and these in turn were mixed with sage, and onward still, till the far-away flat plains of Salmon River were about him, and ever on, tireless, as it seemed, he went, and crossed the canyon of the mighty Snake, and up again to the high, wild plains where the wire fence still is not, and on, beyond the Buffalo Hump, till moving specks on the far horizon caught his eager eyes."
7. **Tell about Coaly-Bay's joining his wild kindred.**
"He lifted up his voice and called to them, the long shrill neigh of his kindred when they bugled to each other on the far Chaldean plain; and back their answer came. This way and that they wheeled and sped and caracoled, and Coaly-Bay drew nearer, called, and gave the countersigns his kindred know, till this they were assurred—he was their kind, he was of the wild, free blood that man had never tamed."
8. **How are hunters able to recognize him?**
They will recognize his enduring strength and lasting beauty. "He is swift and strong among the swift ones, but it is that flowing mane and tail that mark him chiefly from afar."
9. **Tell about his life on the free plains.**
He lives among the wild sage, facing stormy nights and winter snows; wolves and grizzlies are his enemies and no man-made pastures of grain await him—only "wild, hard hay, the wind and open plains, but here at last he found the thing he craved—the one worth all the rest."
10. **What is the author's wish for him?**
"Long may he roam—this is my wish, and this—that I may see him once again in all the glory of his speed with his black mane on the wind, the spur-galls gone from his flanks, and in his eyes the blazing light that grew in his far-off forebears' eyes as they

spurned Arabian plains to leave behind the racing wild beast and the fleet gazelle—yes, too, the driving sandstorm that o'erwhelmed the rest, but strove in vain on the dusty wake of the desert's highest born."

Outline for Testing Silent Reading

(For appropriate student responses to this outline, check the responses to "Questions For Silent Reading.")

The Willful Beauty

(a) The scene of the story. (b) Coaly-Bay, his appearance and his nature. (c) The owner's experience in breaking him for riding. (d) Coaly-Bay's trick. (e) The ranchman's bargain. (f) The new owner's experience with Coaly-Bay and his neighbor's vegetable garden. (g) Settling with the gardener. (h) The sign at the gate.

The Bear Bait

(a) The band of hunters. (b) Coaly-Bay sold for bear bait. (c) The horse's attempt to escape and his capture.

His Destined End

(a) Coaly-Bay being driven to the bear glade. (b) Ernest Thompson Seton's feeling for the horse. (c) The crack of the rifle. (d) Coaly-Bay's escape. (e) Joining his wild kindred. (f) Life on the free plains. (g) The author's wish.

SATAN, THE WAR DOG THAT SAVED A TOWN, P. 41

1. **In what war did the incident related in this story occur?**
The incident occurred in World War One.
2. **What made the situation of the French garrison unbearable?**
They were running out of ammunition without hope of replenishments since the enemy controlled the roads. All outside communication with the garrison had been cut off including telephones, telegraphs, and homing pigeons that had been shot. The Germans were positioned to "pour a deadly fire into the French town." All hope seemed lost.
3. **How did Satan save the town?**
He brought a homing pigeon that enabled them to send a message asking that the German guns pinning them down be silenced.
4. **What did Satan bring besides the message?**
He carried two small baskets carrying homing pigeons.
5. **What happened to the homing pigeons?**
With messages attached to their legs, they departed for the distant troops. One pigeon was shot down by German fire, but the other escaped "and flew straight to his loft" where an officer retrieved the message and the town was saved.
6. **How does this story prove that "animals have personalities like humans"?**
Satan would not quit his important mission though he was wounded. He was loyal to his owner even in the face of enemy fire.
Commit to memory Browning's lines on page 23 that express this same thought.
"God made all the creatures and gave them our love and fear, To give sign we and they are his children, one family here."
7. **Read again what is said in "Literature and Life," pages 17 and 18, about the three joys of reading; which of these joys has the reading of this story given you?**
The three joys of reading include: "the joy of sharing in the adventures of men in bygone times and in far-distant lands"; "the joy of gaining your full portion of the wisdom that mankind has stored up through the ages"; "the awakening of your feelings to the wonders that lie all about you in the great outdoor world." Student responses will vary.
8. **Find in the glossary the meaning of: garrison, mongrel, voila, mon ami, terse.**
9. **Pronounce: isolated, aluminum.**

Class Reading

(See page 16.) The description of Satan, page 42, line 16, to page 43, line 12; the rest of the story, page 43, line 14, to the end.

Outline for Testing Silent Reading

Student responses should be drawn from the following information: (a) The condition of the French garrison; "But now their ammunition was giving out, and there was no way of getting more, for the enemy was in possession of every road. Worst of all, the Germans had managed to plant a battery on the left in a position from which it could pour deadly fire into the French town. Owning to the shortage of shells, only a weak reply could be made by the garrison. If the latter could only let the French army know the position of that battery, it might yet be silenced in time. But there was no way of letting it know. The telephone and telegraph wires had been cut, the last homing pigeons had been killed by a bursting shell, and every other means of communication was destroyed." (b) Satan and his message; Satan was "swift-limbed, intelligent, and absolutely fearless under fire." Those qualities, along with his intense love for his master, enabled Satan to speed through fire, take a German bullet, and race on to his master to deliver the message he carried. The message taken from a metal tube attached to his collar read, "For God's sake, hold on. Will send troops to relieve you tomorrow." Along with that message Satan carried two small baskets containing homing pigeons by which the garrison could send word for assistance. (c) The homing pigeon and the silencing of the German battery. The officer wrote a message to "Silence the battery on our left," along with directions showing the enemy positions and released the pigeons to carry their message. They took to the air, and though one was shot down by enemy fire, the other one flew safely through the bullets and back to his home where his message was found by an officer. Because of Satan and the pigeon, the garrison soon "heard the deep roar of the big French guns which smothered with bursting shells the German battery on their left, and they knew that the town was saved."

Library Reading

Several suggested readings are listed in the students' Reader, many of which are no longer in print. However, students should be encouraged to read Jack London's classic *The Call of the Wild*.

THE THUNDERING HERD, P. 46

1. **The events narrated in this story took place, it is said, in 1871. Describe the caravan and tell where the family was going.**

   The caravan consisted of Mr. and Mrs. Anderson and two young men, Thomas and Benjamin. Their meager belongings included two dilapidated mules, one old cow, and a dog. They were leaving Indiana to resettle on "the frontier beyond the Mississippi."

2. **How long had they been traveling when the incident of the thundering herd occurred?**

   They had been on the trail for two days.

3. **Where did the event occur, and under what conditions?**

   The event occurred on a barren stretch of "desert-like prairie" where the "watercourses and the cottonwoods were half a day's journey apart, and an intolerable thirst was over all the landscape."

4. **What does this story tell you of the number of buffaloes on the plains at that time?**

   The story suggests that there were still thousands of buffaloes roaming the plains at that time.

5. **Find in the glossary the meaning of: dilapidated, inadequate, coulee, eminence, incredulous, butte, annihilation, frontlet, buffer, domicile, veered, diminution, dissipated.**

6. **Pronounce: coyote, ally, amicable, undulating, pall, impotent, respite, irreparable.**

Class Reading

The plan of escape, page 47, line 13, to page 48, line 3; the description of the approach of the herd, page 48, lines 4 to 23; the passing of the herd, page 48, line 24, to the end.

Outline for Testing Silent Reading

Make an outline to guide you in telling the story.

A sample outline could include the following: (a) The journey; (b) They discover the approaching herd; (c) Preparing to protect themselves; (d) The stampede arrives; (e) The loss of the mule and cow; (f) The stampede's end.

Library Reading

Encourage the students to locate similar stories of animal adventures in the *Reader's Guide to Periodical Literature* as outlined in "Magazine Reading" in their Readers.

Extended Activities:

The following activities can be used with any of the stories in this section.

1. Students should be well acquainted with the elements of a short story that follow the design of a pyramid and usually consist of five main parts: the *exposition* explains the background and setting of the story including any of the following: who, what, when, where; the *rising action* introduces the conflicts and action in the story; the *climax* is the turning point, the highest part of the pyramid from which the reader can begin to make accurate predictions about the story's end; the *falling action* wraps up the conflicts; the *resolution* is the satisfying end of the story when all the problems are solved. On the enclosed pyramid outline have students tell the plot line of any of the stories in this section.

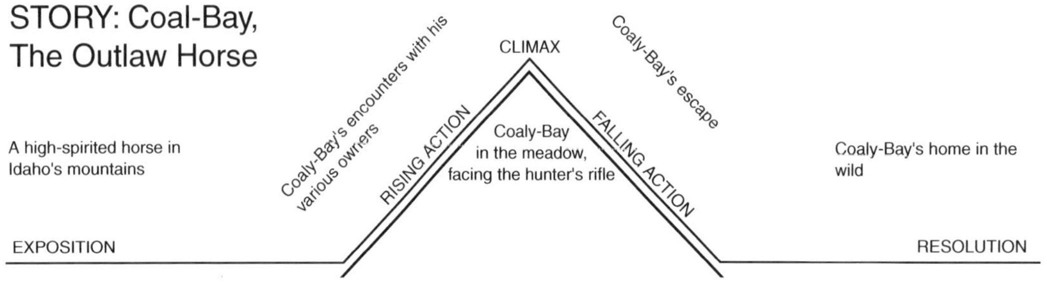

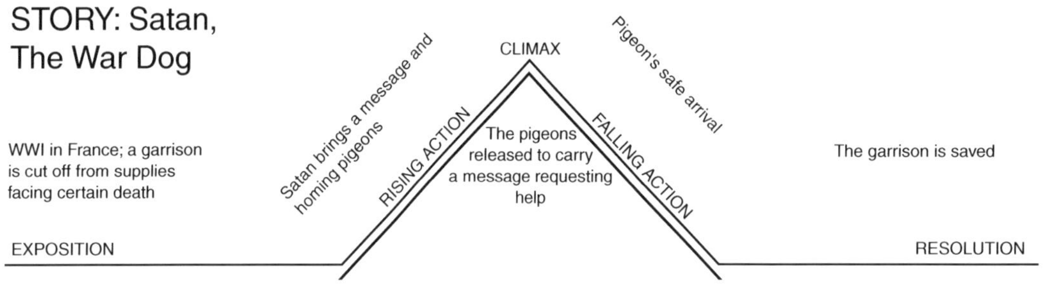

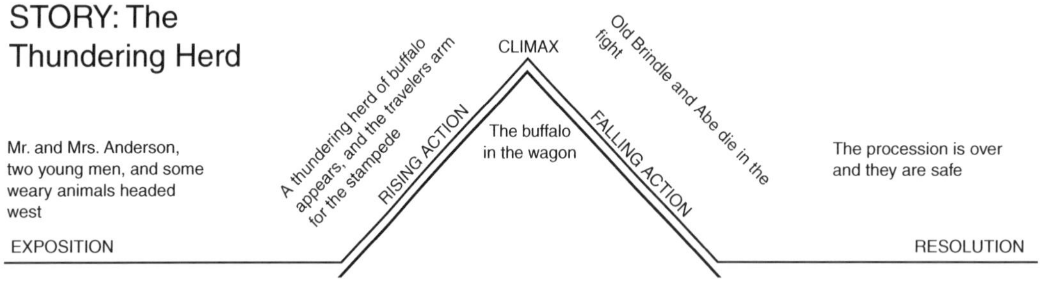

2. After students have read the stories, have them choose one title and prepare a book cover to summarize the story. The cover should include: the front cover including design and title, the inside front flap containing a summary of the story, the inside back flap introducing the author, and the back cover containing endorsements from the readers.

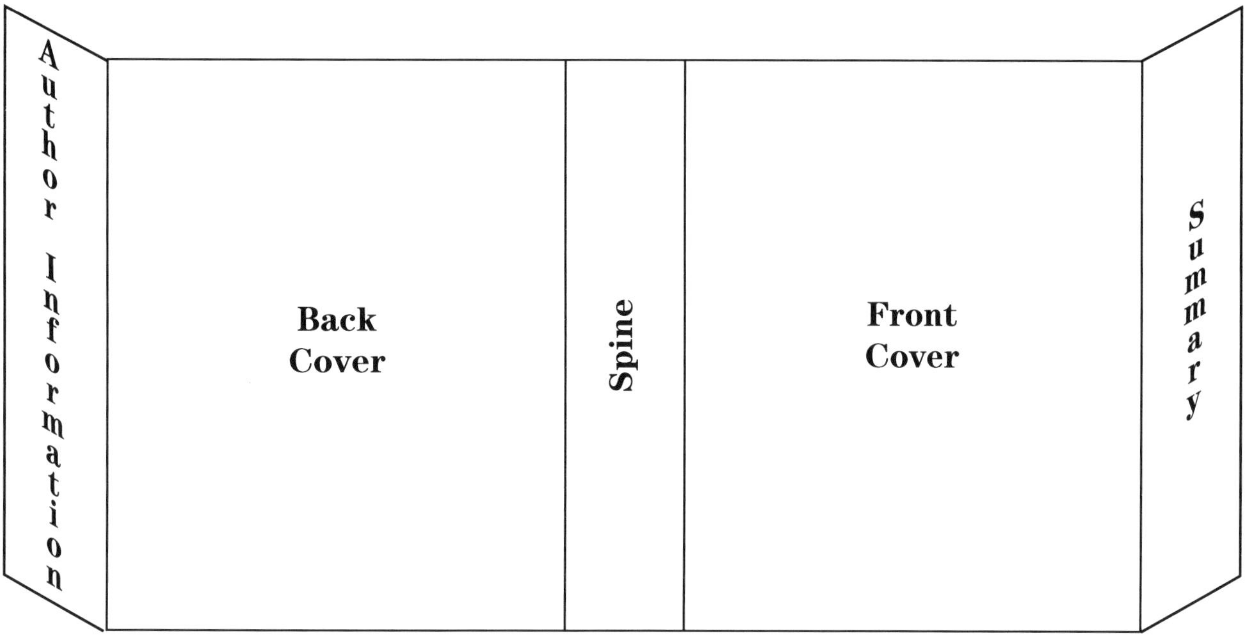

3. In the "Introduction," students read that "animals have personalities like human beings." After reading the three stories describing the animal's human characteristics and behavior, have students complete the following chart with details from the story that reinforce that idea.

Title of Story	Animals' Human Personalities	How Animals Helped Humans	What Humans Learned from Animals
Coaly-Bay, the Outlaw Horse	loved to race, glories in his speed, rebellious, clever, cunning, vicious, independent	----------------------	that animals also value freedom
Satan, The War Dog That Saved a Town	intelligent, fearless, dependable, loyal	he delivered the message that saved the men of the town	to value loyalty and obedience, even in the face of death
The Thundering Herd	loyalty from the family dog and mule	mule defended the wagon by kicking at the thundering herd	the mule's loyalty left an "irreparable loss," Tommy was comforted by the dog licking his hands

NAME______________________________ **CLASS**__________ **DATE**____

THE THUNDERING HERD, P. 46

1. **You should be well acquainted with the elements of a short story that follow the design of a pyramid and usually consist of five main parts: the *exposition* explains the background and setting of the story including any of the following: who, what, when, where; the *rising action* introduces the conflicts and action in the story; the *climax* is the turning point, the highest part of the pyramid from which the reader can begin to make accurate predictions about the story's end; the *falling action* wraps up the conflicts; the *resolution* is the satisfying end of the story when all the problems are solved. On the enclosed pyramid outline tell the plot line of any of the stories in this section.**

STORY:

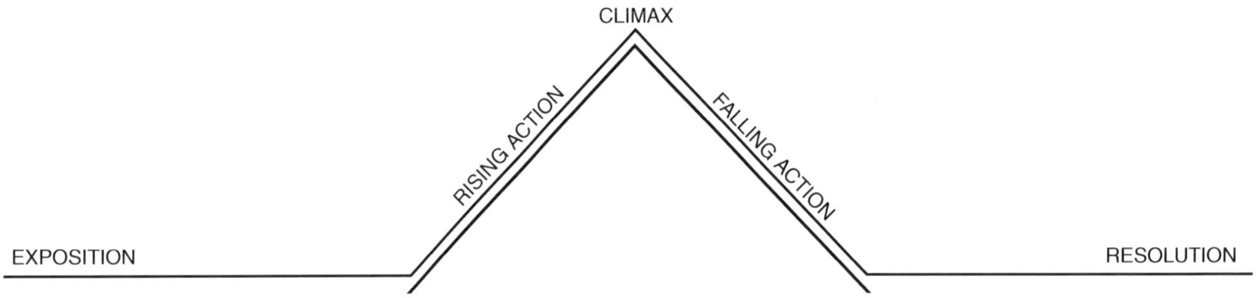

STORY:

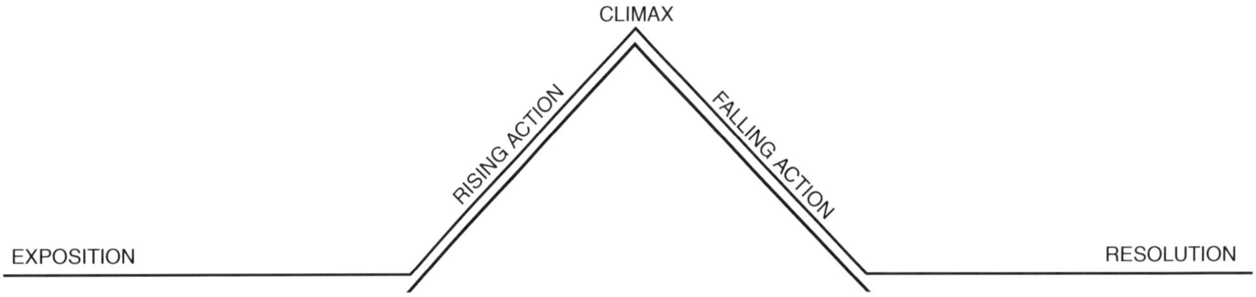

STORY:

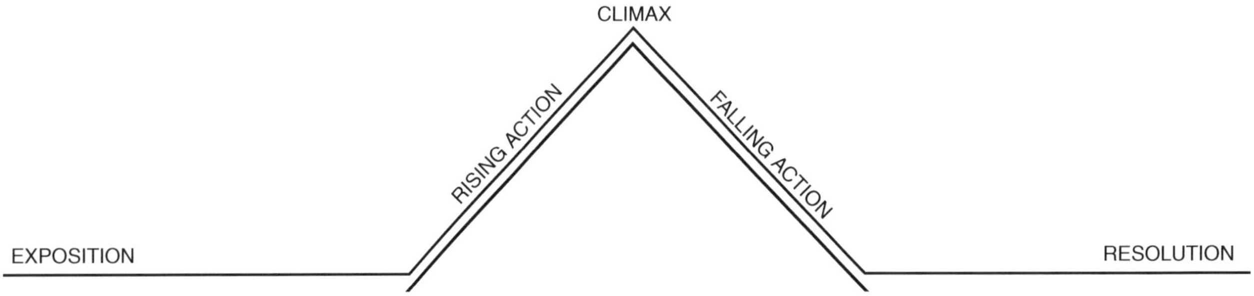

2. **After you have read the stories, choose one title and prepare a book cover to summarize the story. The cover should include: the front cover including design and title, the inside front flap containing a summary of the story, the inside back flap introducing the author, and the back cover containing endorsements from the readers.**

3. **In the "Introduction," you read that "animals have personalities like human beings." After reading the three stories describing the animal's human characteristics and behavior, complete the following chart with details from the story that reinforce that idea.**

Title of Story	Animals' Human Personalities	How Animals Helped Humans	What Humans Learned from Animals
Coaly-Bay, the Outlaw Horse			
Satan, The War Dog That Saved a Town			
The Thundering Herd			

Birds

To a Waterfowl, p. 56

1. **After a good reader has read this entire poem in class, tell under what circumstances it was written.**

   Have students read the biography of Bryant under "Notes and Questions." They will discover that Bryant, on a foot journey to Massachusetts, "felt forlorn and desolate, and the world seemed big and cold. On his way he paused, impressed by the beauty of the sunset, and saw a solitary wild-fowl wing its way along the horizon until it was lost in the distance." His hope was renewed, and when he stopped for the night, he penned this poem.

2. **How does the poet speak of the sunset?**

   He speaks of the sunset's rosy depths that color "the heavens with the last steps of the day."

3. **What characteristics did Bryant show in stopping to enjoy the sunset and to watch the bird?**

   Among other characteristics, students will want to note his ability to look beyond his gloom and enjoy the simple beauty around him. Through nature he gained new hope.

4. **What was the appearance of the bird against the sky?**

   He described the bird as "darkly painted on the crimson sky."

5. **What words used in the fourth stanza emphasize the thought that there is no path or road for the bird to follow through the air?**

   He uses the phrases, "pathless coast" and "illimitable air" to show the bird's free flight.

6. **Find the lines that tell what toil is referred to in the sixth stanza.**

   His toil in flight, his lone wandering, his fanning wings in the "cold, thin atmosphere" will end soon.

   When will the bird's toil end?

   His toil will end when he arrives at his summer home.

   What will follow toil?

   He will rest and "scream among thy fellows; reeds shall bend soon o'er thy sheltered nest."

7. **How does the thought that the bird is guided help the poet?**

   He takes hope that He who guides the bird "Will lead my steps aright."

8. **What comparison does he make between his life and the flight of the bird?**

He compares the bird's flight "through boundless sky" to "the long way that I must tread alone."

9. **What did you learn in "Literature and Life," page 20, about literature that interprets life?**

This passage refers to the great writers who have observed nature and described life through literature to help us enjoy "the riches that lie all about us in the commonest of things," remind us of "life's uncertainties," encourage us to do acts of "service to others," and breathe "a message of hope and faith to all mankind," all of which "interpret the spirit of human brotherhood that makes life worthwhile."

Can you show that this poem is such a piece of literature?

Students should be encouraged to explain how Bryant's poem is such a piece.

10. **Find in the glossary the meaning of: plashy, marge, desert.**
11. **Pronounce: illimitable, abyss.**

Class Reading

Bring to class and read other lyrics by Bryant.

Bryant's poems mentioned in his biography, "Robert of Lincoln," and "To the Fringed Gentian," can be found in *The Elson Readers, Book Seven.* "March" and "The Death of the Flowers" can be found in *The Elson Readers, Book Six.* "The Gladness of Nature" and "The Yellow Violet" can be located in *The Elson Readers, Book Five.* Many of Bryant's poems can be located on the Internet by researching William Cullen Bryant.

Newspaper Reading

See page 59 for student activities using a newspaper.

The Skylark, p. 60

1. **To whom is the poem addressed?**
The poet addresses the "Bird of the wilderness."
2. **What different names does the poet give to the bird?**
The poet calls him "Bird of the wilderness," "emblem of happiness," and "Musical cherub."
3. **What claim has the skylark to the first of these names?**
He flies over "moorland and lea," references to wasteland and meadow.
4. **What word refers to the lark's morning song?**
The glossary defines "matin" as a "morning song."
5. **What line in the second stanza tells you that it is early morning?**
Line 10: The poet's reference to a "dewy wing" tells us it is early morning.
6. **Find a line that tells how high the lark flies while singing.**
Lines 13-17 describe his flight over fountains, mountains, sunrise, clouds, and the rainbow.
7. **Where does the lark make its nest?**
He makes his nest "Low in the heather blooms."
8. **What word used by the poet in describing the lark's nest tells his country?**
He uses the word "heather," which the glossary defines as "small blossoming evergreen shrubs" found in Hogg's Scotland.
9. **Where do you think the shepherd poet was when he heard the lark? Could other shepherds have received happiness or strength from the song of the lark, even though they could not express their thoughts in poetry?**
Students are encouraged to discuss where a poet could best experience nature's beauty presented in this poem. Certainly other shepherds could experience the exhilaration of nature without expressing it in poetry.
10. **What must you have in yourself in order to enjoy the song of a bird as the poet enjoyed it?**
Answers will vary.
11. **Read again the discussion of lyrics on page 58, and tell why you think this is lyric poem.**
A lyric poem is defined as a short poem that expresses the poet's personal feelings about his subject. Have students identify the words/phrases that express the poet's personal reflections about the skylark.
12. **Find in the glossary the meaning of: lay, fell, heather.**

To a Skylark, p. 61

1. **How did Wordsworth feel toward the skylark, according to line 1?**
The poet saw the skylark as a mysterious traveler.
2. **In what two ways was he thinking of the bird?**
He thought of the skylark as an "ethereal minstrel" (a songbird) and a "pilgrim of the sky" (a traveler).
3. **What claim has the skylark to the title "ethereal minstrel"? To the title "pilgrim of the sky"?**
As an "ethereal minstrel" he lifts one's spirits with his song; as a "pilgrim of the sky" he travels where he pleases, unhindered by the cares of earth.
4. **What questions does the poet ask the skylark?**
"Dost thou despise the earth where cares abound? Or, while the wings aspire, are heart and eye Both with thy nest upon the dewy ground?"
How did James Hogg answer these questions in the first stanza of his poem?
He refers to the skylark as a "bird of the wilderness" whose dwelling place is in desert and cloud.
5. **Find a line of Wordsworth's poem that tells where the nest is made.**
Line 4 refers to "thy nest upon the dewy ground."
What words used by James Hogg show that he thought of the "dewy ground"?
He refers to the "fell and fountain sheen," references to Wordsworth's "dewy ground."
6. **The darkness of night hides the nightingale; what does Wordsworth say hides the skylark?**
The skylark is hidden in "A privacy of glorious light," defined in the glossary as "you are all alone, having flown too high for other birds to follow you."
7. **What habit makes the lark "true to Heaven"?**
He is "true to Heaven" when he can "pour upon the world a flood of harmony" through his songs.
What habit makes him "true to Home"?
He is true to Home when he returns to his "nest which thou canst drop into at will, those quivering wings composed, that music still!"
Which habit is a type of our longing to do good and great things?
Our longing to "pour up on the world a flood of harmony" is one of the "kindred points of Heaven."

Which habit is a type of the faithful performance of common duties?

Our faithful performance of common duties where we may "soar but never roam" is one of the "kindred points of Home."

8. **What feeling led Wordsworth to write this lyric?**

Have students discuss Wordsworth's mood that may have inspired this lyric.

9. **You will enjoy hearing these lines read in class by a good reader.**

10. **Read again what is said in "Literature and Life" on page 18 about literature that interprets life; can you show that this poem is such a piece of literature?**

This passage refers to the great writers who have observed nature and described life through literature to help us enjoy "the riches that lie all about us in the commonest of things," remind us of "life's uncertainties," encourage us to do acts of "service to others," and breathe "a message of hope and faith to all mankind," all of which "interpret the spirit of human brotherhood that makes life worthwhile." Students should be encouraged to explain how Wordsworth's poem is such a piece.

11. **Wordsworth's life was enriched by an appreciation of nature. What did you learn on page 26 of the "Introduction" about the wonders of nature?**

This passage suggests that "Nature is full of many wonders," wonders that include secrets of brooks, forests, birds, sunrise and sunset, spring and winter, as well as living creatures. "Through science, and through what poets and other keen observers have set down for us in books, we shall be able to make our way about and to add beauty and interest to our lives."

12. **What are some of the wonders that "add beauty and interest to our lives"?**

Encourage students to identify the wonders they have observed.

13. **Find in the glossary the meaning of: aspire, composed, instinct.**

To A Skylark, p. 63

1. **By what name is the skylark addressed in the first line?**
   The skylark is addressed as a "blithe Spirit."
2. **What characteristics of the lark's song and flight made the poet say, "Bird thou never wert"?**
   From his lofty position "from heaven, or near it," he poured out his heart "In profuse strains of unpremeditated art."
3. **Find a line in the second stanza that shows the energy and enthusiasm with which the lark begins its flight; why should this sudden spring of the bird make the poet think of fire?**
   Line 6: "Higher still and higher from the earth thou springest." The lark reminds the poet of a flame leaping into the air.
4. **What question does the poet ask in the seventh stanza?**
   "What is most like thee?"
   In what stanzas does he try to answer the question?
   In stanzas 8 to 11, the poet compares the lark to a poet, a high-born maiden, a golden glow-worm, and a rose.
5. **Is he satisfied with any of the comparisons he has made? Find the lines which tell us that the song of the lark is sweeter and more joyous than any of these things.**
   He is not satisfied with those comparisons. Stanza 12, line 4 says, "All that ever was joyous and clear and fresh, thy music does surpass."
6. **In which stanzas does the poet compare music produced by man with music of the lark's song?**
   Stanzas 13 and 14 describe the lark's "flood of rapture so divine, " a song that surpasses even our best wedding hymns and triumphal chants.
   How does our music seem when compared to the song of the lark?
   Our music seems "But an empty vaunt, a thing wherein we feel there is some hidden want."
7. **What question is asked in lines 16 and 17, on page 65?**
   "What objects are the fountains of thy happy strain? What fields or waves of mountains? What shapes of sky or plain?" The poet seems to be asking for whom the lark sings so majestically.
8. **In the questions that follow, the poet suggests what the lark may be singing about; what things does he suggest?**
   The questions that follow are, "What love of thine own kind? What ignorance of pain?" They suggest the lark may be singing of love and freedom.

9. **From what does the poet say the lark has never suffered?**
The lark has never suffered from "languor" or "shadow of annoyance."

10. **How are we affected by "hate and pride and fear"?**
"We look before and after, and pine for what is not; our sincerest laughter with some pain is fraught; our sweetest songs are those that tell of saddest thought."

11. **The poet tries to imagine how we would feel if we were not affected by hate or pride or fear and knew no sorrow; does he think we would then feel joy as great as the lark's? Find the line in which he tells us.**
He does not believe we could ever feel the lark's intense joy. Stanza 19, line 10: "I know not how thy joy we ever should come near."

12. **What does the poet ask of the bird in the last stanza?**
"Teach me half the gladness That thy brain must know."
Why does he want to know this gladness?
"The world should listen then—as I am listening now."

13. **Compare this poem on the skylark with those of Wordsworth and Hogg. What impressed each poet most in the skylark?**
Each poet mentions the lark's great musical charm. Hogg speaks of the lark as a "musical cherub," Wordsworth refers to his "flood of harmony," and Shelley mentions his "profuse strains of unpremeditated art." Students should be encouraged to find other similarities.

14. **What did you learn in "Literature and Life" on page 20 about true literature?**
This passage refers to the great writers who have observed nature and described life through literature to help us enjoy "the riches that lie all about us in the commonest of things," remind us of "life's uncertainties," encourage us to do acts of "service to others," and breathe "a message of hope and faith to all mankind," all of which "interpret the spirit of human brotherhood that makes life worthwhile."
This poem was written more than one hundred years ago; can you tell why men "treasure it and will not let it die"?
Encourage students to discover the timeless truths that this poem presents.

15. **Find in the glossary the meaning of: even, wrought, unbeholden, deflowered, vernal, chaunt, languor, fraught.**

16. **Pronounce: aerial, hymeneal, satiety.**

Hark! Hark! the Lark, p. 68

1. **At what time of day does the lark sing "at heaven's gate"? What lines tell you that it is morning?**
   Line 2 says the lark begins to sing in the morning when "Phoebus 'gins arise." Phoebus is the god of the sun.
2. **By what other name is Phoebus known?**
   The glossary says Phoebus is also known as Apollo.
3. **For what was the watering of the steeds a preparation?**
   Living in a horse-drawn culture, Phoebus may have been preparing his steeds for the day's travels.
4. **The use of "lies" in the song is old English idiom; what does it add to the poem?**
   Archaic words often contibute an atmosphere of past times. Encourage students to discuss the use of the word in this setting.
5. **What is added to the picture by the poet's choice of marigolds as opening flowers?**
   Budding marigolds preparing to open suggest the opening of a new day.
6. **Which lines do you think are the most beautiful in this little song?**
   Answers will vary.
7. **Which lines sing themselves to you? The Schubert music of this lyric is particularly pleasing.**
   Answers will vary.
8. **Have you heard this lyric rendered by a good singer? You would enjoy listening to the phonograph records of it by Gluck, Williams, and others.**
   Answers will vary.
9. **Who can memorize these lines in the shortest time?**
10. **Find in the glossary the meaning of: chaliced.**

Extended Activity:

Have students listen to various pieces of classical music and select a piece that best fits the mood of this poem. Students should explain the connection, either in a written essay or in a speech.

NAME______________________________CLASS__________DATE____

HARK! HARK! THE LARK, p. 68

Listen to various pieces of classical music and select a piece that best fits the mood of this poem. Explain the connection, either in a written essay or in a speech.

THE MOCKINGBIRD, P. 69

1. **The first two paragraphs describe the place where the bird lives; how does the description of the second paragraph differ from that of the first?**

   While the first paragraph describes the various plants of the land, the second paragraph describes the behavior of the mockingbird as he courts his mate.

2. **How does the author imply that the richness of the plant life of this region is reproduced in the bird's song?**

   The author says in this land "these bounties of nature (plant and bird) are in the greatest perfection." They complement each other.

3. **How does Audubon say the musical powers of the mockingbird compare with those of the nightingale?**

   To compare the nightingale "to the finished talent of the mockingbird is, in my opinion, quite absurd."

4. **You will enjoy hearing Victor records: "Mocking Bird," Gluck, with bird voices by Kellogg; "Bird Chorus" and "Songs of Our Native Birds," Kellogg; "Songs and Calls of Our Native Birds," Gorst; also Columbia record, "Bird Calls, " Avis.**

   While these items may no longer be available, information and music of the mockingbird can be located on the Internet. One such site is http://dhr.dos.state.fl.us/symbols/bird.html

5. **In the "Introduction" on pages 27 and 28 you read that some selections present the facts of nature as interpreted through the poets' imagination, while others show what men of scientific training have observed; which does this story represent?**

   This story represents nature through both the poet's imagination and the scientist's keen observation.

6. **Find in the glossary the meaning of: diversified, hautboy, modulations, derived, imparted, resort, essays.**
7. **Pronounce: bignonias, genial, species, foliage, ruffian, Mozart.**

Outline for Testing Silent Reading

Make an outline to guide you in telling the main thoughts of this selection.

Library Reading

"A Mocking Bird," Bynner, and "The Mocking Bird," Stanton (in *Melody of Earth*); "Bob, the Mocking Bird," Lanier (in *The Lanier Book*); selections from *Our Humble Helpers,* Fabre.

Suggestions For Theme Topics

See the Reader for a possible student project related to birds.

Extended Activity:

The following activities can be adapted to further enhance students' exposure to these important authors.

With the exception of William Shakespeare, all the authors in this section were born and lived in the same general time span of history. They share many similarities, as well as differences. Have students read each biography and complete the following chart. When the chart is complete, have the students list the similarities and differences they have noted in the chart.

	date of birth/death	place of birth	education (if listed)	profession/interests	claim to fame
Bryant	1794-1878	western Massachusetts	district school, studied law	wrote poetry, editor of the *New York Evening Post*	one of America's most-loved poets
Hogg	1770-1835	Ettrick, Scotland		shepherd, cowherd, songwriter	published *The Queen's Wake*
Wordsworth	1770-1850	Cumberland Highlands of Northern England		simple life and nature	beauty of the country inspired him
Shelley	1792-1822	Field Place, Essex, England	Eton, a famous English boarding school and Oxford University		long and short pieces and lyrics
Shakespeare	1564-1616	Stratford-on-Avon, England		wrote poems and plays, was an actor, shareholder in a theater	creation of dramatic literature
Audubon	1780-1851	near New Orleans, Louisiana	educated in France, studied drawing and French artists	studied natural history, especially birds	wrote *The Birds of North America*, made the life-size drawings himself

NAME______________________________**CLASS**__________**DATE**____

THE MOCKINGBIRD, P. 69

With the exception of William Shakespeare, all the authors in this section were born and lived in the same general time span of history. They share many similarities, as well as differences. read each biography and complete the following chart. When the chart is complete, list the similarities and differences you have noted in your chart.

	date of birth/death	place of birth	education (if listed)	profession/interests	claim to fame
Bryant					
Hogg					
Wordsworth					
Shelley					
Shakespeare					
Audubon					

Flowers and Trees

Morning-Glories, p. 75

1. **The poet has made a compound word by using the name Shakespeare gave to a fairy or sprite with the word "airy." What do you think was his purpose in doing this?**

   Arial-airy is defined in the glossary as having "the light movements of Ariel, a spirit of the air, in Shakespeare's 'The Tempest.'" The poet used this compound word to reinforce the image of the lightness of the morning glories swinging airily from the trellis.

2. **When is the name of the flower first mentioned?**

   The name "morning-glory" first appears in stanza five.

3. **What reason do you think the poet had for not telling it earlier?**

   Students should be encouraged to discuss the author's reasons for identifying the flower later in the poem.

4. **Who told the poet this story?**

   Stanza 2, line 7: "And the rose told me the story."

5. **How can you learn to know flowers as this poet knew them?**

   In the author's biography, students will read that "He spent his life learning her (Nature's) ways and describing them in poetry full of rich imagery." One can only learn to know the flowers when one takes time to examine and learn from them.

6. **What poems have you read in which the poet talks to a bird or flower?**

   Answers will vary; however, in the poem entries under "Birds" students will find poets who speak to birds in "To A Waterfowl"; "The Skylark"; "To A Skylark," by Wordsworth; "To A Skylark," by Shelley; and "Hark! Hark! the Lark." In this section of poems about flowers and trees, several poets address their subjects including Brooke, Emerson, and Tennyson.

7. **Why does the poet think of the fairies as fleeing at cockcrow?**

   Since in legends fairies usually come out at night, one would expect them to flee "at cockcrow" when daylight arrives.

8. **Compare this poem with Keat's "Sweet Peas" (in *The Elson Readers, Book Seven,* page 80).**

Sweet Peas
by John Keats

Here are sweet peas, on tiptoe for a flight,
With wings of gentle flush o'er delicate white,
And taper fingers catching at all things,
To bind them all about with tiny rings.
Linger awhile upon some bending planks
That lean against a streamlet's rushy banks,
And watch intently Nature's gentle doings;
They will be found softer than ringdove's cooings.
How silent comes the water round that bend!
Not the minutest whisper does it send
To the o'erhanging sallows; blades of grass
Slowly across the checkered shadows pass.

Both poems reflect on the stillness of nature's beauty. Cawein speaks of "the morning glory's tendrils" and Keats mentions the sweet peas' "taper fingers catching at all things." Have students find other similarities in these poems.

9. **Find in the glossary the meaning of: Ariel-airy, aromatic, fay, elfin.**
10. **Pronounce: jessamine, Titania.**

Class Reading

Bring to class and read: "The Flowerphone," Brown (in *Melody of Earth*).

Extended Activity:

Alliteration refers to the repetition of same beginning sounds. Cawein scatters alliterative lines throughout his poem. Have students identify all the alliterations in this poem. Answers should include:

"Ariel-airy ease; And their aromatic honey"; "the story that the jessamine told the rose"; "And fairy feet on the flowers Fell"; "and the fairies fled in fear"; petticoats, purple and pink."

NAME________________________________ CLASS__________ DATE____

MORNING-GLORIES, P. 75

Alliteration refers to the repetition of same beginning sounds. Cawein scatters alliterative lines throughout his poem. Identify all the alliterations in this poem.

____

____

____

____

____

____

____

____

____

____

____

____

____

____

____

____

____

____

____

____

____

Pine-Trees and the Sky: Evening, p. 77

1. **What cause did the poet think the evening sky would have for sorrowing?**
   The evening sky was sorrowing because the day was over.
2. **Why did the setting sun bring the thought that "the best is over"?**
   "The best is over" for the "silly lover" who could only "remember now, and think, and sigh."
3. **How did the cry of the sea-gull affect the poet?**
   "The sea-gull's mocking cry" made the poet "tired and sick that all was over."
4. **The changing western sky made the poet think how life had changed for him; the fading color made him think of joys that were gone forever; what did he see when he turned to the north? Can you tell why he was comforted by the sight?**
   "I saw the pines against the white north sky, very beautiful, and still, and bending over their sharp black heads against a quiet sky." He was comforted because "there was peace in them."
5. **Can you tell why he felt brave and strong when he looked at the white sky and the quiet trees?**
   Encourage students to discuss how the sky and quiet trees could generate feelings of bravery and strength in the observer.
6. **Compare this poem with Bryant's "To A Waterfowl"; what likenesses do you find?**
   Answers may vary but should include the following: the setting of both poems occurs in the evening; as the "Fowler's eye" seeks to harm the flight of the waterfowl, so the "sea-gull's mocking cry" tries to discourage the poet's dreams; both poets find strength in the beauty of the waterfowl and the pine trees.

Class Reading.

Bring to class and read: "The Soldier," Brooke; "The Island of Skyros" (a poem in memory of Brooke), Masefield.

The Rhodora, p. 78

1. **Under what circumstances did the poet find the rhodora?**
   "When sea winds pierced our solitudes, I found the fresh rhodora in the woods."
2. **What tells you that the flower grew in a lonely place?**
   The flower was "Spreading its leafless blooms in a damp nook, To please the desert and the sluggish brook."
3. **What comparison does the poet make between the color of the bird and the color of the flower?**
   The poet says the "purple petals" of the flower cheapen the redbird's array.
4. **Why is the poet not troubled at the thought of the rhodora's wasting its loveliness?**
   He says, "If eyes were made for seeing, The beauty is its own excuse for being."
5. **Mention ways in which we show that there is use for beauty in the satisfaction it gives the eye.**
   Students should mention that beauty comes in many forms: the artist's strokes, nature's brilliant colors, a mother's gentle smile.
6. **Who can memorize these lines in the shortest time?**
7. **Read the fourth and last stanzas of "To A Waterfowl"; compare the thought in these stanzas with the thought in the last line of "The Rhodora."**
   The fourth and last stanzas of "To A Waterfowl" are:

   There is a Power whose care
   Teaches thy way along that pathless coast—
   The desert and illimitable air—
   Lone wandering, but not lost.

   He who from zone to zone
   Guides through the boundless sky thy certain flight,
   In the long way that I must tread alone
   Will lead my steps aright.

   The last line of "The Rhodora" states:

   "The selfsame power that brought me there brought you."

Both poems acknowledge a power greater than their own that will guide their "steps aright."

8. **Find in the glossary the meaning of: blooms, cheapens.**

Flower in the Crannied Wall, p. 79

1. **What do you find in the first three lines that tells you the flower was small and not firmly rooted?**

   "Flower in the crannied wall, I pluck you out of the crannies; I hold you here, root and all, in my hand." This indicates that the flower's roots were fragile and not firmly planted.

2. **Why does the poet make the insignificance of the flower so plain to us?**

   He compares the mystery of the small flower in our hands to the mystery of our insignificance in God's hands.

3. **To whom is the poet talking?**

   The poet is talking to the "flower in the crannied wall."

4. **What does his use of the words, "little flower," tell you of Tennyson's feeling for flowers?**

   It suggests the tenderness he feels toward flowers.

5. **What other poems have you read that show how birds and flowers speak to those who have learned to listen?**

   Answers will vary but may include lines from the following poems: "The Rhodora"; "Pine-trees and the Sky: Evening"; To A Skylark," Shelley; "To A Waterfowl," Bryant.

6. **If Tennyson had known all he wanted to know about that little flower, he would have known what no mortal knows of the great mysteries of life and death. What did you learn on pages 25 and 26 about the belief ancient peoples had concerning the mysteries of life and the origin of flowers?**

   "Many peoples have believed that even the kindly aspects of nature were influenced by supernatural powers. There were divinities of the harvest, of the rain, of the months and seasons. The wood and the water were inhabited by deities of less importance. The origin of the flowers were explained by this religion of nature."

7. **On page 26 it is stated that we "have won from Nature many of her secrets." Mention some of the "secrets" that men of science have recently learned.**

   Have students scan recent newspapers, magazines, and newscasts to learn the "secrets" of nature.

8. **What great secret does this poem tell us has never been discovered?**

   We have never discovered the secret of God and man.

9. **In "Literature and Life," page 19, you read that there are poems of such enduring charm that men treasure them and "will not let them die"; why do you think that this**

little poem is one that men will always treasure?

Answers will vary but may reflect the poem's timeless message of man's eternal quest for meaning.

10. **Compare with this poem by Tennyson these lines from one of Wordsworth's great poems: "To me the meanest flower that blows can give thoughts that do often lie too deep for tears."**

Both lines refer to the smallness of the flower and the importance of its message.

Extended Activity:

This series of poems presents a variety of vivid images. Have students choose a line from any poem that paints a picture in their minds and create an illustration of the line that depicts the image.

NAME______________________________**CLASS**__________**DATE**____

FLOWER IN THE CRANNIED WALL, p. 79

This series of poems presents a variety of vivid images. Choose a line from any poem that paints a picture in your mind and create an illustration of the line that depicts the image.

Spring and Autumn

The Coming of Spring, p. 81

1. **How did the settlers on Sun Prairie feel at the coming of spring? Why?**
   Spring to the settlers felt "like a pardon to imprisoned people" because "for five months they had been shut closely within their cabins."
2. **What was the first outdoor work of the spring? Can you give any reason for why this would be the first work done?**
   The first outdoor work was "digging ditches and chopping canals in the ice so that the barn would not be inundated by the spring rains." During the day, there was "sawing and splitting the pile of logs which Mr. Stewart had been hauling during the open days of winter." Encourage students to explore why these tasks would be done first.
3. **Would you like to do the boys' part of this work? Give reasons for your answer.**
   The boys' work consisted of "cows to milk and drains to keep open," "to pile the wood behind the men as they sawed and split the large logs into short lengths." Answers will vary.
4. **Would the maple logs interest you as much as they interested Lincoln? Explain why.**
   The maple trees were appealing for the sap they produced, and the boys "wore their tongues to the quick, licking the trickle from the rough wood. Answers will vary.
5. **What does the fact that Lincoln watched the migrating birds tell you about his interest in nature?**
   The author says nature "was always a pleasure," to Lincoln; he knew its birds and their habits and "could imitate their cries, and often caused them to turn and waver in their flight, by uttering their resounding cries."
6. **What work was the boy called upon to do at this time that he disliked very much? Find the sentence that tells why he did not complain about it.**
   Lincoln was called upon to "fan up the seed wheat," a job which "the boys hated…because it was a dusty and monotonous job." Page 84, line 33 says: "It was of no use to cry out; the work had to be done."
7. **What experiences did Lincoln have that you would enjoy? What experiences that you would not enjoy?**
   Answers will vary.

8. **What qualities made Lincoln a worthy home member and a good American citizen?**

Students should be encouraged to identify his qualities, identifying such characteristics as hard work, discipline, ability to entertain himself, fair play with friends, and an uncomplaining attitude toward work.

9. **Is such a life as his necessary to produce these qualities?**

These qualities can be produced under any circumstances.

10. **What would be the result if all boys and girls would persevere in unpleasant duties as Lincoln did?**

Encourage students to identify the effects of perseverance in the tasks they face.

11. **How would our country be helped if all its citizens worked in this way?**

We would be a stronger nation if all our citizens would work cooperatively as Lincoln did.

12. **On page 86, lines 14 to 25, the author compares the boys' picnic to the ancient celebration of spring by primitive peoples. What did you learn on pages 25 and 26 about the influence of nature upon early people?**

Early people often thought that aspects of nature were influenced by supernatural powers. "Thus men in all ages have felt the influence of nature upon them and have sought to explain it, in art and song and story, as well as in religion."

13. **In the "Introduction" on page 26 you were told that an important part of our business in life is "to establish relations with the world in which we live." Can you show that the boys of this story had established such relations, and that this added great enjoyment to their lives?**

The boys felt a kinship with all nature around them: the call of the birds, the coming of spring, the stories of Jack, the hired man. Nature for them held "a singular charm," "no sweeter sound," "something primeval and splendid."

14. **What were you told in "Literature and Life," pages 19 and 20, about literature as a source of learning the "facts of life"? How does this selection give you a clearer idea of the "facts of life" on a midwestern farm than you could gain from your history or geography or from an encyclopedia?**

"Literature and Life" states that "all through life you will find pleasure and increased understanding if you will supplement books of this latter kind (geography, history, or encyclopedias) by the literature of great authors who have recorded their observation of events and peoples in language of such endearing charm that men treasure it and will not let it die." While reference books can provide us with "facts of life" in location and history, authors of stories such as these can bring us "facts of life" about real people.

15. **Find in the glossary the meaning of: inundated, conical, transitory, swales, infallible, ecstasy, confiscated.**
16. **Pronounce: exquisite, horizon, jocund, savor, primeval.**

Class Reading

Bring to class and read: "The Call of Spring," Noyes (in *High Tide*).

Outline for Testing Silent Reading

Make an outline to guide you in telling the story.

Library reading

A Son of the Middle Border, Garland.

Information on this work by Garland can be researched on the Internet at http://xroads.virginia.edu/~HYPER/HNS/Garland/ Sudents who enjoyed this piece on the coming of spring by Garland may enjoy his story, "The Great Blizzard," in *The Elson Readers, Book Seven.*

Suggested Theme Topic

Life on a modern farm as compared with the life led by boys of this story.

Home-Thoughts, From Abroad, p. 88

1. **Browning wrote this poem while in Italy; read the lines that show his longing for England.**
Lines 1 and 2: "Oh, to be in England, now that April's there!"
2. **What word gives the idea that spring comes suddenly in England?**
Line 8: "In England—now!"
3. **What are the signs that the poet associates especially with early spring?**
He describes the "tiny leaf" of "the lowest boughs and the brushwood sheaf" and the song of the chaffinch on "the orchard bough."
4. **Commit to memory the lovely description of the thrush's song.**
Line 14: "he sings each song twice over, lest you should think he never could recapture the first, fine careless rapture."
5. **Notice the beautiful setting given to the thrush; which words add especially to the beauty of the picture?**
Line: 11: "Hark, where my blossomed pear tree in the hedge leans to the field and scatters on the clover blossoms and dewdrops—at the bent spray's edge that's the wise thrush."
6. **How will "noontide wake anew the buttercups"?**
After the "hoary dew" of morning, the sun's warmth will "wake anew the buttercups."
7. **Tell why buttercups are "the little children's dower."**
A dower is defined in the glossary as a "treasure; gift, wealth, or property which a bride brings to her husband." They are, perhaps, the treasures the children pick for their mothers.
8. **To what flower in Italy is the buttercup compared?**
The buttercup is "far brighter than this gaudy melon-flower."
9. **Describe in a few lines what you love best in the springtime at your home.**
Answers will vary.
10. **Contest: who can read the entire poem most effectively?**
11. **What did you learn in "Literature and Life," page 21, about literature that makes beauty evident to us? Can you show that this poem is such a piece of literature?**
"There is the literature that makes evident to us the beauty that our more prosaic eyes might fail to note....When you have read in this book Browning's 'Home-Thoughts, from Abroad,' springtime will come to you filled with new delights."
12. **Find in the glossary the meaning of: bole, whitethroat, rapture, dower.**

13. Pronounce: elm-tree, chaffinch, dewdrop, anew, gaudy.

Class Reading

The sources of the readings listed in the reader may be out of print except for "Apple Blossoms," Martin (in *The Elson Readers, Book Six*). Compare that poem with "Home-Thoughts, from Abroad."

A Vagabond Song, p. 90

1. **To what does the poet say his heart keeps time?**
His heart keeps time with "the yellow and the purple and the crimson" of Autumn.
2. **Where does he see these colors?**
He sees them "from every hill of flame."
3. **How does the color of the maples affect him?**
They "can shake me like a cry of bugles going by."
4. **What connection do you see between scarlet and the sound of bugles?**
Answers may vary but may include the idea that both scarlet and bugles catch one's attention.
5. **What color were the asters that appeared like smoke?**
The poet describes the asters as "frosty," perhaps the gray-white color of smoke.
6. **Whom does the poet say he must follow?**
"There is something in October sets the gypsy blood astir; we must rise and follow her."
7. **What gives the appearance of flame to the hills?**
The flame of the hills are the brilliant colors of "yellow and the purple and the crimson" leaves.

Class Reading

Bring to class and read: "Indian Summer," Teasdale (in *Rivers to the Sea*).

Teasdale was a popular poet at the turn of the twentieth century. Information about her and *Rivers to the Sea* may be located on the Internet at: http://authorsdirectory.com/biography_online or http://www.selfknowledge.com422au.htm

See "Suggested Problems" in the reader for extended activities that enhance these selections.

Extended Activity:

In this section the authors paint word pictures using similes, comparing two unlike things using "like" or "as." Have students skim the works in this section and identify all the similes, explaining how the things compared are similar.

"The Coming of Spring": "the cloudless sky was blue as a plowshare"; "the ice outspread like a burnished share"; the ducks "covered the ground like some strange, down-dropping storm from the sky, and when alarmed they rose with a sound like the rumbling of thunder."

"A Vagabond Song": "my heart is like a rime"; "scarlet of the maples can shake me like a cry of bugles"; "frosty asters like smoke upon the hills."

NAME______________________________CLASS__________DATE____

A VAGABOND SONG, P. 90

In this section the authors paint word pictures using similes, comparing two unlike things using like or as. Skim the works in this section and identify all the similes, explaining how the things compared are similar.

NAME____________________________ **CLASS**__________ **DATE**______

Story	***Find in the glossary the meaning of:***
Reader p. 29	**foal**__________
	careering__________
	vestige__________
	bucking__________
	hobbling__________
	superb__________
	limpid__________
	caracoled__________
	harry__________
Reader p. 41	**garrison**__________
	mongrel__________
	voila__________
	mon ami__________
	terse__________
Reader p. 46	**dilapidated**__________
	inadequate__________
	coulee__________
	eminence__________
	incredulous__________
	butte__________
	annihilation__________
	frontlet__________
	buffer__________
	domicile__________
	veered__________
	diminution__________
	dissipated__________
Reader p. 56	**plashy**__________
	marge__________
	desert__________
Reader p. 60	**lay**__________
	fell__________
	heather__________
Reader p. 61	**aspire**__________
	composed__________
	instinct__________
Reader p. 63	**even**__________
	wrought__________
	unbeholden__________

deflowered____________________________
vernal____________________________
chaunt____________________________
languor____________________________
fraught____________________________
Reader p. 68 **chaliced**____________________________
Reader p. 69 **diversified**____________________________
hautboy____________________________
modulations____________________________
derived____________________________
imparted____________________________
resort____________________________
essays____________________________
Reader p. 75 **Ariel-airy**____________________________
aromatic____________________________
fay____________________________
elfin____________________________
Reader p. 78 **blooms**____________________________
cheapens____________________________
Reader p. 81 **inundated**____________________________
conical____________________________
transitory____________________________
swales____________________________
infallible____________________________
ecstasy____________________________
confiscated____________________________
Reader p. 88 **bole**____________________________
whitethroat____________________________
rapture____________________________
dower____________________________

Pronounce:
Arab, corral, indomitable, Salmon, subtly, isolated, aluminum, coyote, ally, amicable, undulating, pall, impotent, respite, irreparable, illimitable, abyss, aerial, hymeneal, satiety, bignonias, genial, species, foliage, ruffian, Mozart, jessamine, Titania, exquisite, horizon, jocund, savor, primeval, elm-tree, chaffinch, dewdrop, anew, gaudy.

Part II: The World of Adventure

In This Section—

Objectives—

By completing "Part II," the following objectives will be met.

1. The student will use effective reading strategies to construct meaning and identify the purpose of a text including:
   a. using illustrations
   b. defining unfamiliar words
   c. scanning for details
   d. retelling and summarizing
2. The student will determine the main idea or essential message and identify relevant supporting details and facts of a text.
3. The student will read and organize facts from the text and other sources to make a report, outline, and perform an authentic task.
4. The student will prepare for writing by focusing on the topic and organizing supporting details in a logical sequence.
5. The student will draft and revise writing.
6. The student will produce final documents that have been edited for correct spelling, punctuation, and grammar.
7. The student will write for a variety of audiences and purposes.
8. The student will write in a variety of genres including narrative and poetic.
9. The student will use reference materials (dictionaries, encyclopedias, maps, charts, and the Internet).
10. The student will use speaking strategies effectively such as eye contact, gestures, and visuals that engage the audience.
11. The student will identify the development of plot and how conflicts are resolved in a story.
12. The student will identify and understand similarities and differences among the characters, settings, and events presented in various texts.
13. The student will identify the author's purpose and point of view.
14. The student will identify and use literary terminology such as alliteration and simile.
15. The student will respond critically to fiction and poetry.
16. The student will respond to a text by explaining how the motives of the characters or events compare with those in his or her own life.
17. The student will use context clues to understand words and ideas.
18. The student will predict events that may occur in the text and explain the reasoning behind the prediction.
19. The student will understand the qualities necessary for people to become good citizens and apply those qualities to his or her personal life.
20. The student will understand the qualities necessary to develop good character and apply those qualities to his or her personal life.

Stories of the Supernatural

The Masque of the Red Death, p. 99

1. **What is said in the "Introduction" on page 97 about purely imaginary stories of adventure? How does Poe make the events of this story seem as if they really happened?**
   "Adventure is an experience out of the ordinary." Through imagination the "poet was able to picture the scenes so vividly that he seemed to have been present." In other words, the poet, Poe, was able to describe the events so vividly that they seemed real.
2. **What two kinds of adventure are mentioned on page 97? Which of these kinds is narrated in "The Masque of the Red Death"?**
   Two kinds of adventure are mentioned on page 97. The first kind of adventure is adventure that is purely imaginary and the second kind of adventure is adventure that has a partial foundation based on fact. "The Masque of Red Death" has a partial foundation in fact.
3. **Name several stories dealing with this kind of adventure that you read in "Part I."**
   Several other stories with this kind of adventure are "Coaly-Bay The Outlaw Horse," "Satan, The War Dog," and "The Thundering Herd."
4. **What other imaginative stories by Poe have you read?**
   Answers will vary.
5. **Look up in the glossary the meaning of: sagacious, depopulated, bizarre, perforce, grotesque, decorum, habiliments, tangible.**
6. **Pronounce: eccentric, august, courtiers, ballet-dancer, suite, disconcert, fete, piquancy, robust, illimitable.**

Class Reading

Read aloud the paragraphs of the introduction, trying to suggest by your reading Poe's purpose in writing them; the paragraphs that contain the development of the main incident, trying to suggest what Poe has so powerfully suggested in his story—the terrible fear under all the seeming gayety, and its final outburst;

the paragraph that gives the climax, striving to suggest by your reading the increasing fear and final horror; selected sentences that exemplify Poe's imaginative and poetic style, such as in the descriptions of the clock and of the dancers, and in the last paragraph, particularly the last sentence; selected descriptions that give you the most vivid pictures, noting especially the sentence in each that is most poetically expressed; examples showing the careful selection of words especially fitted to express the thought.

Outline for Testing Silent Reading

Make an outline to guide you in telling the story.

Library Reading

"A Descent into the Maelstrom," Poe.

Suggestions for Theme Topics

(Two-Minute Talks.)

1. A great plague of which I know or have read.
2. The Black Death in the fourteenth century. (Use encyclopedias or other library sources.)
3. Contrast the behavior of Prospero with that of Surgeon-General William C. Gorgas, who fought yellow fever in Panama and who rescued Cuba from disease. (*The Mentor,* November, 1920; use *The Readers' Guide* to find other material.)
4. Father Damien and his work among the lepers on the island of Molokai. (*A Treasury of Heroes and Heroines,* Edwards.)
5. Experiences of Dr. Wilfred C. Grenfell as a medical missionary, from his autobiography, *A Labrador Doctor.* (*Who's Who in America* will tell you simple facts about the author's life.)

Extended Activities:

1. Have students create masks that might have been worn at the ball. Display them.

2. Have students mark at least fifteen adjectives describing the ball. Using these adjectives have students create a poem that interprets the mood of the ball.

NAME______________________________CLASS__________DATE____

THE MASQUE OF THE RED DEATH, P. 99

1. **Create a mask that might have been worn at the ball.**

2. **Mark at least fifteen adjectives describing the ball. Using these adjectives create a poem that interprets the mood of the ball.**

The Raven, p. 109

Discussion

1. **Do you think this poem was written to tell a story or to give expression to feeling?**

   While this poem tells a story, it most vividly gives expression to feeling.

2. **Tell the incidents of the story contained in the poem.**

   The poem begins with the speaker reading in his chamber when he hears a "tapping" at the door. He opens the door to find no one there. He continues to hear a tapping and thinks it is some visitor. He describes his feelings of sadness for his lost Lenore, and the sound on the door instills fear in him. He opens the door and there is "Darkness." He hears tapping again, and again describes the feelings welling up inside him. He finally opens the shutter to allow a raven to enter. This raven perches atop the chamber door. The speaker questions the raven about its wanderings to which the raven consistently replies, "Nevermore." The speaker then grows very anxious and mournful of his Lenore. The raven does not seem to help the speaker ease these feelings, but rather the raven inspires the feelings to grow more intense. At the end of the poem the raven is still sitting "on the pallid bust of Pallas just above" his chamber door.

3. **What does the poet say he had hoped to find in his books that December night?**

   He hoped to find "the morrow" "surcease of sorrow." He was looking for some respite from his depression.

4. **What sound aroused him?**

   A "tapping" at his chamber door aroused him.

5. **What reasons can you give for the terror that seized him at the sound?**

   He was nearly asleep and deep in thought when the tapping started. Possibly in this state of mind, he was startled and thought it was Lenore at the door. He was not expecting a visitor.

6. **Why does the raven seem to bring more gloom and sorrow to the room?**

   The raven is black. Black symbolizes death and sadness, and adds an eerie atmosphere to the story.

7. **What do you think the "never flitting" raven symbolizes or represents?**

   The "never flitting" could symbolize the memories of Lenore that continue to haunt the speaker.

8. **What other poems or stories have you read that show Poe's**

love of the mysterious and terrible?

In *The Elson Readers, Book Eight,* the story of the "Masque of the Red Death" shows Poe's love of the mysterious and terrible. Students may have read other stories as well.

9. **Have you ever enjoyed reading something you could not understand? Did you enjoy it because your imagination was excited or because you liked the sound of the words?**

Answers will vary.

10. **Find lines in the poem that you like although you cannot explain them; can you tell why you like them?**

Answers will vary. Students may look for lines that have a nice sound to them.

11. **Find examples of alliteration in the poem, that is, the repetition of the same letter or sound at the beginning of two or more words in close succession, as "nodded, nearly napping."**

Other examples of alliteration are: "filled me with fantastic terrors never felt before," "silken, sad, uncertain," "entreating entrance," "doubting dreaming dreams," "flirt and flutter," "ebony bird beguiling," "Ghastly grim," "Followed fast and followed faster," "velvet violet," "tempest tossed," "Horror haunted," and "rare and radiant."

12. **Find words that give or suggest the sound described.**

Words that give or suggest the sound described is called onomatopoeia. Some words in the poem are: "tapping," "rapping" "rustling," "beating," and "flutter."

13. **What lines in the first stanza rhyme? What are the end words of these lines?**

The lines that rhyme in the first stanza are lines 2, 4, 5, and 6. The end words of these lines are "lore," "door," "door," and "more."

14. **What lines in the second stanza rhyme? What are the words of these lines.**

The lines that rhyme in the second stanza are lines 2,4,5, and 6. The end words are "floor," "Lenore," "Lenore," and "forevermore."

15. **Study each stanza to find the lines that rhyme and the end words in each.**

All the stanzas in the poem follow the same rhyme scheme: ABCBBB.

16. **What have you learned about these end words?**

The words follow a pattern.

17. **What rhyme do you find in the first line of the first stanza? In the third line?**

In the first line the rhyme is "dreary" and "weary," and in the third line the rhyme is "napping" and "tapping." Words that rhyme within a line are called internal rhymes.

18. Find a word in the fourth line that rhymes with the last word in the third line.

The word in the fourth line that rhymes with the last word in the third line is "rapping." It rhymes with "tapping."

19. Study each of the stanzas in this way to find the rhymes of the lines.

20. With which of the two kinds of adventures mentioned in the "Introduction" on page 97 does this seem to deal?

This poem seems to represent adventure that is pure imagination.

21. Is it an imaginative story, or has it some basis of fact of legend?

It has some basis of fact. Refer to question 22.

22. "Lenore" represents Poe's young wife, who, it was certain could not live long. In this poem, written two years before her death, Poe imagined what his feelings would be at her death. Point out lines that express these feelings.

Lines that express these feelings are: "vainly I had sought to borrow From my books surcease of sorrow—sorrow for the lost Lenore," "On the morrow he will leave me, as my Hopes have flown before," "—is there balm in Gilead?"

23. What were you told in the "Introduction" on page 98 about the value of creative reading, or reading in such a way as to see the story in action through your imagination?

If one reads creatively, he will be able to see the story as if it were a play and such reading is a never-ending source of delight.

24. Which of these narratives by Poe can you see the more clearly?

Answers will vary.

25. Find in the glossary the meaning of: surcease, beguiling, craven, divining, censer, nepenthe.

26. Pronounce: obeisance, decorum, placid, ominous, respite.

Class Reading

Bring to class and read "Annabel Lee" and "The Bells," Poe.

Magazine Reading

Bring to class and read, or make a brief oral report on the best story of mystery that you have read in a magazine.

Extended Activity:

Have students write to create a feeling.

Name______________________________**Class**__________**Date**____

The Raven, p. 109

Write to create a feeling.

Narratives in Verse

Bonnie George Campbell, p. 115

Discussion

1. **Who can read this poem so well that the listeners may gain the thought of the story?**
2. **Who is the hero?**

   "Bonnie George Campbell" was the hero.
3. **Note that this ballad suggests an emotion, but not the poet's; whose emotion is suggested?**

   The poem mentions the emotions of "his auld mother" and "his bonnie bride."
4. **Their grief is told by the effects of the hero's failure to return home; what are these effects?**

   His mother was "greeting fu' sair"—"weeping bitterly"; his bride was "riving her hair"—"tearing" her hair.
5. **Notice that the details of the hero's death are left to the readers' imagination.**

   One of the characteristics of ballads is that "they merely tell the main facts of the story, leaving details to the imagination of the reader." Encourage students to discuss the possible causes of the death of "Bonnie George Campbell."
6. **Who is speaking in the fourth stanza?**

   Those words may have been spoken by his mother and bride.
7. **Make a list of the Scotch words that you could understand from the context; of those that it was necessary for you to look up.**

   The Scotch words are: Tay, Bonnie, rade, hame, cam, guid, auld mither, fu' sair, riving, toom.
8. **What characteristics of the folk ballad does this poem have? How have the old ballads come down to us?**

   Students will find information on the ballad under "Notes and Questions." In short, this ballad has no known author, tells a story, and uses the language of the people, not the kings. Ballads such as these were handed down orally from generation to generation until finally, with the coming of the printing press, they were collected and written down for our enjoyment.
9. **What other old ballad have you read?**

   The Elson Readers, Book Seven includes another folk ballad, "Sir Patrick Spens."
10. **You will enjoy hearing phonograph records of modern ballads such as Kipling's "Fuzzy-Wuzzy," "Gypsy Trail," "On the Road to Mandalay," etc.**

JOHN GILPIN, P. 118

1. **How does the poet's language add to the humor of the poem?**
   The poet uses descriptive imagery that paints pictures in the reader's mind.
2. **Find stanzas in which the humor is furnished entirely by the poet's manner of telling something.**
   Answers will vary but the students will probably enjoy the stanzas that describe his ride to the calendar's home and back to his own home again.
3. **What expression in line 12, page 118, shows that this is not a very modern poem?**
   "All in a chaise and pair" suggests that they rode in carriages pulled by two horses.
4. **What do you think was the poet's purpose in writing this ballad?**
   One purpose of literature like this may be the sheer joy of entertainment that requires readers to exercise their sense of imagination. Encourage students to discuss other purposes a ballad such as this may have.
5. **Have you read any other poems that amuse and entertain you as this ballad does?**
   Answers will vary.
6. **Can you name an American poet who has written humorous poems?**
   Answers will vary but may include authors such as Oliver Wendell Holmes and Hawthorne. One later poet of humor is Shel Silverstein.
7. **What good does such a poem as this do?**
   Refer to responses given in question 4. After students have determined the purpose of the poem, have them decide what value the poem has for the reader.
8. **The story of this poem is a good one to test your power of visualizing incidents and scenes, as you were advised to do in the "Introduction" on page 97. Make a list of the pictures that would be contained in your "private moving picture show" for this story. Where in this series would you place the picture on page 115?**
   Answers will vary.
9. **Find in the glossary the meaning of: trainband, calendar, agog, trice, gambol, guise, bootless, posting, amain.**
10. **Pronounce: tedious, comely.**

Magazine Reading

Bring to class and read, or make a brief report on, the most interesting narrative in verse that you have read in a magazine.

The Highwayman, p. 128

1. **Where is the scene of this story laid? At what time? How can you tell?**
   The scene of this story begins in an inn at evening when "the wind was a torrent of darkness," "the moon was a ghostly galleon," and "the road was a ribbon of moonlight."
2. **How did people travel at that time?**
   The people traveled by foot and horseback.
3. **How do you think the highwayman expected to get his "prize"?**
   Highwaymen were robbers, sometimes robbing the rich to help the poor. This highwayman probably expected to get his "prize" from some rich person he was about to rob.
4. **Whom does he mean when he says, "If they press me sharply"?**
   He is referring to the "redcoat troop," King George's men who protected the country.
5. **What are we to imagine that Tim, the ostler, did?**
   Since Tim saw and heard what the highwayman told the landlord's daughter, he probably warned the redcoats about the highwayman since Tim also loved her.
6. **How does the poet want you to feel toward Tim?**
   He paints a negative picture of Tim in the readers' mind: "his eyes were hollows of madness, his hair like moldy hay," "dumb as a dog he listened."
7. **What did the troopers expect the highwayman to do?**
   They expected him to return to Bess, so they gagged her and tied her to a musket.
8. **How was he warned?**
   She managed to free her fingers from the knots with which she was bound, and when she heard the highwayman coming, "her finger moved in the moonlight, her musket shattered the moonlight; shattered her breast in the moonlight and warned him—with her death."
9. **Why did he not remain in hiding after his escape?**
   He returned to avenge her death "shrieking a curse to the sky, with the white road smoking behind him, and his rapier brandished high!"
10. **Does it seem fitting that the highwayman should meet a violent death? Why?**
    Since he made his living through violence, it seems fitting that he died a violent death.

11. **What comparisons are made in the first stanza? Which of these can you picture most clearly?**

    The poet begins with three metaphors: "The wind was a torrent of darkness"; "The moon was a ghostly galleon"; "The road was a ribbon of moonlight."

12. **How does the poet suggest the movement of the horse?**

    "Over the cobbles he clattered and clashed" suggests the hurried pace of the horse.

    How does he suggest the movement of the troopers?

    "A redcoat troop came marching-marching-marching."

13. **What is added to the story by the last two stanzas of the poem?**

    By repeating the first two stanzas, the poet seems to suggest that the ghost of the highwayman still roams at night, looking for his lost love at the inn just as he did when he was alive.

14. **Read again what is said of this poem in the "Introduction" on page 97; mention other poems you have read that were based on an old legend?**

    The "Introduction" says this poem is "based upon old legends dealing with events that have only a partial foundation of fact." "Paul Revere's Ride" by Longfellow, found in this Reader, may be another poem such as this.

15. **Compare your "private moving picture show" of this story with that of "John Gilpin"; which do you see the more clearly?**

16. **Find in the glossary the meaning of: plaiting, harry, casement, looping, priming.**

17. **Pronounce: moor, breeches, rapier, ostler.**

Class Reading

Bring to class and read aloud "Kilmeny" (in *The Elson Readers, Book Seven*), and other narrative poems by Noyes.

Lochinvar, p. 133

1. **What geographical references tell you that the scene of this story is laid in Scotland?**
The poet refers to the Esle River, Netherby (a reference to their clansmen), the Solway, and Cannobie Lee.
2. **What names mentioned do you recognize as Scotch names?**
Lochinvar, Netherby, Graemes, Forsters, Fenwiks, and Musgraves are Scotch names.
3. **Find a line in the first stanza that sums up the character of Lochinvar.**
Line 5: "So faithful in love, and so dauntless in war."
4. **Find a line in the second stanza that describes the character of the bridegroom.**
Line 11: "A laggard in love, and a dastard in war" is defined in the glossary as an "unworthy suitor" and a "coward," respectively.
5. **Find a line in the third stanza that adds to the picture of the bridegroom given in the second stanza.**
Line 16: "The poor craven bridegroom said never a word" reinforces his image as a coward.
6. **How is the reader affected by the contrast between the two men.**
The reader will admire the bold, "dauntless" Lochinvar and dislike the cowardly, speechless bridegroom.
7. **Find the question asked by the bride's father. Why was his hand on his sword as he asked it?**
Line 17: "Oh, come ye in peace here, or come ye in war, or to dance at our bridal, young Lord Lochinvar?" The bride's father was prepared to fight with Lord Lochinvar should he have come "in war."
8. **What impression did Lochinvar give the bride's father by his answer?**
Lochinvar responded that he came "with this lost love of mine to lead but one measure, drink one cup of wine. There are maidens in Scotland more lovely by far that would gladly be bride to the young Lochinvar." Stanza 6 says "her father did fume."
9. **Do you think Lochinvar was sincere in his response?**
Answers will vary; students should support their answers with details from the poem.
10. **Describe the picture the sixth stanza makes you see.**
Stanza 6 describes Lochinvar's stately form and the bride's lovely face as they danced, the bridegroom's helpless dangling, the mother's fretting, and the father's fury.

11. What did Lochinvar accomplish by means of the dance?

He touched her hand, whispered in her ear, led her to the door, and escaped with her on horseback.

12. What were we told in the first stanza that explains Lochinvar's escape?

"His steed was the best."

13. Who are mentioned as the pursuers?

The pursuers included the Netherby clansmen—the Forsters, Fenwicks, and Musgraves; guests at the wedding.

14. What do you know of the methods of travel and communication before 1800?

Answers will vary but may identify horseback for travel and communication by word of mouth.

15. What two kinds of adventure are mentioned in the "Introduction" on page 97? Which of these kinds does this story narrate?

The "Introduction" mentions adventures "based on real happenings" and adventures "based on old legends with events that have only a partial foundation of fact." Students will read in the biography that this adventure is based on an old ballad handed down by word of mouth, with "only a partial foundation of fact."

16. In this poem Scott has imitated the old ballad style; point out some of the passages that show this.

Have students refer to the development of ballads as told in "Notes and Questions" following "Bonnie George Campbell."

They will note that a ballad such as this tells "us something of the life, the history, and the standards, superstitions, and beliefs of distant times." Encourage students to identify the passages that support that statement.

17. Find in the glossary the meaning of: border, brake, measure, bar, galliard, bonnet, croup, scar.

18. Pronounce: Lochinvar, dauntless, gallant.

Class Reading

Bring to class and read Longfellow's ballad "The Skelton in Armor" (in *The Elson Readers, Book Seven*), noting the similarity of theme.

The Leap of Roushan Beg, p. 135

1. **Describe in your own words Roushan Beg's perilous position before the leap.**
Student responses should reflect the description in stanza 5: "Suddenly the pathway ends; sheer the precipice descends; loud the torrent roars unseen; thirty feet from side to side yawns the chasm; on air must ride he who crosses the ravine."
2. **What do you think has brought him to this peril?**
He is referred to in stanza 1 as a "son of the road and bandit chief." He was being pursued by "Reyhan the Arab of Orfah."
3. **Find lines that show his love for his horse.**
Stanza 2: " More than maiden, more than wife, more than gold, and next to life Roushan the Robber loved his horse."
4. **Find lines that tell how he gained his wealth.**
Stanza 3: "Plundered khan, or caravan journeying north from Koordistan, gave him wealth and wine and food."
5. **What shows Kyrat's intelligence.**
Stanza 10 says Kyrat "paused a moment on the verge, measured with his eye the space, and into the air's embrace leaped as leaps the ocean surge."
6. **To what does the poet compare the leap of the horse?**
Stanza 11: "As the ocean surge o'er sand bears a swimmer safe to land, Kyrat safe his rider bore."
7. **To which one of the two, Roushan Beg or Kyrat, does the greater part of the credit belong for the leap? Why?**
The greater credit belongs to Kyrat who safely made the leap after Roushan urged Kyrat to rescue him.
8. **To whom did the watching Arab give the credit?**
In the last stanza the Arab stated, "In all Koordistan lives there not so brave a man as this Robber Kurroglou!"
9. **How did the bearing of Roushan Beg after the leap influence the Arab?**
Roushan's bearing left the impression of a phantom: "Thus the phantom horseman passed and the shadow that he cast leaped the cataract underneath. Reyhan the Arab held his breath while this vision of life and death passed above him."
10. **Describe the appearance of Kyrat.**
Roushan Beg described Kyrat as follows: "Round and slender as a reed"; "Soft thy skin as silken skein; soft as woman's hair thy mane; tender are thine eyes and true; all thy hoofs like ivory shine, polished bright."

11. Compare Kyrat with Coaly-Bay; what likenesses do you find?

Students will recall the story of Coaly-Bay in "Part One." Encourage students to create a list of the similarities in these two horses.

12. Why would you call this poem a ballad?

As noted before, ballads may be short stories that tell of "stirring subjects, with battle, adventure." This poem is one of adventure.

13. What other ballads by Longfellow have you read?

Answers will vary.

14. Find in the glossary the meaning of: fourscore, livery, housings, verge.

15. Pronounce: Roushan, khan, chasm, forehead.

Class Reading

Bring to class and read "Muleykeh," Browning.

"How They Brought the Good News From Ghent to Aix," p. 139

1. **This poem is without historical basis; the ride occurred only in the mind of the poet; what does this tell you of Browning's power of imagination?**
   His imagination is rich and vivid; through precise sensory images he paints pictures in the reader's mind.
2. **Does he tell what he imagined the good news was?**
   The good news is never stated.
3. **Why do you think three riders started to carry this good news?**
   The glossary states that the two towns, Ghent and Aix, were one hundred miles apart. Perhaps three riders were needed in case, as we see in the poem, the horses collapsed on the ride.
4. **How does the beginning of the poem give you the impression of haste?**
   The first stanza says they "sprang to the stirrup," and "I galloped, Dirck galloped, we galloped all three"; the watchman cried, "Good Speed!" and "Speed!" echoed the wall to us galloping through."
5. **At what time did the messengers start?**
   Stanza 3 states: "'Twas moonset at starting."
6. **How is the passing of time noted by the riders?**
   "Not a word to each other; we kept the great pace neck by neck stride by stride; never changing our place." They galloped through the night, heard the cocks crow and saw the sun rise in the morning. Still they rode on.
7. **When did the rider see his horse for the first time during the ride? Why had he not seen him before?**
   He first saw his horse when "up leaped of a sudden the sun." He had not seen his horse in the black of night.
8. **Would the news which you imagine the messengers were carrying require such haste as is described in the poem?**
   Answers will vary. Encourage students to speculate what the message may have been and what caused its urgency.
9. **Which stanza gives the most vivid impression of haste? Which gives the impression of endurance? Which is the expression of desperation?**
   Stanza 1 describes their haste; stanza 5 shows Roland's endurance; stanza 6 describes Dirck's desperation when his horse went down. Students may choose other stanzas using images from the stanzas to support their answers.

10. To whom does the rider give the credit for carrying the message?

The rider gave credit to his horse "who brought the good news from Ghent."

11. Find in the glossary the meaning of: abreast, slacker, butting, bluff, askance, peer, burgess.

12. Pronounce: Ghent, Aix, pique.

Incident of the French Camp, p. 142

1. **Find lines that verify the statements made in the "Introduction" on page 97 about this poem.**
The statements in the "Introduction" state that poems such as "Incident of the French Camp" "are based on real happenings. The poet did not himself pass through the adventures; yet through his imagination, he was able to picture the scenes so vividly that he seemed to have been present." The poet uses first person pronouns as though he was at the scene. Lines that lead the reader to think the poet was there include: Line 1: "You know, we French stormed Ratisbon;" Line 3: "On a little mound, Napoleon stood on our storming deck."
2. **What does the expression, "we French," tell you about the speaker?**
"We French" indicates that the speaker was sympathetic to the French cause, in fact, considered himself a Frenchman.
3. **Where was Napoleon at the time Ratisbon was "stormed"?**
He was "A mile or so away, on a little mound."
4. **Describe in your own words the position in which he stood.**
Napoleon was standing on a mound "with neck out-thrust...legs wide, arms locked behind."
5. **What were Napoleon's thoughts as he stood on the mound?**
"My plans that soar, to earth may fall, let once my army-leader Lannes waver at yonder wall."
6. **Why is his sentence not finished?**
He is stopped in mid-sentence by the arrival of "A rider, bound on bound full-galloping; nor bridle drew until he reached the mound."
7. **What would Napoleon think when he saw a horse galloping toward him?**
He expected news of the war—perhaps defeat.
8. **At what was he surprised?**
He was surprised to see a smiling boy dismount.
9. **What lines make us feel his shock of horror?**
"You looked twice e'er you saw his breast was all but shot in two."
10. **What was the boy's message?**
"Emperor, by God's grace we've got you Ratisbon! The Marshal's in the market-place, and you'll be there anon to see your flag-bird flap his vans where I, to heart's desire, perched him!"
11. **Had he reason for his "smiling joy"?**
Yes, he brought good news to Napoleon, good news which he had personally helped to procure, though he was dying.

12. Why does the poet repeat the words, "The chief's eyes flashed"? What did the flashing of the eye show?

The poet uses repetition to emphasize the hope that the news brought him: "his plans soared up again like fire."

13. What different thought caused his eye to soften?

His eye softened when he saw that the young man was wounded.

14. To what does the poet compare the softening of Napoleon's eye?

His eyes softened "as sheathes a film the mother-eagle's eye when her bruised eaglet breathes."

15. Why does the thought of the eagle seem appropriate in connection with Napoleon?

Napoleon was a great military genius with a sharp eye for weakness among his enemies. He knew when and where to attack them at their weakest points. Like an eagle he soared above the common man in his military brilliance.

16. Who is the hero of this story?

The boy who delivered the message is the hero; he died for the French cause.

17. What thought gave him power to smile in spite of his terrible pain?

He had defended the "flag-bird," the French flag, "to heart's desire."

18. Read the lines from Tennyson on page 95. Why are they especially fitting to introduce a group of selections that includes many stories of heroic adventure?

Tennyson's lines are as follows: "Great deeds cannot die They with sun and moon renew their light Forever blessing those that look on them." These are appropriate words because they remind us that heroic deeds such as the young soldier's in this story, never die.

19. Find in the glossary the meaning of: prone, oppressive, flag-bird, van.

Suggestions for Theme Topics

(Two-Minute Talks.)

1. A true war incident, preferably of World War One.
2. A story illustrating devotion to a leader and a cause.
3. A description of Napoleon's personal appearance.

A Ballad of John Silver, p. 144

1. **To whom does "We" refer?**
   "We" refers to "the pig-tailed, quidding pirates and the pretty pranks we played."
2. **What do the skull and cross-bones signify?**
   The skull and cross-bones were the symbols of piracy.
3. **What was the black Jolly Roger?**
   In the glossary the black Jolly Roger is defined as "the black banner of pirates."
4. **What body of water was known as the Spanish Water, or Spanish Main?**
   The Spanish Water referred to the Caribbean Sea.
5. **How was the ship armored?**
   "We'd a long brass gun amidship, like a well-conducted ship."
6. **How were the sailors armed? For what purpose?**
   "We had each a brace of pistols, and a cutlass at the hip." Their arms were used to attack and destroy "the goodly merchant-men."
7. **What did they do to the merchant ships? What did they do to the crews?**
   "She was boarded, she was looted, she was scuttled till she sank." The crews were killed, wounded, or drowned.
8. **How did the pirates amuse themselves?**
   "Then, having washed the blood away, we'd little else to do than to dance a quiet hornpipe as the old salts taught us to."
9. **Mention several modern inventions that have forced the pirate to give up his business.**
   Have the students brainstorm inventions that have eliminated the danger of pirates.
10. **The character of John Silver is found in the greatest of pirate stories, *Treasure Island;* have you read the book?**
11. **Find in the glossary the meaning of: lissome, brace, aboard, scuttled, salts.**

Class Reading

Bring to class and read "The Tarry Buccaneer," Masefield (in *Salt-Water Ballads*).

Suggested Theme Topic

How the American navy put an end to the Tripolitan piracy.

FLEURETTE, P. 146

1. **Who is speaking in this poem?**
   The "wounded Canadian" was speaking.
2. **Why does he speak so lightly of the loss of his leg?**
   The loss of his leg was not as disturbing to him as the loss of his facial appearance.
3. **Why does the nurse refuse to give him a mirror?**
   She didn't want him to see his disfigured face that others saw, shuddered, and turned away from in distress.
4. **Who was Caliban?**
   The glossary defines the Caliban as "an ugly creature half man, half monster in Shakespeare's "The Tempest."
5. **What comparison could there be between the soldier's face and Caliban's?**
   The soldier's face was "ravaged and raw and red," dreadful to look at, as the Caliban's may have been.
6. **What did the French soldier tell his sister about the Canadian?**
   The French soldier told her "How I'd smothered a bomb that fell into the trench, and so none of my men were hit, though it busted me up a bit."
   What shows that she was impressed by the story?
   "I fancied that I heard her sigh."
7. **What feeling must a story of self-sacrifice inspire?**
   Such stories inspire the best in humanity, eliciting respect and honor for those who have sacrificed themselves so heroically.
8. **What caused the great light that shone in the girl's eyes?**
   The great light was the respect and honor with which she looked at him.
9. **How did she show him that he was not "a thing of dread"?**
   "When gently she bent her head: 'May I kiss you, sergeant?' she said. Then she kissed my burning lips, with her mouth like a scented flower."
10. **The French sentence, page 147, lines 30 and 31, means "It is you, it is you, Mercel! My brother, how happy I am!"**
    Find in the glossary the meaning of other French words in the poem, and of: gargoyle, linnet.
    Other French words in the poem are: poilu (French soldier), malheureax (unhappy man).
11. **Pronounce: Fleurette.**

Class Reading

Bring to class and read "Grand Pere" (another war poem), Service.

Newspaper Reading

Not all heroic deeds of adventure occur on the battlefield. Bring to class and read an item from your daily newspaper, telling of a brave action by someone.

Suggested Theme Topic

How crippled and disfigured soldiers of the World Wars were marvelously helped by surgery and fitted with artificial legs, arms, etc., so that they could carry on useful occupations.

Extended Activity:

1. As students read these narrative poems, they will find the poets expressing a variety of moods and figurative language. Review the following terms with the students.

mood: the feeling the poem gives the reader such as sadness, happiness, or peacefulness.

sensory images: images that come to us through the five senses, touch, sight, sound, taste, or smell

simile: compares two unlike things saying one is like or as the other

metaphor: compares two unlike things saying one is the other

personification: giving human actions to nonhuman objects

onomatopoeia: words that sound like their meaning such as whoosh, boom, zip

Assign the poems to pairs of students and have them complete the chart identifying as many of the terms as they can find in their poem. (Not all the poems may have all the terms.)

TITLE____________________________________

mood	sensory images	simile	metaphor	personification	onomatopoeia

2. With lengthy, narrative poems such as these, it is helpful to stop reading after each stanza and quickly review and summarize what has happened. To assist the students in understanding and clarifying meaning as they read, have them complete the following chart, summarizing each stanza as they read and making predictions about what may occur ahead.

TITLE______________________________________

Stanza #_____	>	Stanza #_____	>	Stanza #_____
Stanza #_____	>	Stanza #_____	>	Stanza #_____
Stanza #_____	>	Stanza #_____	>	Stanza #_____

NAME________________________________CLASS__________DATE____

FLEURETTE, P. 146

1. As you read these narrative poems you will find the poets expressing a variety of moods and figurative language. Review the following terms.

   mood: the feeling the poem gives the reader such as sadness, happiness, or peacefulness.

   sensory images: images that come to us through the five senses, touch, sight, sound, taste, or smell

   simile: compares two unlike things saying one is like or as the other

   metaphor: compares two unlike things saying one is the other

   personification: giving human actions to nonhuman objects

   onomatopoeia: words that sound like their meaning such as whoosh, boom, zip

   Complete the chart identifying as many of the terms as you can find in your poem. (Not all the poems may have all the terms.)

TITLE____________________________________

mood	sensory images	simile	metaphor	personification	onomatopoeia

2. With lengthy, narrative poems such as these, it is helpful to stop reading after each stanza and quickly review and summarize what has happened. Complete the following chart, summarizing each stanza as you read and making predictions about what may occur ahead.

TITLE______________________________

Stanza #_____

Stanza #_____

Stanza #_____

Stanza #_____

Stanza #_____

Stanza #_____

Stanza #_____

Stanza #_____

Stanza #_____

Stanza #_____

Stanza #_____

Stanza #_____

Stanza #_____

Stanza #_____

Stanza #_____

A Story of Christmas

A Christmas Carol, p. 151

STAVE ONE

1. **What is the central idea or purpose of this story?**
The central idea or purpose of this story is to show the true meaning of giving. If one gives of himself, he will find greater joy in life. There is more to life than material possessions. The story is about a man who through a series of adventures changes from a stingy miser to a loving, thoughtful person.
2. **What does the author tell us about Scrooge's character at the beginning of the story.**
We learn in the beginning of the story that Scrooge is a "tight-fisted" man. He is a "squeezing, wrenching, grasping, scraping, clutching, covetous old sinner." The author also tells us Scrooge was as "secret and self-contained, and solitary as an oyster."
3. **If Dickens had not told us anything before, what would we learn of Scrooge from his conversation with his nephew?**
We would learn that Scrooge valued money over family ties. He refused his nephew's invitation to Christmas dinner with a "humbug."
4. **What would we learn from the visit of the gentleman who asked for a contribution?**
Scrooge would not give freely to help others. He thought the government institutions and laws established to help the poor were all the generosity that needed to be given to the destitute. Scrooge said, "I can't afford to make idle people merry."
5. **What does his treatment of the carol singer tell us?**
Scrooge threw a ruler at the young carol singer. This tells us that he was bitter toward Christmas and those who wished to spread cheer.
6. **What does his treatment of his clerk tell us?**
Scrooge treated his clerk as if he were a slave rather than an employee. It is as if the clerk should have been grateful for the ever so slight generosity of Scrooge to provide him with a job. Scrooge obviously thought he owed the world nothing and the world owed him everything.
7. **Has the author any reason for making the weather so unpleasant?**
The weather personifies Scrooge's attitude about Christmas. The weather is dark, bleak, and cold.

8. **What reason do you think the author had for making Scrooge's room so gloomy?**
   Like the weather, Scrooge's gloomy room shows the content of his heart.
9. **In what respect do we feel that Scrooge needs to change?**
   Scrooge needs to recognize that helping others and being kind to others are virtues. Marley tells him that he is doomed to roam the earth "…and witness what it cannot share, but might have shared on earth, and turned to happiness." Marley hopes to help Scrooge avoid the same fate.
10. **What is the author's plan for reforming him?**
    The author's plan for reforming is Scrooge is to have three spirits visit him during the night. Each might find a way to change Scrooge's heart.
11. **Find in the glossary the meaning of: stave, 'Change, palpable, Bedlam, Poor Law, Saint Dunstan, corporation, Belshazzar, ward.**
12. **Pronounce: ironmongery, simile, homage, Parliament, inexplicable.**

Class Reading

Description of Scrooge, page 152, line 25, to page 153, line 22; the nephew defending Christmas, page 155, lines 15 to 28; the clerk leaving the counting house, page 159, line 25, to page 160, line 15; description of Marley, page 163, line 35, to page 164, line 8, Marley and Scrooge, page 164, line 17, to page 169, line 29.

STAVE TWO

1. **Describe the Ghost of Christmas Past.**
   The Ghost of Christmas Past is described on page 172. He is a "strange figure—like a child; yet not so like a child as like an old man viewed through some supernatural medium which gave him the appearance of having receded from the view, and being diminished to a child's proportions. Its hair, which hung about its neck and down its back, was white as if with age; and yet the face had not a wrinkle on it." "The arms were very long and muscular; the hands the same, as if its hold were of uncommon strength. Its legs and feet, most delicately formed, were, like those upper members, bare. It wore a tunic of the purest white; and round its waist was bound a lustrous belt, the sheen of which was beautiful. It held a branch of fresh green holly in its hand; and, in singular contradiction of that wintry emblem, had its dress trimmed with summer flowers. But the strangest

thing about it was that from the crown of its head there sprang a bright, clear jet of light, by which all this was visible…"

2. **What did the ghost say was its purpose in visiting Scrooge?**
The ghost said its purpose in visiting Scrooge was "Your (Scrooge's) welfare."

3. **What did it first show Scrooge?**
The ghost first showed Scrooge the place where he was bred.

4. **How soon did Scrooge show that he was affected by what he saw?**
Scrooge was soon affected by what he saw. When the boys on the horses went by "he rejoiced beyond all bounds to see them." Then he sobbed knowing he as a child was sitting alone at the schoolhouse.

5. **What stories was the boy, Ebenezer Scrooge, reading? How do you know?**
The stories the boy, Ebenezer, was reading were *The Arabian Nights* or the *Thousand and One Nights,* of which the stories of Ali Babba and Aladdin are a part. The boy also makes reference to Robinson Crusoe. We know this because he names the characters of the stories.

6. **Of what did this vision of himself when a boy make Scrooge think?**
This vision of himself made Scrooge think of the boy caroler. He wishes he would have given him a little something.

7. **How did the vision of the happy Christmas Eve at Mr. Fezziwig's affect Scrooge? Of whom did it make him think?**
During the visit to Mr. Fezziwig's Scrooge "had acted like a man out of his wits. His heart and soul were in the scene, and with his former self." It made him think of his clerk, and he wished he could say a word or two to him.

8. **Which of all the "shadows" made him feel most keenly what he had missed in life?**
Of all the shadows that he saw the one that made him most keenly feel what he had missed in life was seeing his old girlfriend. It affected him so greatly he asked the ghost why he delighted in torturing him and cried, "No more. I don't wish to see it. Show me no more!"

9. **Find in the glossary the meaning of: ferret, visitation, supplication, remonstrated, sweep, apprenticed, aspiration, dowerless, pinioned, brigand.**

10. **Pronounce: opaque, vestige, jocund, Genii, gainsay, corroborated.**

Class Reading

Description of the spirit, page 172, line 20, to page 173, line 13; the Fezziwigs, page 179, line 27, to page 182, line 18; Scrooge and his former sweetheart, page 183, line 20, to page 185, line 17.

STAVE THREE

1. **Describe the Ghost of Christmas Present.**

   The Ghost of Christmas Present "was clothed in one simple deep green robe, or mantle, bordered with white fur. This garment hung so loosely on the figure that its capacious breast was bare… Its feet…were also bare, and on its head it wore no other covering than a holly wreath set here and there with shining icicles. Its dark brown curls were long and free; free as its genial face, its sparkling eye, its open hand, its cheery voice, its unconstrained demeanor, and its joyful air. Girded round its middle was an antique scabbard; but no sword was in it, and the ancient sheath was eaten up with rust."

2. **Describe his throne.**

   His throne was made of "turkeys, geese, game, poultry, brawn, great joints of meat, sucking pigs, long wreaths of sausages, mince pies, plum puddings, barrels of oysters, red-hot chestnuts, cherry-cheeked apples, juicy oranges, luscious pears, immense twelfth-cakes, and seething bowls of punch."

3. **Where did it take Scrooge; where did they stay longest?**

   The Ghost took Scrooge to London on Christmas morning. They went first to Bob Cratchit's house, then to a miner's house, a lighthouse, then to his nephew's house. They stayed the longest at his nephew's house.

4. **Which of these visits did you enjoy most? Why?**

   Answers will vary. Have students use excerpts from the text to support their opinions.

5. **What feelings were awakened in Scrooge by these sights?**

   Scrooge was feeling nostalgia and longing at these sights.

6. **What effect did the spirit have upon those whom it visited?**

   The spirit gave those they visited extra Christmas cheer.

7. **Select passages that made you smile as you read them.**

8. **Give instances which show that the Cratchits were a contented family and pleased with each other.**

   There are many instances which show that the Cratchits were a contented family and pleased with each other. When the two young Cratchits rushed in from outside they were full of cheer. Martha entered and her mom kissed her a "dozen times." All the children helped each other and were happy with the tiny goose. They also, regardless of how horrible Scrooge had treated them, toasted him.

9. **Why did the spirit show Ignorance and Want to Scrooge?**
The spirit showed Scrooge Ignorance and Want so that he would realize what happens to people when others do not give. The spirit told Scrooge that Ignorance and Want belong to all men and Scrooge was responsible for their existence.
10. **Find in the glossary the meaning of: intervention, brawn, twelfth-cakes, intricate, broad-girthed, squab, "bob," threadbare, steeped, copper, cant, baleful, furze, capital, catch.**
11. **Pronounce: manslaughter, predicament, lolling, bedight, bow, elicited, almshouse.**

STAVE FOUR

1. **Describe the last of the spirits.**
The last of the spirits was "shrouded in a deep black garment, which concealed its head, its face, its form, and left nothing of it visible save one outstretched hand."
2. **What did this spirit show Scrooge?**
This spirit showed Scrooge some businessmen and some workers. The businessmen were discussing the death of one of their colleagues and the workers were discussing the death of their employer. At the end of the stave, the spirit shows Scrooge a grave.
3. **What was its "hidden purpose" in having Scrooge overhear the conversation of former business associates.**
The spirit wanted Scrooge to realize the effect he had on his co-workers. They cared not for him and despised his selfishness. Scrooge was to conclude that the dead man was himself.
4. **What was the effect upon Scrooge of seeing people carry away his goods and of listening to the dialogue of Joe, the laundress, the charwoman, and the undertaker's man?**
Scrooge's reaction was one of horror. Scrooge "viewed them with a detestation and disgust which could hardly have been greater, though they had been obscene demons marketing the corpse itself."
5. **What did the visit to Caroline's home and to Bob Cratchit's show Scrooge?**
The visit to Caroline's home and Bob Cratchit's home showed Scrooge that, though sad at his death, their hearts were lighter.
6. **When the spirit took him to the churchyard, why was Scrooge anxious to know whether what he had seen were things that will be or that may be?**
Scrooge at this point was wanting a second chance. He was hoping that what he has seen are things that may be.
7. **Did he receive any answer to his pleading?**

Scrooge did not receive an answer to his pleading.

8. **What promises did he make?**
   Scrooge promises to keep the Christmas spirit. He says, "I will honor Christmas in my heart."
9. **Did Scrooge need the visit of this last spirit? Why?**
   Yes, Scrooge needed the visit of this last spirit to finalize his transformation.
10. **Find in the glossary the meaning of: charwoman, repleted.**
11. **Pronounce: gills, disgorged, brooch, inexorable.**

Class Reading

Thoughts on death, page 219, line 28, to page 220, line 2; in the churchyard, page 225, line 23, to page 226, line 35.

STAVE FIVE

1. **How did Scrooge know he was alive?**
   Scrooge knew he was alive because when he awoke, he touched his bedpost and curtains. Everything in his room was as he remembered. He heard the church bell and opened his window in which golden sunlight streamed into the room.
2. **What tells you that he had really suffered through the night?**
   When Scrooge awoke, the readers know he suffered through the night because he had tears on his cheeks.
3. **How did he express his joy at being alive?**
   He expressed his joy at being alive by laughing, whooping, and dancing.
4. **Who received his first attention?**
   The boy outside the window received his first attention. Scrooge asked him what day it was.
5. **How do you account for the "wonderful happiness" at the nephew's?**
   Those at his nephew's house delighted in Scrooge's presence.
6. **How did Scrooge show that his repentance was real?**
   He showed his repentance by donating money to the poor, giving Bob Cratchit a raise in pay, and keeping the Christmas spirit.
7. **Turn again to the picture on page 96. Why is this picture appropriate in connection with the lesson that Scrooge learned?**
   Sir Galahad lived a life of serving others, without regard for self; after his transformation, so did Scrooge.
8. **What did you learn in "Literature and Life" on pages 17-18 about literature that interprets life? What does this story interpret?**
   True literature is "the expression of the facts of life, or of the

interpretation of life, or of the beauty of life, in language of such enduring charm that men treasure it and will not let it die." "A 'Christmas Carol' interprets the spirit of human brotherhood that makes life worthwhile."

9. Find in the glossary the meaning of: Laocoon, piping, malady.

10. Prounounce: unanimity, feign, borough, abstinence.

Class Reading

The next morning, page 227, line 1, to page 230, line 5; Scrooge and the portly gentleman, page 230, line 15, to page 231, line 6; Scrooge and his nephew, page 231, line 13, to page 232, line 5; Scrooge and Bob Cratchit, page 232, line 6, to page 233, line 8.

Outline for Testing Silent Reading

Read the story through silently at one sitting if possible. For testing your understanding of the story, you may use, as an outline, scenes given in the dramatization on page 237; or, you may make an outline, using the subtitles of the five staves as topics, adding subtopics for each. An interesting social exercise may be made by dividing the class into five groups, and assigning to each group one stave of the story. Each group will prepare an outline and select one member to tell the substance of the stave to the class, following the outline.

Library Reading

"Solomon Crow's Christmas Pockets," "The Freys' Christmas Party," "Duke's Christmas," Stuart (In *Solomon Crow's Christmas Pockets and Other Tales*); *Ten Boys from Dickens and Ten Girls from Dickens,* Sweetser; *Short Plays from Dickens,* Browne; *The Birds' Christmas Carol,* Wiggin.

Magazine Reading

Bring to class, or make a brief report on, the best Christmas story that you have read in a magazine.

Suggestions for Theme Topics

1. Compare the condition of workers in this story with working conditions at the present time.
2. Compare the loyalty of Bob Cratchit to his employer with that of some modern worker of whom you have heard or read.
3. In your study of civics you have learned of laws that your state has enacted for the improvement of working conditions in industry; make a list of these and report upon them to the class.

4. Make a report on Cruikshank's illustrations of Dicken's characters and of Arthur Rackham's illustrations for *A Christmas Carol*, showing the class some of these pictures.

A Suggested Problem

Dickens called this story a "Christmas carol in prose"; compare its message with that of the original Christmas carol "Peace on earth, good will toward men." Why did Dickens divide the story into "staves" instead of chapters? After you read *A Christmas Carol* through silently and have enjoyed the class readings and discussions, you will find pleasure in dramatizing it for a Christmas program. The conversation in the story will furnish you with ideas for dialogue. Use the words of Dickens whenever possible. The descriptions and the story itself offer suggestions for costumes and acting. The scenes indicated below afford a large number of pupils an opportunity to take part; the different scenes may be assigned to groups and worked out independently of each other.

Act I. Scrooge on Christmas Eve.
Scene 1. In Scrooge's countinghouse. A visit from the nephew.
Scene 2. In Scrooge's room. Appearance of Marley's ghost.

Act II. The Spirit of Christmas Past, showing Scrooge's "shadows of the things that have been."
Scene 1. The school of Scooge's childhood.
Scene 2. Christmas at Fezziwig's.

Act III. The Spirit of Christmas Present, showing Scrooge the universal happiness at Christmas time.
Scene 1. Christmas at Bob Cratchit's.
Scene 2. Christmas at the nephew's.

Act IV. The Spirit of Christmas Yet to Come, showing Scrooge the horrors atttending the death of an unloved man.
Scene 1. In Joe's shop.
Scene 2. In the churchyard.

Act V. Scrooge awakes transformed on Christmas morning.
Scene 1. In his room giving orders for Christmas cheer.
Scene 2. At his newphew's.
Scene 3. Next morning at the countinghouse.

Extended Activities:

1. Have students make a mobile. For the hanging items, have students either illustrate each of the five staves or find a symbol for each of the five staves.

2. Have students create a chart or venn diagram comparing and/or contrasting Scrooge's character at the beginning of the story with his character at the end of the story. Explain to students that characters who change are called dynamic. Characters who do not change are considered static. Have students identify those characters in the story who are static.

3. One of the elements that characterizes Dicken's work is his commentaries on poverty. Have students watch a cartoon version of the story. Discuss with students how the elimination of or downplaying of poverty in the story changes the way the viewer/reader reacts to Scrooge.

NAME______________________________CLASS__________DATE____

A CHRISTMAS CAROL, P. 151

1. Make a mobile. For the hanging items, either illustrate each of the five staves or find a symbol for each of the five staves.

2. Create a chart or venn diagram comparing and/or contrasting Scrooge's character at the beginning of the story with his character at the end of the story. Identify those characters in the story who are static.

A Midsummer Night's Dream, p. 238

Discussion

1. **Make a list of the characters mentioned in the story.**
   Egeus—the father of Hermia
   Hermia—a maiden in love with Lysander
   Lysander—a man in love with Hermia
   Helena—Hermia's best friend and a maiden in love with Demetrius
   Demetrius—a man promised to Hermia; In the end he loves Helena
   Theseus—the reigning duke of Athens
   Oberon—the king of the fairies
   Titania—the queen of the fairies
   Puck—Oberon's favorite counselor, Puck is a mischievous fairie.
2. **Which are the principal characters?**
   The main characters are Hermia, Lysander, Helena, Demetrius, Oberon, and Puck.
3. **What complaint did Hermia's father make to the duke? What was the duke's decision?**
   Egeus complains that Hermia will not marry Demetrius. According to law the duke can put Hermia to death for disobeying her father's wishes regarding marriage. Hermia is given four days to change her mind.
4. **What plan for the safety of Hermia and himself did Lysander make? To whom was this plan told?**
   Lysander decides that they should escape to his aunt's house. Hermia tells their plan to Helena who in turn tells Demetrius.
5. **Tell who Oberon, Titania, and Puck are.**
   Oberon is the king of the fairies, Titania is the queen of the fairies, and Puck is Oberon's "chief favorite and counselor."
6. **What flower did Oberon send Puck to find? What magic was in it?**
   Oberon sent Puck to find the purple "love-in-idleness" flower. The flower, when put in someone's eyes, would make that person love the first thing they see after waking.
7. **What did Oberon tell Puck to do with the juice of the flower?**
   Oberon tells Puck to squeeze out the juice so he can use it on his queen.
8. **Who is the Athenian youth that Oberon asks Puck to find?**
   Oberon told Puck to put the juice of the flower into the young Athenian's eyes. Oberon is referring to Demetrius. Oberon tells Puck he can recognize the youth by his Athenian clothes.

9. **Who is the youth that Puck finds?**
   Puck finds Lysander rather than Demetrius.
10. **What happens when Lysander awakes?**
    Lysander wakes and falls in love with Helena.
11. **What does Oberon do with the juice of the flower? Account for the presence in the woods of Helena and Demetrius.**
    Oberon puts the juice of the flower in his queen's eyes. She falls in love with a clown with an ass's head. Helena and Demetrius are in the woods because Demetrius is following Hermia and Helena is following Demetrius.
12. **By what means did Oberon try to gain possession of the boy? How did he succeed?**
    By tricking Titania into loving the clown, she becomes embarrassed and gives in to Oberon's request to make the boy his page.
13. **How did Puck make amends for his mistake?**
    Puck, to make amends, puts the juice of another flower in Lysander's eyes so he will again love Hermia and allow Demetrius to continue loving Helena.
14. **What did Lysander and Hermia say about "the adventures of the night"?**
    Lysander and Hermia said that during the night they must have been "dreaming the same bewildering dream."
15. **What did Egeus consent that Demetrius should do?**
    Egeus consented that Demetrius should marry Helena and that Hermia was free to marry Lysander.
16. **To whom were the four lovers indebted for their peace and happiness?**
    The four lovers were indebted to Puck for their peace and happiness.
17. **Find in the glossary the meaning of: refractory, forsworn, swain, potent, enamored, amiable, antidote, pretensions, nuptials.**
18. **Pronounce: revels, courtier, dexterously, thyme, hazarding, counterfeit, dotage.**

Outline for Testing Silent Reading

Make an outline to guide you in telling the story.

Library Reading

Other stories in *Tales from Shakespeare,* Lamb.

Extended Activities:

1. Have students create a character relationship map. A relationship

map is a visual way for students to remember characters and their role in the story. An example is given.

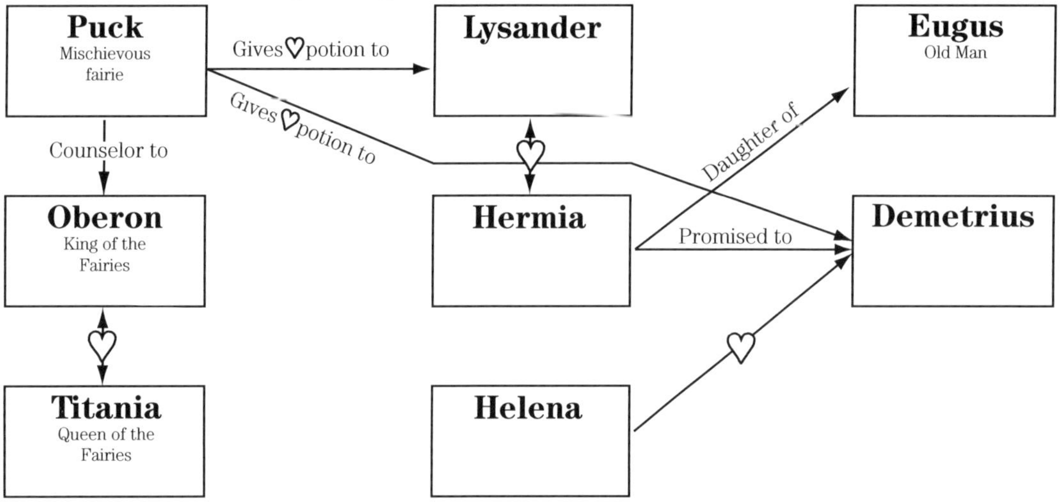

2. Using pictures, have students create a character map of any of the characters. Character maps help students analyze each character individually. Drawing pictures helps visual learners. These organizers can be simple or complex. The example given is just a start to what a character map could look like. More can be added.

3. After character maps have been drawn and discussed, have students choose one character and select a popular song that best describes that character. Have students either present orally or write their reasoning for their song selection.

4. Have students write an essay discussing the ethics of Puck and Oberon's decision to keep the juice of the purple flower in Demetrius's eyes. How would students feel if they were Helena and found out that Demetrius loved them because of a potion?

NAME______________________________**CLASS**__________**DATE**_____

A MIDSUMMER NIGHT'S DREAM, P. 238

1. **Create a relationship map. A relationship map is a visual way to remember characters and their role in the story.**

2. Using pictures, create a character map of any of the characters. Character maps help you analyze each character individually.

3. After character maps have been drawn and discussed, choose one character and select a popular song that best describes that character. Present your reasoning for your song selection.

4. Write an essay discussing the ethics of Puck and Oberon's decision to keep the juice of the purple flower in Demetrius's eyes. How would you feel if you were Helena and found out that Demetrius loved you because of a potion?

Name________________________ **Class**__________ **Date**______

Story	***Find in the glossary the meaning of:***
Reader p. 99	**foal**____________________
	sagacious____________________
	depopulated____________________
	bizarre____________________
	perforce____________________
	grotesque____________________
	decorum____________________
	habiliments____________________
	tangible____________________
Reader p. 109	**surcease**____________________
	beguiling____________________
	craven____________________
	divining____________________
	censer____________________
	nepenthe____________________
Reader p. 118	**trainband**____________________
	calendar____________________
	agog____________________
	trice____________________
	gambol____________________
	guise____________________
	bootless____________________
	posting____________________
	amain____________________
Reader p. 128	**plaiting**____________________
	harry____________________
	casement____________________
	looping____________________
	priming____________________
Reader p. 133	**border**____________________
	brake____________________
	measure____________________
	bar____________________
	galliard____________________
	bonnet____________________
	croup____________________
	scar____________________
Reader p. 135	**fourscore**____________________
	livery____________________

housings____________________
verge____________________

Reader p. 139

abreast____________________

slacker____________________

butting____________________

bluff____________________

askance____________________

peer____________________

burgess____________________

Reader p. 142

prone____________________

oppressive____________________

flag-bird____________________

van____________________

Reader p. 144

lissome____________________

brace____________________

aboard____________________

scuttled____________________

salts____________________

Reader p. 146

gargoyle____________________

linnet____________________

poilu____________________

malheureax____________________

Reader p. 151

stave____________________

‘Change____________________

palpable____________________

Bedlam____________________

Poor Law____________________

Saint Dunstan____________________

corporation____________________

Belshazzasr____________________

ward____________________

ferret____________________

visitation____________________

supplication____________________

remonstrated____________________

sweep____________________

apprenticed____________________

aspiration____________________

dowerless____________________

pinioned____________________

brigand____________________

intervention____________________

brawn____________________

twelfth-cakes____________________
intricate____________________
broad-girthed____________________
squab
"bob"____________________
threadbare____________________
steeped____________________
copper____________________
cant____________________
baleful____________________
furze____________________
capital____________________
catch____________________
charwoman____________________
repleted____________________
Laocoon____________________
piping____________________
malady____________________
Reader p. 238 **refractory**____________________
forsworn____________________
swain____________________
potent____________________
enamored____________________
amiable____________________
antidote____________________
pretensions____________________
nuptials____________________

Pronounce:
eccentric, august, courtiers, ballet-dancer, suite, disconcert, fete, piquancy, robust, illimitable, obeisance, decorum, placid, ominous, respite, tedious, comely, moor, breeches, rapier, ostler, Lochinvar, dauntless, gallant, Roushan, khan, chasm, forehead, Ghent, Aix, pique, Fleurette, ironmongery, simile, homage, Parliament, inexplicable, opaque, vestige, jocund, Genii, gainsay, corroborated, manslaughter, predicament, lolling, bedight, bow, elicited, almshouse, gills, disgorged, brooch, inexorable, unanimity, feign, borough, abstinence, revels, courtier, dexterously, thyme, hazarding, counterfeit, dotage.

Part III: The Great American Experiment

In This Section—

Objectives—

By completing "Part III," the following objectives will be met.

1. The student will use effective reading strategies to construct meaning and identify the purpose of a text including:
    a. using illustrations
    b. defining unfamiliar words
    c. retelling and summarizing
2. The student will determine the main idea or essential message and identify relevant supporting details and facts of a text.
3. The student will read and organize facts from the text and other sources to make a report, outline, and perform an authentic task.
4. The student will prepare for writing by focusing on the topic and organizing supporting details in a logical sequence.
5. The student will draft and revise writing.
6. The student will produce final documents that have been edited for correct spelling, punctuation, and grammar.
7. The student will write for a variety of audiences and purposes.
8. The student will use reference materials (dictionaries, encyclopedias, maps, charts, and the Internet).
9. The student will identify and understand similarities and differences among the characters, settings, and events presented in various texts.
10. The student will identify the author's purpose and point of view.
11. The student will respond critically to fiction, nonfiction, and poetry.
12. The student will respond to a text by explaining how the motives of the characters or events compare with those in his or her own life.
13. The student will use context clues to understand words and ideas.
14. The student will understand the qualities necessary for people to become good citizens and apply those qualities to his or her personal life.
15. The student will understand the qualities necessary to develop good character and apply those qualities to his or her personal life.

The Eternal Spirit of Freedom

Spartacus to the Gladiators, p. 259

1. **Who was Spartacus, and what was the occasion of his speech?**

   If students will read the "Biographical and Historical Notes," they will find that Spartacus "was a Thracian who served in the Roman army. Having deserted, he was taken prisoner, sold as a slave, and trained as a gladiator" in a Roman city. Eventually he escaped, gathering around him many slaves and gladiators who attempted to fight their way back to their homes. However, they were overtaken, and Spartacus was killed, along with six thousand of his followers. He gave this speech after a triumphant day in the arena fighting lions.

2. **To whom was he talking?**

   He was talking to his fellow gladiators.

3. **Of what battles did his grandsire tell one evening? How did these tales of battle affect the young Spartacus?**

   The grandsire told of the battles "of Marathon and Leuctra, and how, in ancient times, a little band of Spartans, in a defile in the mountains, withstood a whole army." The tales affected him so deeply that his "cheeks burned," and his mother had to tear him from the knees of the grandsire.

4. **In *The Elson Readers, Book Seven,* you read of "a little band of Spartans" at Thermopylae; can you tell what these brave Spartans did for the freedom of their people?**

   The Spartans, with a small army of three hundred, defended their country to the death against the powerful Persians. After breaking their javelins, they resorted to fighting with swords and finally their hands and teeth before they were overpowered and slain. Their bravery and obedience were honored with the inscription: "Stranger, go tell the Lacedaemonians (Spartans) that we lie here, obedient to their commands."

5. **Tell the story of Spartacus and his boyhood friend whom he killed.**

   Spartacus compared his early life to a quiet brook by which he played. He learned to trim vines, take care of the sheep, and play the flute. He and his boyhood friend, a neighbor boy, led their flocks to the same grazing fields and shared their simple meals.

When the Romans landed on his shores, they killed his parents. He eventually was taken a prisoner and trained as a gladiator. One day in the arena he killed a man, and when he removed the man's helmet he discovered it was his boyhood friend who recognized Spartacus, smiled at him, gasped, and died; he wore "the same sweet smile that I had marked upon his face when, in adventurous boyhood, we scaled some lofty cliff to pluck the first ripe grapes and bear them home in childish triumph."

6. **What appeal does Spartacus make to his comrades in the last paragraph?**

He appeals to his comrades to fight the enemy as his countrymen did at Thermopylae. "If ye are brutes, then stand here like fat oxen waiting for the butcher's knife; if ye are men, follow me! Strike down yon sentinel, and gain the mountain passes, and there do bloody work as did your sires at old Thermopylae!"

7. **Find a statement in the "Introduction" on page 256 that is particularly appropriate to the thought of this selection.**

"But through all the centuries there have come moments, now in one part of the world and now in another, that have shown how firmly imbedded in the human heart is the conviction that men ought to be free, free to shape their lives according to their desires and their abilities and not according to the command of emperor or king."

8. **Find in the glossary the meaning of: zephyr, arena, belie, Jupiter, venerable, Adonis.**
9. **Pronounce: recesses, sinews.**

THE ISLES OF GREECE, P. 263

1. **What object do you think Byron hoped to gain by bringing the glories of the past so vividly before the modern Greek?**
Perhaps he hoped to inspire in them a respect for "the remnant of our Spartan dead" who died for freedom's sake.
2. **This is an English poet's idea of how a Greek poet might have sung; what line in the first stanza expresses a thought that a Greek poet would hardly admit?**
The poet suggests that the glory of the isles of Greece has set and only the god of the sun, Phoebus, remains.
3. **What do the names Marathon, Salamis, Thermopylae suggest?**
Students will read in the "Historical Note" that at Marathon, "the Greeks defeated a vast Persian army; at Thermoplylae, under Leonidas, a little band of three hundred Spartans gave their lives in defense of a mountain pass; and at Salamis the Greek navy defeated a much larger fleet of the invaders." "Thus the Greeks in ancient times won glory."
5. **Wherein does the poet say the hope of modern Greece lies?**
The poet says "In native swords and native ranks the only hope of courage dwells."
6. **What event in Byron's life makes you know he felt the position of Greece keenly? (It is interesting to note that in December 1823 Daniel Webster introduced a resolution in Congress which is believed to be the first official expression favorable to the independence of Greece uttered by any government of Christendom.)**
Students will read in his biography that Byron was passionate about freedom and, in 1820, went to the aid of the Greeks in their quest for freedom. However, he died "before he had an opportunity to engage in battle."
7. **What did you read in the "Introduction" on page 256 about "ambitious men" who try to keep freedom down? Who were oppressing Greece at the time this poem was written?**
"There have always been ambitious men who have wished to insure their own power by keeping the masses of their followers in subjection. Often they have succeeded." Greece was revolting against Turkey when this poem was written.
8. **What do you know about Greece's part in World War One that tells you how that country regards freedom at the present time?**

Greece fought on the side of the Allies in World War One. They have long stood for individual freedom and justice basic to democracy.

9. **How does a poem such as this aid in the growth of the spirit of freedom?**

The poem inspires freedom for all people, reminding the reader of the Greeks' earliest battles for freedom to the present cry: "Place me on Sunium's marbles steep, where nothing save the waves and I may hear our mutual murmurs sweep."

10. **The music of the poem makes it a pleasure to read it aloud; notice how naturally the emphasis of the rhythm accents the important words.**
11. **Find in the glossary the meaning of: voiceless, lay, degenerate, fettered.**
12. **Pronounce: dearth, bacchanal.**

Class Reading

Bring to class and read "Marco Bozzaris," Halleck. (Marco Bozzaris, the leader of the Greek Revolution, was killed August 20, 1823, in an attack upon the Turks near Missolonghi. His last words were: "To die for liberty is a pleasure, not a pain.")

The poem, "Marco Bozzaris," can be found on the Internet at http://www.bartleby.com/102/8.html

Suggestions for Theme Topics

(Two-Minute talks.)

1. The Battle of Salamis.
2. Miltiades and the Battle of Marathon.
3. The Pass of Thermopylae.

(Use encyclopedias and other library sources; see "Leonidas, the Spartan" in *The Elson Readers, Book Seven.*)

Paul Revere's Ride, p. 267

1. **Read the poem through thoughtfully and be able to tell the story from this outline:**

(a) Understanding as to signals between Paul Revere and his friend;

Paul Revere told his friend that if the British marched that night, April 18, 1775, the friend was to hang a lantern in the belfry of the North Church tower—one lantern if the British came by land and two lanterns if they came by sea. Paul Revere would be on the opposite shore "Ready to ride and spread the alarm to every Middlesex village and farm."

(b) The friend in Boston;

While Paul Revere rowed to the opposite shore, the friend wandered through the streets and alleys, watching for signs of troop movements; he finally heard "The muster of men at the barrack door, the sound of arms, and the tramp of feet, and the measured tread of the grenadiers marching down to their boats on the shore." Climbing to the belfry chamber, he watched as the British troops made their way "On the rising tide." He hung two lanterns to indicate the British were coming by sea.

(c) Paul Revere on the Charlestown side of the river;

"Impatient to mount and ride, booted and spurred, with a heavy tread" Paul Revere paced the opposite shore, watching the belfry tower. At last he saw a speck of light in the tower, leaped to his saddle and turned to see the second lantern burn before he sped into the night with his warning.

(d) The ride.

Paul Revere left the shore and rode through the night to the villagers in Medford, Lexington, and Concord, "A voice in the dark, a knock at the door and a word that shall echo forevermore!" With his warning he roused the sleeping farmers who gave the British "ball for ball from behind each fence and barnyard wall, chasing the redcoats down the lane."

2. **What was Paul Revere's message?**

The poem does not explicitly state his words, only that the villagers heard "a cry of defiance, and not of fear, a voice in the darkness, a knock at the door, and a word that shall echo forevermore." History indicates his words were, "The regulars are out!"

3. **Find the lines that describe the churchyard.**

Stanza 5: "Beneath, in the churchyard, lay the dead in their night encampment on the hill, wrapped in silence so deep and still that he could hear, like sentinel's tread, the watchful night-wind as it went creeping along from tent to tent and seeming to whisper, "All is well!"

4. **How does Longfellow make you feel the hurry of the rider?**
Longfellow mentions the "hurry of hoofs" and "a spark struck out by a steed flying fearless and fleet." In addition, the rhythm of the poem hints at the rapid clatter of hooves striking the earth.
5. **What to you is the most expressive line in the poem?**
Answers will vary.
6. **Read again what is said on page 20 about the value of supplementing history books with literature. How is the story "in the books you have read" of the Battle of Lexington enriched by the story in the poem?**
History books, geography books, and encyclopedias provide facts, "but all through life you will find pleasure and increased understanding if you will supplement books of this latter kind by the literature of great authors who have recorded their observation of events and peoples in language of such enduring charm that men treasure it and will not let it die." The Battle of Lexington as told from a factual or historical point of view may not stir the reader's imagination or emotions as does the story in this poem.
7. **How did Longfellow's prophecy at the end of the poem apply to our country in the World Wars?**
Longfellow's prophecy suggests that Revere's words "shall echo forevermore!" They were words that inspired people to rise and fight for freedom, a call that our country answered in the World Wars.
8. **What statement in the first paragraph of the "Introduction" on page 255 shows you the motive that caused Longfellow to write this poem?**
"These impulses to render patriotic service, this ambition to make your life count—all take you out of your usual self and awaken the best traits of your character."
9. **Draw a map showing the relative positions of Boston, Charlestown, Medford, Lexington, Concord.**
See map on next page.
10. **Suggest a series of pictures that would tell the story of this famous historic ride; where in your series would you place the picture on page 259?**
11. **Find in the glossary the meaning of: grenadier, impetuous, spectral, tranquil, emerge.**
12. **Pronounce: barrack, alder.**

Class Reading

Bring to class and read "The Reveille," Harte; "A Troop of the Guard," Hagedorn (in *The Home Book of Verse*).

Bret Harte's complete works including "The Reveille," can be found on the Internet at various locations. One possibility is http://www.underthesun.cc/Classics/Harte/poetical

Note: *The Home Book of Verse* contains American and English poems from 1580-1920. It is no longer in print but may be available used from various booksellers or copies may be found occasionally at libraries.

Extended Activity:

See question 10. Assign stanzas to various students. Have the students illustrate their stanza and choose one line from their stanza to serve as a caption. When completed have the students organize their stanzas using the illustrations and captions to complete a picture map of the poem.

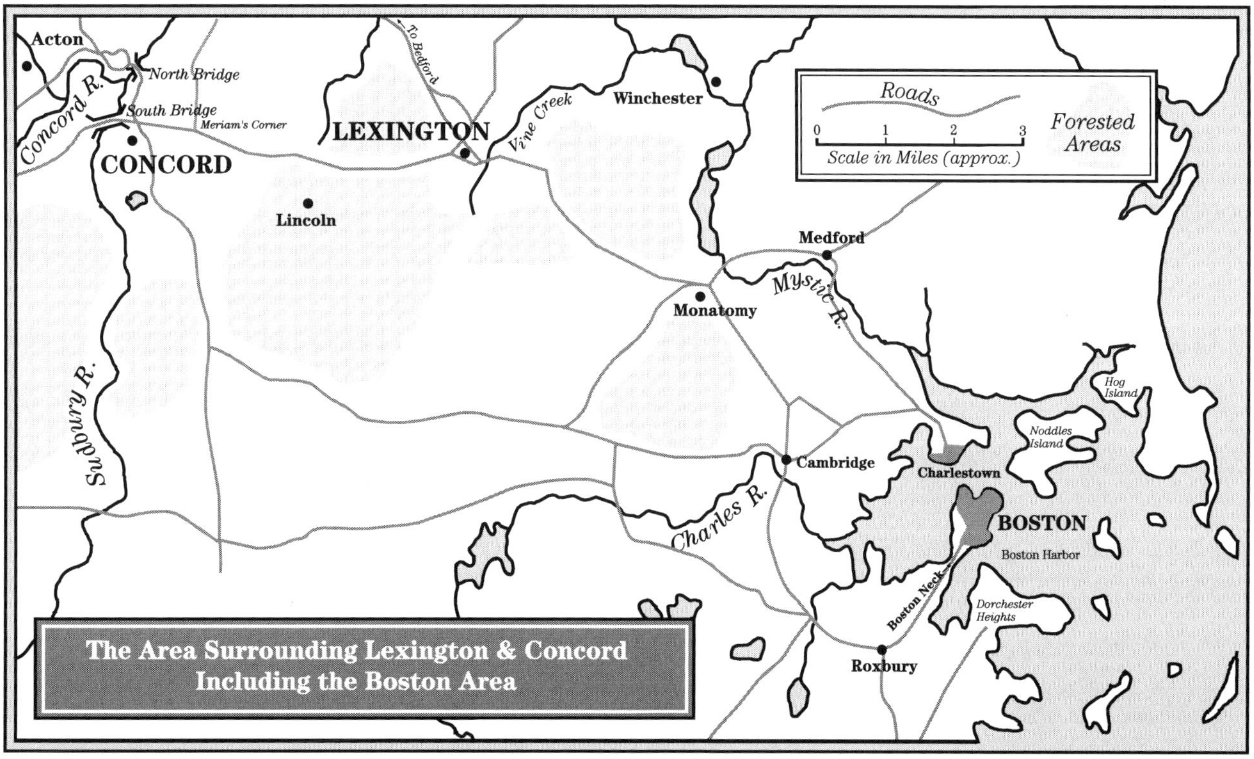

The Area Surrounding Lexington & Concord Including the Boston Area

NAME________________________________**CLASS**____________**DATE**____

PAUL REVERE'S RIDE, P. 267

Illustrate a stanza and choose one line from your stanza to serve as a caption.

Concord Hymn, p. 272

1. **In what sense was the shot "heard round the world"?**
   The shot "heard round the world" was the shot that eventually led to America's freedom from Great Britain, and which created a nation whose influence is felt around the world,and whose belief in freedom was soon to echo throughout much of the Western world as country after country threw off the chains of their governments.
2. **What did this battle mean to the world?**
   From this battle came the development of America as an independent nation, a leader among nations today.
3. **For what purpose does the poet say this "votive stone" is set?**
   The glossary defines a "votive stone" as "a monument sacred to them." The stone was set "That memory may their deed redeem, when, like our sires, our sons are gone."
4. **How does this poem help memory "to redeem the deed"?**
   It reminds the reader of the "foe," and the "conqueror" who died for our freedom.
5. **In what different ways does "memory redeem the deeds" of the World War heroes?**
   Encourage students to explore ways in which memory of past deeds and heroes encourages us to be a better people and nation today.
6. **Why do we observe Memorial Day?**
   Memorial Day was established to honor those who gave their lives in all wars in which Americans fought.
7. **In the prayer in the last stanza the poet tells us to whom the shaft is raised; which of these is greater, the "freemen" or the "Spirit"?**
   The Spirit is greater since it was the Spirit "that made those freemen dare to die and leave their children free."
8. **Find in the glossary the meaning of: arched, embattled, votive.**

Class Reading

Bring to class and read some newspaper item which shows that the spirit of freedom still lives.

I Have A Rendezvous With Death, p. 273

1. **Notice how the beautiful descriptions of nature, contrasted with the grim determination to keep the rendezvous, emphasize the joy of life and of living, and make the keeping of the pledge the more heroic; find lines that bring out sharply this contrast.**

   Line 3: "When Spring comes back with rustling shade and apple blossoms fill the air—I have a rendezvous with Death when Spring brings back blue days and fair." Line 11: "I have a rendezvous with Death on some scarred slope of battered hill when Spring comes round again this year, and the first meadow—flowers appear." Page 274, line 2: "But I've a rendezvous with Death at midnight in some flaming town, when Spring trips north again this year."

2. **This poem expresses a young man's generous consecration of himself to death while love of life is keen; which lines bring out this thought most beautifully?**

   Answers will vary.

3. **What other soldier poets have you learned to know in this book? Do you know of any others?**

   Lord Byron who wrote "The Isles of Greece" was a soldier poet, as was Joyce Kilmer who wrote "Rouge Bouquet."

4. **How does this poem show that the spirit of liberty was the same in the World Wars as it was in the days of Paul Revere?**

   The soldiers who fought in those wars did "not fail that rendezvous."

5. **Pronounce: rendezvous.**

Library Reading

Other poems by the same author (in *Poems*).

ROUGE BOUQUET, P. 275

1. **Where did these fighting men meet death?**
   They met their death in "the wood they call the Rouge Bouquet."
2. **How does the refrain resemble "taps"?**
   The refrain is played by "bugle-notes that softly say: 'Farewell! Farewell! Comrades true, born anew, peace to you! Your souls shall be where the heroes are; And your memory shine like the morning star. Brave and dear, shield us here. Farewell!'" Those words echo the sentiments of "taps" played at memorial services for anyone in America buried with military honors.
3. **Notice how painstakingly the poet worked out exactly the same rhyming scheme in the two stanzas; what interesting fact do you note in the twenty-second line of each stanza?**
   These two stanzas follow this rhyme scheme: AABBCDCDEEEFG GFHIHIJJKLLMMJ In the twenty-second line, K, the line stands alone with no other end rhyming lines; that line contains internal rhyme words that rhyme within the line rather than at the ends of lines. Each third syllable within the line rhymes.
4. **What part of "taps" do these lines imitate?**
   "Taps" is played with a bugle or trumpet calling "Put out the lights. Go to sleep." In "Rouge Bouquet" a bugle also calls, "Go to sleep! Go to sleep!" Encourage students to research the history of "taps." Information on the Internet can be found at http://www.mdw.army.mil/FS-H06.HTM
5. **Why does the poet say "There is no worthier grave"?**
   Dying for one's country is considered the worthiest "grave."
6. **Notice that this group of selections is called "The Eternal Spirit of Freedom"; what famous struggles for liberty are mentioned?**
   These selections were written to remember the struggles of Spartacus against the Romans, Greeks against Turks, Americans against Great Britain, and Americans and French in the World War.
7. **Find in the glossary the meaning of: meter, aureole, Gael.**
8. **Pronounce: Rouge Bouquet, stalwart.**

Class Reading

Bring to class and read "Main Street"; "Roofs"; "The Snowman in the Yard"; "Trees"; "To A Blackbird and His Mate Who Died in the Spring"; "Dave Lilly"; Joyce Kilmer (in *Poems, Essay, and Letters, Vol. 1*). *The Bookman,* October, 1918, has a portrait of

Joyce Kilmer; try to get a copy to show your classmates.

Joyce Kilmer's poems can be found at: http://www.everypoet.com/archive/poetry/Joyce_Kilmer.

A Suggested Problem

In the "Introduction" on page 256 you read that the selections in this group "are only a few out of many such stories and poems that express this eternal spirit of freedom." Be prepared to contribute to a program of additional selections found in outside reading.

Extended Activity:

1. Poets use a variety of rhyme schemes when writing their poems. In the poem "Rouge Bouquet" the students were asked to note the poet's painstaking rhyme scheme. (See question 3.) Have them choose another poem from any of these selections and identify the rhyme scheme to show the variety of schemes poets use to design their poems.

"The Isles of Greece": ABABCC DEDEFF, etc.

"Paul Revere's Ride": AABBA CDCDEEFFFGGHHIIIJJ. Challenge students to identify the rhyme scheme of all his stanzas. His pattern is not consistent from stanza to stanza.

"Concord Hymn": ABAB CDCD EFEF GHGH

"I Have A Rendezvous With Death": ABBCAC DDAEAEFF GHGAFAHFII

2. The selections in "The Eternal Spirit of Freedom" all refer to the themes of patriotism and freedom shown by citizens in various countries and centuries. After reading these selections, have students brainstorm on the importance of freedom and patriotism, how they were shown in these stories, and how they are expressed today. The students should then create an essay expressing what freedom and patriotism mean to them and how they can appropriately express those concepts today. The essay should be edited for correct grammar and punctuation and rewritten in a final copy.

NAME______________________________CLASS__________DATE____

ROUGE BOUQUET, P. 275

1. Poets use a variety of rhyme schemes when writing their poems. In the poem "Rouge Bouquet" you were asked to note the poet's painstaking rhyme scheme. Choose another poem from any of these selections and identify the rhyme scheme to show the variety of schemes poets use to design their poems.

   Title________________________

   Rhyme Scheme____

2. The selections in "The Eternal Spirit of Freedom" all refer to the themes of patriotism and freedom shown by citizens in various countries and centuries. After reading these selections, brainstorm on the importance of freedom and patriotism, how they were shown in these stories, and how they are expressed today. Then create an essay expressing what freedom and patriotism mean to you and how you can appropriately express those concepts today. Use correct grammar and punctuation.

America's Experiment in Free Government

Supposed Speech of John Adams, p. 278

1. **What was the vote under discussion at the time of this supposed speech?**
   Delegates to the Continental Congress were divided in their sentiments regarding the wisdom of declaring independence from England. In this "supposed speech," Adams, a strong proponent for independence, summed up the discussion: "The injustice of England has driven us to arms; and, blinded to her own interest, she has obstinately persisted, till independence is now within our grasp. We have but to reach forth to it, and it is ours. Why, then, should we defer the declaration."
2. **Why, in the opinion of the speaker, must the colonists carry on the war?**
   If the colonists were to give up the war, they, in essence, "submit and consent that we shall be ground to powder, and our country and its rights trodden down in the dust. I know we do not mean to submit. We never shall submit! The war, then, must go on; we must fight it through. And if the war must go on, why put off the declaration of independence?"
3. **What advantages does he say they will gain by the Declaration of Independence?**
   "That measure will strengthen us. It will give us character abroad. Nations will then treat with us, which they never can do while we acknowledge ourselves subjects in arms against our sovereign."
4. **Whom does he address as "Sir"?**
   A specific person is not identified in the speech; however, the reader can assume that he is addressing the president of the Continental Congress.
5. **What plan does he suggest for making the declaration known to the people?**
   "Read this declaration at the head of the army...Publish it from the pulpit...Send it to the public halls."
6. **What results does he expect will come from this action?**
   "Every sword will be drawn, and the solemn vow uttered to maintain it or perish on the bed of honor...religion will approve it, and the love of religious liberty will cling around it, resolved to stand with it, or fall with it....the very walls will cry out in its support."

7. Show that the speaker has considered the possible consequences of signing the declaration.

"You and I, indeed, may rue it. We may not live to see the time this declaration shall be made good. We may die; die colonists; die slaves; die, it may be, ignominiously, and on the scaffold. Be it so; be it so."

8. What prophecy does he make concerning the day on which the declaration was signed? Has this prophecy been fulfilled?

"Through the thick gloom of the present I see the brightness of the future, as the sun in heaven. We shall make this a glorious, an immortal day. When we are in our graves, our children will honor it. They will celebrate it with thanksgiving, with festivity, with bonfires, and illuminations. On its annual return they will shed tears, copious tears, gushing tears; not of subjection, and slavery, not of agony and distress, but of exaltation, of gratitude, and of joy." Encourage students to discuss how this prophecy has been fulfilled in our July fourth celebrations that honor Independence Day.

9. Point out lines in the speech that seem to you to be the most stirring.

Answers will vary.

10. The signing of the Declaration of Independence was the first great step in America's experiment in free government; why was it of great moment?

The signers of the Declaration of Independence were steering through uncharted waters. They had no models, only strong resolve to succeed. Its success depended on their courage, foresight, and commitment; indeed, in the closing words of the Declaration, the signers vowed, "And for the support of this Declaration, with a firm reliance on the protection of divine Providence, we mutually pledge to each other our Lives, our Fortunes, and our sacred Honor."

11. Find in the glossary the meaning of: eradicated, ignominiously, copious.

Extended Activity:

1. Differing views on independence from England sparked this supposed speech. Encourage students to research what hesitations those opposing independence held and what reasons the proponents of independence held. Set up a mock debate for students to argue both sides of the independence issue.

2. As noted in the closing words of the Declaration of Independence,

many of the signers indeed lost their lives, fortunes, and honor. Have students research the lives of several of the signers of the document to learn what their commitment cost them.

NAME________________________________CLASS__________DATE____

SUPPOSED SPEECH OF JOHN ADAMS, P. 278

1. Differing views on independence from England sparked this supposed speech. Research what hesitations those opposing independence held and what reasons the proponents of independence held. Set up a mock debate to argue both sides of the independence issue.
2. As noted in the closing words of the Declaration of Independence, many of the signers indeed lost their lives, fortunes, and honor. Research the lives of several of the signers of the document to learn what their commitment cost them.

Liberty and Union, p. 281

1. **Picture to yourself our country in Washington's time with reference to thc extent of territory, the cities, and the means of transportation and communication; why is our unity of government even more remarkable today than it was in 1797?**

America has grown incredibly in our territory, population, system of transportation, and communication. From horse-drawn carriages to instant messaging, from citizens of largely English descent to citizens from every continent on earth, our system of government as designed by our founding fathers, has withstood the astronomical changes, providing us a stable foundation on which to build the United States.

2. **What means of changing the Constitution have we?**

According to Washington, "The basis of our political systems is the right of the people to make and to alter their Constitution of Government"; we alter the Constitution by making amendments to it.

3. **What changes have been made by amendments?**

Encourage students to research the twenty-seven amendments to the Constitution to discover the changes that have been made. Various Internet sites are available including: http:/www.house.gov/Constitution/Amend.html

4. **In line 10, page 282, Washington warns against "external" enemies. What reason is mentioned in the "Introduction" on page 257 for the hostility of some European governments?**

"The older governments of Europe thought such an experiment (that men should govern themselves) would surely fail. They wanted it to fail, for with its success no throne would be secure."

5. **In the "Introduction" on page 258 you read a definition of the American idea of free government. What advice on page 283 shows that Washington had the same view of a successful democracy?**

The American idea of free government is "the idea of a government controlled by all the people, because they realized that unrestrained liberty is anarchy, and that free government means 'a liberty connected with order.'" Washington said, "The very idea of the power and the right of the people to establish government presupposes the duty of every individual to obey the established government."

6. **What are the "pillars of human happiness" according to Washington?**

   "Of all the dispositions and habits which lead to political prosperity, religion and morality are indispensable supports. In vain would that man claim the tribute of patriotism, who should labor to subvert these great pillars of human happiness, these firmest props of the duties of men and citizens."

7. **Why did Washington think education so necessary in a democracy?**

   "Promote, then, as an object of primary importance institutions for the general diffusion of knowledge. In proportion as the structure of a government gives force to public opinion, it is essential that public opinion should be enlightened."

8. **How did our course in World War One prove that we were guided "by an excellent justice"?**

   As President of the United States, Woodrow Wilson engaged America in the World War "to make the world safe for democracy." In defeating Germany, the Allies proved that they were guided "by an excellent justice."

9. **In "Literature and Life" on page 18 you read that the "second joy of reading will give you the power to ripen your judgment by the accumulated wisdom left as an inheritance by the world's greatest minds." What wise advice have you gained from this selection?**

   Answers will vary.

10. **Find in the glossary the meaning of: apprise, covertly, insidiously, palladium, alienate, local, efficacious, acquiescence, maxim, hypothesis, usurpation, subvert, felicity, impostures.**
11. **Pronounce: address, artifice, essay, precedent, inveterate, amicable, solicitude.**

Suggestions for Theme Topics

1. The relations of the United States to Cuba.
2. Our relations to Puerto Rico.
3. Our relations to Hawaii.
4. Our relations to the Philippines.

Extended Activity:

Question three asked the students to learn what changes have been made by amendments. After they have identified the twenty-seven amendments, have them choose one amendment that most directly affects their lives. In a short essay have them describe the concerns that may have given rise to that specific amendment and how it affects them today.

NAME______________________________CLASS__________DATE____

LIBERTY AND UNION, P. 281

Question three asked you to learn what changes have been made by amendments. After you have identified the twenty-seven amendments, choose one amendment that most directly affects your life. In a short essay describe the concerns that may have given rise to that specific amendment and how it affects you today.

The American Experiment, p. 286

1. **This selection is taken from an address, "The Character of Washington," delivered at a public dinner in Washington on February 22, 1832, the centennial of George Washington's birthday; why was a discussion of the "American experiment" especially appropriate on such an occasion?**

   As general of the Revolutionary War that won freedom from British rule, first president of the United States, and president of the Constitutional Convention responsible for creating the Constitution, Washington was truly one of America's greatest statesmen and a chief contributor to the "American experiment." Honoring him in this way was appropriate.

2. **How does Daniel Webster in the first paragraph define this experiment?**

   He defines the American experiment as "A government established, without a throne, without an aristocracy, without castes, orders, or privileges—and this government, instead of being a democracy existing and acting within the walls of a single city, was to be extended over a vast country of different climates, interests, and habits, and of various communions of our common Christian faith."

3. **Explain the two distinctive features of this experiment.**

   Equal representation and delegated power, defined in the glossary as the "power of one to act or vote for others, with their permission," were distinctive features that had never been tried before.

4. **Why was the use of "the principle of representation or delegated power" so necessary in the American experiment in free government?**

   It was the vehicle through which the world would see a society "maintain its own peace and good government, carry forward its own great interests, and conduct itself to political renown and glory" through power derived not from kings and overlords, but from the common people.

5. **In the second paragraph Webster reviews the situation with reference to political liberty in Europe; what change in France within the century does he note?**

   "A recent occurrence in the French chamber shows us how public opinion on these subjects is changed. A minister had spoken of the 'king's subjects.' 'There are no subjects,' exclaimed hundreds of voices at once, 'in a country where the people make the king!'"

6. **Can you mention any like changes that have occurred in Europe since Webster's time?**
   Students should be reminded of the fall of the Berlin Wall that divided Germany and the fall of communism in Russia.
7. **In the last paragraph what prophecy does Webster make?**
   "The spirit of human liberty and of free government, nurtured and grown into strength and beauty in America, has stretched its course into the midst of the nations. Like an emanation from Heaven, it has gone forth, and it will not return void. It must change, it is fast changing, the face of the earth."
8. **To what extent has this prophecy come true?**
   Encourage students to discuss ways in which this prophecy is being fulfilled. They will recognize that America is a world leader in democracy and freedom.
9. **Read again what is said in the first paragraph in the "Introduction" of page 257 about the "Great American Experiment." What similar ideas do you get from the first paragraphs of Webster's speech?**
   The "Introduction" states that "It was an 'experiment,' because it was based on the idea that a nation made up of men from all parts of the world, living in a territory of vast extent, and under very different conditions of climate, occupation, and degree of wealth, might, through representatives chosen by all its citizens, determine its own plan of government." Webster's speech describes the American experiment as "A government established, without a throne, without an aristocracy, without castes, orders, or privileges—and this government, instead of being a democracy existing and acting within the walls of a single city, was to be extended over a vast country of different climates, interests, and habits, and of various communions of our common Christian faith."
10. **Find in the last paragraph lines that you think aptly express America's situation in the world today.**
    Answers will vary.
11. **Find in the glossary the meaning of: conception, void, stable.**
12. **Pronounce: ally, benignity.**

The Poor Voter on Election Day, p. 289

1. **What does the poor voter mean when he says, "Today a king of men am I"?**
"Alike are great and small, the nameless and the known. My palace is the people's hall; the ballot box my throne!" The voter makes decisions made by kings elsewhere.
2. **What sentence in the Declaration of Independence does this poem help make clear?**
"We hold these truths to be self-evident, that all men are created equal, that they are endowed by their Creator with certain inalienable Rights, that among these are Life, Liberty, and the pursuit of Happiness."
3. **What are some of the "griefs that seek redress" and "rights to need my vote" at the present time?**
Encourage a class discussion of the "griefs" and "rights" in the students' communities.
4. **What progress along these lines has been made by legislation since Whittier's time?**
Students should consider local, as well as national, legislation that has brought about changes in their communities, including civil rights for minorities.
5. **Why is it so important in a democracy that there be no "slackers" among the citizens who have the qualifications to vote?**
The success of democracy depends on all citizens becoming involved in their local communities, voting for honorable leaders, and supporting their government.
6. **In some communities voters are "tagged" at the polls in order to make those who have not voted conspicuous and ashamed; what is the situation in an ideal community?**
Have students define what an "ideal community" would look like and how its citizens might behave.
7. **What are some of the advantages of living in a democracy where one voter counts for the same as another?**
Whittier identifies the advantages of democracy as those who serve voting beside those who are served, those who are wealthy voting beside those who are poor, those who are weak voting beside those who are strong. Wealth and power do not decide alone, but voting puts us all on equal footing.
8. **In a democracy, why is voting on election day a citizen's duty?**
Encourage students to discuss the value of voting.

9. **Find in the glossary the meaning of: pedant, clouted.**
10. **Pronounce: pretense, redress.**

Newspaper Reading

Bring to class editorials that urge reforms in some of the things that Whittier calls "wrongs to sweep away."

GETTYSBURG ADDRESS, P. 291

1. **In a speech delivered in Independence Hall in 1861, just before he became president, Lincoln said, "I have never had a feeling, politically, that did not spring from the sentiments embodied in the Declaration of Independence...It was not the mere matter of the separation of the colonies from the motherland, but that sentiment in the Declaration of Independence which gave liberty, not alone to the people of this country but, I hope, to the world, for all future time"; what is the sentence in the Declaration of Independence to which Lincoln refers?**

   The opening sentence of the Declaration refers to our inalienable rights of Life, Liberty, and the pursuit of Happiness. It goes on to say, "That whenever any form of Government becomes destructive of these ends, it is the Right of the People to alter or to abolish it, and to institute a new Government, laying its foundation on such principles and organizing its powers in such form, as to them shall seem most likely to effect their Safety and Happiness." Lincoln considered that not only an American right, but a human right, regardless of country or nationality.
2. **Is there anything in this address that you can apply to the World Wars?**

   The Gettysburg Address is remembered for its timeless message; we must resolve that from every "honored dead" from any war "we take increased devotion to that cause for which they gave the last full measure of devotion."
3. **Memorize the address.**
4. **Find in the glossary the meaning of: conceived, proposition, hallow, detract, measure.**

Class Reading

Bring to class and read "O Captain! My Captain," Whitman (in *The Elson Readers, Book Seven*).

Library Reading

"The Perfect Tribute," Andrews.

Magazine Reading

You will be interested in seeing the established version of the "Gettysburg Address." Draw from the library and bring to class "Lincoln's Gettysburg Address," *The Century,* for February

1894; note Lincoln's handwriting; compare the three versions of the address: Lincoln's first draft, the Associated Press report, and Lincoln's revised autograph. Show the accepted version to the class. Information on Lincoln's various drafts of the address can be researched at http://lcweb.loc.gov/exhibits/gadd.

Extended Activity:

1. Before students read the address, have them research the Battle of Gettysburg by completing the following outline. (Answers provided for teacher reference.)

Location of the Battle: Gettysburg, PA; the dates of the Battle: July 1-3, 1863; generals who led the Battle: Union troops led by Gen. George G. Meade and the Confederate troops led by Gen. Robert E. Lee; victor of the battle: the Union troops held while the Confederate troops retreated; number of men who died at the Battle: estimated at around 8,000 men; the date of this address: November 19, 1863; location of this address: Soldier's National Cemetery in Gettysburg; the occasion of the address: dedication of the cemetery; the people's response to the address: the speech was highly controversial with Republicans (Lincoln's party) giving it high praise and Democrats denouncing it as silly and shameful; its place in historical speeches: considered among the greatest American speeches of all time.

2. Have students bring in pictures from books or magazines of various types of weapons used in the Civil War, along with pictures of weapons used in modern warfare; compare and contrast the differences in the types of weapons and fighting between these wars.

NAME______________________________**CLASS**__________**DATE**____

THE GETTYSBURG ADDRESS, P. 291

1. Before you read the address, research the Battle of Gettysburg by completing the following outline.

Location of the battle:____

The dates of the battle:____

Generals who led the battle:

Union____

Confederate____

Number of men who died at the battle:____________________________

The date of this address:______________________________________

Location of this address:______________________________________

The occasion of the address:___________________________________

The people's response to the address:____________________________

____

Its place in historical speeches:_________________________________

2. Bring in pictures from books or magazines of various types of weapons used in the Civil War, along with pictures of weapons used in modern warfare; compare and contrast the differences in the types of weapons and fighting between these wars.

____

____

____

____

____

____

____

____

____

____

____

____

____

ABRAHAM LINCOLN, P. 293

1. **How does Lincoln's life demonstrate "the vigor of democracy"?**
"The vigor of democracy" is seen "where every door is open, in every hamlet and countryside, in city and wilderness alike, for the ruler to emerge when he will and claim his leadership in the free life." Lincoln's life began in humble surroundings, but he emerges to "claim his leadership in the free life."
2. **Discuss "Genius is no snob."**
"It does not run after titles or seek by preference the high circles of society. It affects humble company as well as great. It pays no special tribute to universities or learned societies or conventional standards for greatness, but serenely chooses its own comrades, its own haunts, its own cradle even, and its own life of adventure and of training."
3. **What sentence in the second paragraph describes Lincoln? What do you think of this sentence as an example of saying much in a few words?**
The third sentence describes his "great heart that seemed to comprehend all mankind in its catholic and benignant sympathy, the mind that sat enthroned behind those brooding, melancholy eyes whose vision swept many an horizon which those about him dreamed not of—that mind that comprehended what it had never seen, and understood the language of affairs with the ready ease of one to the manner born."
4. **What are some of the "mysteries of democracy" which Lincoln's life expressed?**
Lincoln's life began in obscurity and poverty, "from soils which no man has prepared and in circumstances amidst which they are the least expected." The "mysteries of democracy" give every man the opportunity to rise to greatness regardless of his origins. Encourage students to research Lincoln's childhood and contrast it with his enduring fame as one of America's greatest presidents.
5. **How do your school and other democratic institutions help you "to make the most of every gift and power you possess"?**
Answers will vary.
6. **How does Mr. Wilson explain his feeling that Lincoln was "permanently at home nowhere"?**
"The question where he was is of little significance, that it is always what he was that really arrests our thought and takes hold of our imagination."

7. **What is the "test of every American"?**
"The test of every American must always be, not where he is, but what he is."
8. **In what way were Washington and Lincoln typical Americans?**
"Lincoln and Washington were typical Americans in the use they made of their genius."
9. **Why does Mr. Wilson feel that Lincoln was "a lonely spirit"?**
"It was a very lonely spirit that looked out from underneath those shaggy brows and comprehended men without fully communing with them, as if, in spite of all its efforts at comradeship, it dwelt apart, saw its visions of duty where no man looked on."
10. **In what way might "this cabin" keep alive the hopes of mankind even better than "constitution, doctrines of right, and codes of liberty"?**
The cabin might be "an altar upon which we may forever keep alive the vestal fire of democracy as upon a shrine at which some of the deepest and most sacred hopes of mankind may from age to age be rekindled."
11. **What is your opinion of people who are willing to enjoy the privileges but are not willing to share the duties of the society to which they belong?**
Answers will vary.
12. **What is expected of "real democrats"?**
Real democrats are "servants of mankind, ready to give our very lives for the freedom and justice and spiritual exaltation of the great nation which shelters and nurtures us."
13. **Which sentence best visualizes for you the occasion—the cabin and the crowd listening to the President?**
Answers will vary.
14. **Be prepared to read to the class a sentence selected because it seemed especially significant to you.**
15. **Find in the glossary the meaning of: significant, democracy, aristocracy, fealty, catholic, consummation, depict, familiars, communing, vestal, transmute.**
16. **Pronounce: haunts, dominant, validity, benignant, reassurance, permeating, sovereign.**

Library Reading

He Knew Lincoln, Tarbell; *Boy's Life of Lincoln,* Nicolay.

Magazine Reading

See *Collier's* for September 9, 1916, for an illustrated description of the acceptance of the memorial.

Suggestions for Theme Topics

1. Other great Americans of humble origin.
2. The best "intimate" story I know about Lincoln.

Extended Activity:

After reading this selection given at the dedication of Lincoln's boyhood home, have students research Lincoln's early childhood to appreciate his humble beginnings. Information is readily available at various Internet sites including http://school.discovery.com/homeworkhelp/worldbook/atoz.

NAME______________________________**CLASS**__________**DATE**____

ABRAHAM LINCOLN, P. 293

After reading this selection given at the dedication of Lincoln's boyhood home, research Lincoln's early childhood.

Home and Country, p. 298

1. **What does the author consider "the germ of the best patriotism"?**
"The germ of the best patriotism is in the love that a man has for the home he inhabits, for the soil he tills, for the trees that give him shade, and the hills that stand in his pathway."
2. **The love of home forms the basis for the love of the homeland; why does the author regard this as "the saving principle of our government"?**
"The love of home—deep-rooted and abiding" will be transformed to love and sacrifice for our country.
3. **Which is the greater in saving the Republic, the patriotic citizen, or the drumbeat, the flag, and the barracks?**
"The citizen standing in the doorway of his home, contented on his threshold, his family gathered about his hearthstone...shall save the Republic when the drumtap is futile, and the barracks are exhausted."
4. **Can you tell how every sacrifice endured and every service rendered in the home "will deepen the glory of the Republic"?**
As the home goes, so goes the Republic. If our homes are strong, "consecrated to humanity," our Republic will be strong.
5. **What ways to exalt the citizen are suggested in the last paragraph?**
The exalted citizen will be given opportunities to develop self-respect, self-reliance, responsibility, independence, and humility; that citizen will be encouraged to become upright, fearless, free, loving, loyal, and earnest.
6. **The author defines the relation in America between the home and the homeland; why is this a suitable conclusion to a group of selections dealing with America's experiment in free government?**
Encourage a group discussion of the correlation between strong homes and free nations. How does one affect the other? How are they interrelated?
7. **Find in the glossary the meaning of: dimpling, provincial, unbartered, allegiance.**

Citizenship and Service

You Are the Hope of the World, p. 301

Note to the teacher: These questions are reflective in nature and will have varying responses. Use them as discussion starters rather than seeking specific answers.

1. **Why do you think boys and girls take "baseball or crêpe de Chine" more seriously than the "gorgeous experiment" of democracy?**
2. **What practical training in taking active part in a democracy does your school offer?**
3. **How do boys and girls respond when responsibility for order in the halls or care of equipment, for instance, is placed on them?**
4. **In your opinion, what does America stand for?**
5. **Which of the shortcomings listed by the author have you noticed in your community?**
6. **What efforts are you or your school making to remedy some of these things now?**
7. **Hermann Hagedorn seems hard on the "elders"; what purpose may he have in his remarks?**
8. **What are the standards of success in your school and community?**
9. **What characters in history or in your circle of acquaintances do you know who have had other aspirations than dollars?**
10. **What is the new standard of success?**

    "We must learn that success consists not in what we have but in what we are, not in what we hold in our pockets but in what we hold in our heads and our hearts, not in our skill to buy low and sell high, but in our ability greatly to dream, to build, to battle, to kindle, to serve."
11. **How can boys and girls put into practice in school these high ideals—"greatly to dream, to build, to battle, to kindle, to serve"?**
12. **What can you do, because you love American democracy, to make these ideals the standards by which the popularity of boys and girls in your school is judged?**
13. **Read again what is said in the "Introduction" on page 258 about "the spirit of service" that every good citizen must have; why is this spirit so necessary in a free government?**

"The spirit of service" is one of "brotherhood, of cooperation of all for the good of all, without which no free government can endure."

14. Find in the glossary the meaning of: materialistic, sordid, corruption, stodgy, mandate.

15. Pronounce: abhor, exaltation, individualistic.

Outline for Testing Silent Reading

Make an outline to guide you in telling the main thoughts of this selection.

Library Reading

Other chapters from *You Are the Hope of the World.*

Newspaper Reading

Bring to class and read the best editorial you can find urging some needed improvement in citizenship.

Suggestions for Theme Topics

1. A school experiment in self-government.
2. Things in my school that tend to make pupils social, that is, to develop in them a spirit of cooperation (team work) and service (helpfulness to others).
3. How a school by its organization and discipline may help to realize a true democracy.
4. A report on the George *Junior Republic* (*Junior Republic,* George).
5. How a school composed of many nationalities typifies our Republic.
6. How the presence of different nationalities in a school helps the students to become more intelligent, more sympathetic, more tolerant, and more democratic.
7. How the Boy Scouts, the Camp Fire Girls, the Girl Scouts, and similar organizations promote the spirit of democracy.
8. Book reviews of *The Promised Land,* Antin; *How the Other Half Lives,* Riis; *From Alien to Citizen,* Steiner.

A Suggested Problem

Write out a list of things you can do to make your town or neighborhood a better community. Keep a record for a week of the particular thing you have done each day, such as helping to beautify your school grounds or your home, picking up waste paper, etc. Or make a program for a "Good Health Day" discussion.

The Heritage of Noble Lives, p. 306

1. **Give the topic of each paragraph.**
   Possible topics may include: paragraph 1: America's greatest worthies—Washington and Lincoln; paragraph 2: material effects of their leadership; paragraph 3: their heritage of words and deeds; paragraph 4: our inheritance; paragraph 5: heritage of evil men; paragraph 6: positive influence of men of character.
2. **Arrange these topics in the form of an outline and listen while six pupils give the substance of the selection, each giving the thought of one paragraph in his own words.**
3. **Give another title to the selection.**
   Encourage students to collaborate on a new title for the selection.
4. **Why is the influence of men who speak in deeds greater than that of those who speak only in words?**
   Deeds have a greater lasting influence on the observer than mere words because deeds materially affect change.
5. **In what ways have the lives of Washington and Lincoln influenced the nation?**
   "Without Washington we should probably never have won our independence of the British crown, and we should almost certainly have failed to become a great nation...Without Lincoln we might perhaps have failed to keep the political unity we had won."
6. **What debt do all citizens owe these men for their noble example of service?**
   Encourage students to reflect on their personal debt to these great leaders.
7. **Find in the glossary the meaning of: worthies, sunder, material, jangling, prevalent, unscrupulous, sectional, consciousness.**
8. **Pronounce: dauntless, incalculable, demagogue.**

Library Reading

The Boys' Life of Theodore Roosevelt, Hagedorn.

Letter to Mrs. Bixby, p. 310

1. **Of what fine qualities in President Lincoln does this letter give evidence?**

   One sees the qualities of empathy for the common person's grief, respect for the sacrifice of others, and charity for the widow.

2. **Memorize these words from Lincoln's second inaugural address: "With malice toward none, with charity for all, with firmness in the right, as God gives us to see the right, let us strive on to finish the work we are in; to bind up the nation's wounds; to care for him who shall have borne the battle, and for his widow and his orphan—to do all which may achieve a just and lasting peace among ourselves, and with all nations."**

3. **Do these words from Lincoln's inaugural address support Roosevelt's characterization of him in the first paragraph of "The Heritage of Noble Lives"?**

   Encourage students to read the passage again and point out words that support Roosevelt's characterization of Lincoln.

4. **Find in the glossary the meaning of: beguile, bereavement.**

5. **Pronounce: adjutant, sacrifice.**

YUSSOUF, P. 311

1. **Where do you think the scene of this poem is laid? Give the reason for your answer.**
   Based on the references to a sheik, tent, and nomadic life, the story seems to take place in a desert among Arabs. Encourage students to support their responses with lines from the passage.
2. **What do you know of the habits of people who live in tents?**
   Answers will vary.
3. **What virtues should men living in this way most admire? Why?**
   Virtues may include trust, generosity, and nobleness because a nomadic life of necessity does not include locks on goods nor secure homes.
4. **How do you think Yussouf had won his title of "The Good"?**
   Have students discuss the deeds he may have done to earn his title.
5. **To what does the stranger compare himself?**
   He compares himself to one "against whose life the bow of power is bent."
6. **What does the bending of the bow signify?**
   Since he was an "outcast and in dread," perhaps his life was threatened by pursuers bent on his destruction.
7. **To what tribes does the stranger refer?**
   He refers to "all our tribes," the Arab desert people.
8. **What did the stranger expect? What more than he expected did Yussouf do? How did this affect the stranger?**
   He expected shelter and food; Yussouf gave him gold and his swiftest horse. "Kneeling low, he bowed his forehead upon Yussouf's hand, sobbing."
9. **What was the struggle going on in the stranger's mind and heart that is called "self-conquest"?**
   He was at war within himself, deciding whether or not to reveal his true identity to Yussouf.
10. **What emotions made the stranger's face "grand"?**
    "That inward light the stranger's face made grand," when he determined to disclose his true identity.
11. **What do you suppose Yussouf's "one black thought" had been?**
    It may have been a thought to destroy the man who had killed his son.
12. **How did he avenge his son?**

He avenged his son by responding with peace and forgiveness to his murderer.

13. **When does Yussouf show himself most noble?**

He repays the stranger with "thrice the gold" and tells him "never to return," taking the "one black thought" with him.

14. **Which lines in the last stanza are addressed to the stranger and which to the dead son?**

The first three lines are addressed to the stranger: "Take thrice the gold," said Yussouf, "for with thee into the desert, never to return, my one black thought shall ride away from me." The last three lines are addressed to the dead son: "First-born, for whom by day and night I yearn, Balanced and just are all of God's decrees; Thou art avenged, my first-born sleep in peace."

15. **Into which two lines is the thought of the poem condensed?**

Lines 17-18: "As one lamp lights another, nor grows less, So nobleness enkindleth nobleness." These lines are inscribed on the walls of the Library of Congress.

16. **Find in the glossary the meaning of: prying, enkindleth, sheik.**

Class Reading

Bring to class and read "The Shepherd of King Admetus"; "The Finding of the Lyre," Lowell.

A Man's A Man For A' That, p. 313

1. **The first two lines are contracted; what is left out?**
   The full lines would read "Is there a man for honest poverty That hangs his head and all that?"
2. **What does Burns call the person "that hangs his head" because of "honest poverty"?**
   He refers to him as "The coward slave."
3. **Explain the comparison of a person to a coin in lines 7 and 8, page 313.**
   The guinea is defined in the glossary as "an English gold coin no longer in use worth about $5.11." Burns implies that the guinea may be just a coin of little value, but the "man's the gowd [gold] for a' [all] that."
4. **How may we help to realize the poet's prayer expressed in the last stanza?**
   He expresses the idea that we are brothers the world over, regardless of color or creed. We may help to realize that prayer by accepting others of all nationalities and faiths.
5. **Learn this stanza by heart.**
6. **Burns, the humble poet, made the world happier and better through his poems of brotherhood and love; how does he exemplify the spirit of democracy?**
   Students will read in the biography that Burns "was a strong believer in equal rights for everyone. He felt no envy of those who were accounted great, but gloried in the privilege of being independent."
7. **Why do you think men treasure this poem and will not let it die?**
   It carries a timeless message of compassion and brotherhood that surpasses time and national boundaries.
8. **Compare "A Man's a Man For A' That" with Whittier's "The Poor Voter on Election Day"; what resemblances do you find?**
   Students should note the similarity that an independent man is a great man regardless of rank or status.
9. **Pronounce: guinea, marquis.**

Class Reading

Bring to class and read "A Consecration," Masefield (in *Collected Poems*).

IF, P. 315

1. **Which of these "Ifs" seems especially difficult to practice?**
   Answers will vary.
2. **Notice how in the first two examples the conditions are made doubly difficult by the additions, "and blaming it on you" and "But make allowance for their doubting, too."**
3. **What is better than looking good and talking wise?**
   "Being lied about, don't deal in lies; or, being hated, don't give way to hating."
4. **What does Kipling imply should be the aim of dreaming and of thinking?**
   The aim is to "not make dreams your master...and not make thoughts your aim."
5. **How does he regard Triumph and Disaster?**
   He regards them as "two impostors."
6. **Which "If" embodies advice especially good for athletes?**
   Students may select a variety of lines, but lines 19-20 may be especially good: "And lose, and start again at the beginnings and never breathe a word about your loss."
7. **Which one makes a fine motto when a difficult task is before you that you must see through to the end?**
   "If you can force your heart and nerve and sinew to serve your turn long after they are gone, and so hold on when there is nothing in you except the will which says to them: 'Hold on.'"
8. **How might "loving friends" hurt one?**
   Encourage students to define ways they have been hurt by "loving friends."
9. **Which "If" suggests making good use of one's time?**
   "If you can fill the unforgiving minute with sixty seconds' worth of distance run."
10. **Is the reward worth striving for?**
    "Yours is the Earth and everything that's in it, and—which is more—you'll be a Man, my son."
11. **Find in the glossary the meaning of: impostor, knave.**

Library Reading

The Iron Trail, Beach. (Compare the hero with that of Kipling's "If.")

COLUMBUS, P. 317

1. **Do you like the way this poem opens?**
   Answers will vary. Students should explain why they chose the answer they gave.
2. **Why did not the poet start his narrative with the beginning of the voyage?**
   The setting of the poem, as it is, sets the stage for the tension under which he sailed.
3. **What are the Gates of Hercules?**
   The glossary defines the Gates of Hercules as "Gibraltar." Have the students find the Straits of Gibraltar on a map.
4. **To whom did the mate expect to repeat what Columbus said?**
   He planned to repeat Columbus's words to the crew.
5. **How had a crew been secured for this voyage?**
   Contrary to popular myths, Columbus's crew consisted mostly of honest, seafaring men rather than cutthroats and criminals. The Internet provides a variety of resources for student research on the crew including: http://www1.minn.net/~keithp/crew.htm; www.jsc.nasa.gov/er/seh/crews.htm; http://community.wow.net/300history/02/04.html
6. **How did the men stand the test of the voyage?**
   They grew weary of the endless, "shoreless seas" and begged to return to their homes.
7. **What report of them did the mate give to Columbus?**
   "My men grow mutinous day by day; my men grow ghastly wan and weak."
8. **What did he want Columbus to do if they should "sight naught but seas at dawn"?**
   "The stout mate thought of home" and wanted Columbus to turn back.
9. **What made the mate think that God had gone from those seas?**
   "These very winds forget their way."
10. **When did the events narrated in the fourth stanza take place?**
    The events occurred on the last night at sea when the mate had given up all hope of ever seeing land.
11. **What is the last question asked by the mate? How did Columbus answer the question?**
    "What shall we do when hope is gone?" The words leaped like a leaping sword: 'Sail on! sail on! and on!'"

12. **What thought does the "leaping sword" give you?**
A "leaping sword" represents hope and victory.

13. **Does the description of Columbus with which the last stanza opens seem in contrast with the "leaping sword"?**
Yes, the last stanza describes Columbus as "pale and worn" rather than as a man of victory.

14. **What did Columbus see that night?**
He saw "a speck a light! A light! A light! A light!"

15. **What did that light tell him?**
It told him that land and hope were ahead. "It grew, a starlit flag unfurled!"

16. **What does the poet mean when he says "It grew"?**
The faint light of the new day became brighter and brighter, along with Columbus's vision of a new world.

17. **What is the "starlit flag"?**
The "starlit flag" represents the nation that eventually developed from Columbus's discovery.

18. **What lesson did Columbus teach that world?**
"He gave that world its grandest lesson: 'On! Sail on!'"

19. **How has the poet made us feel the wonder, the triumph, and the thankfulness of Columbus when the light appeared?**
The poem's climactic ending of light contrasts with the poem's beginning of "shoreless seas" when "the very stars are gone." The reader can sense the changing mood of the poem with the appearance of light.

20. **Why does the poet stop at this point?**
He wants the reader to experience the thrill that Columbus experienced when he saw light and land.

21. **What "grandest lesson" did Columbus give to the world?**
One should never give up, no matter how dark the prospects for victory.

22. **How do you value perseverance and courage such as Columbus exemplified?**
Answers will vary.

23. **Compare the lesson this poem teaches with that of Kipling's "If"; with that of Burns's "A Man's a Man for A' That"; with that of Lowell's "Yussouf."**
Each of the poems reflects the persistence and dedication necessary to success.

24. **Find in the glossary the meaning of: blanched, very, dread.**

25. **Pronounce: Joaquin.**

The Bugle Song, p. 319

1. **Find the two lines in the last stanza that express the heart of the poem.**
"Our echoes roll from soul to soul, and grow forever and forever."
2. **The echoes of the bugle die; what becomes of the echoes of our words and actions?**
Our words and actions echo forever.
3. **What lines in Lowell's poem "Yussouf" (page 311) express the same thought?**
"As one lamp lights another, nor grows less, so nobleness enkindleth nobleness."
4. **Can you give an illustration from your school experience of the fact that a good example is contagious? How about selfish conduct? What opinion does Roosevelt express on this point in "The Heritage of Noble Lives" (page 306)?**
Answers will vary. Roosevelt states that "every American is richer by the heritage of the noble deeds and noble words" of our founding fathers. By the same token, "we are the worse for the deeds and words of those who have striven to bring evil to the land."
5. **Notice that the first stanza describes a beautiful setting for the blowing of the bugle; and the third is the poet's interpretation of the echoes, which he expresses to one whom he loves and who perhaps is with him at the moment.**
6. **Does the poet succeed in making you see a beautiful picture in the first four lines of the poem?**
Answers will vary.
7. **To what does the poet compare the echoes in the second stanza?**
He compares the echoes to "the horns of Elfland, faintly blowing."
8. **What words in the poem are particularly expressive?**
Encourage students to identify the words they find expressive.
9. **Notice how the choice of words, the varied and interesting rhymes, and the alliteration all contribute to the music of the poem.**
10. **Read again the note about lyric poetry on page 58, and then tell why this poem is called a lyric. Have you heard a phonograph record of it?**
A lyric poem is "a musical poem appropriate for song." The repetition of words and phrases, along with the rhythm of the poem, make it a lyric poem.

11. It is interesting to notice that Rupert Brooke in "Pine-Trees and the Sky," Bryant in "To a Waterfowl," and Tennyson in this poem follow the same plan—first stating a fact and then following with an interpretation of it, beautifully expressed.
12. You will enjoy listening to a good reader in your class who is able to bring out the beauty of the imagery, the music of the lyric, and the contrast between "our echoes" and those of the bugle.
13. Memorize the poem.

The Chambered Nautilus, p. 321

1. **In what stanzas does the poet talk to us about the nautilus?**
The poet describes the nautilus in stanzas 1 to 3.
2. **In what stanza does he address the shell?**
He addresses the shell in stanza 4.
3. **Which stanza tells the message brought by the shell?**
The message of the shell appears in stanza 5.
4. **Why was it necessary for the poet to tell us the history of the shell before he interpreted its message?**
To understand the message, one must understand how the nautilus is formed. Have students read the "Note" regarding the nautilus to clarify the poet's comparison.
5. **What made it possible for the poet to hear the message brought by the shell?**
He heard the message "through the deep caves of thought."
6. **Does this help you understand what kind of boy Oliver Wendell Holmes must have been?**
Oliver Wendell Holmes must have been an astute observer of nature, as well as a deep thinker able to draw comparisons between nature and life.
7. **To what old belief concerning the nautilus does the poet refer in the first stanza?**
He refers to the nautilus as a ship which sails on the surface in the waters where "the cold sea-maids" who rose "to sun their streaming hair."
8. **What things mentioned show that the poet is thinking of the warm waters in which the nautilus lives?**
He mentions the "gulfs enchanted" and the "coral reefs" which are warm water areas.
9. **Do you like the use of the word "wrecked" in connection with the nautilus? Why?**
Answers will vary.
10. **Who was the "frail tenant"?**
The "frail tenant" was the sea animal that lived in the shell.
11. **What does the broken shell reveal?**
The broken shell reveals the chambers in which the animal has lived.
12. **Find lines in the third stanza which tells how the cells are formed and why they were "sunless" as long as the shell was unbroken?**
"Still, as the spiral grew, he left the past year's dwelling for the new, stole with soft steps its shining archway through, built up its

idle door, stretched in his last-found home, and knew the old no more." Each chamber is closed behind the animal; no sunlight enters it until it is broken.

13. **How may the soul build more lofty mansions? What thoughts will help? What actions will help?**

Encourage a class discussion of the actions and thoughts that "build lofty mansions."

14. **What does the poet mean by the "outgrown shell" of the soul?**

Just as the nautilus shell is eventually outgrown and left behind on the seashore, so one's soul will outgrow its "low-vaulted past" and leave its shell "by life's unresting sea!"

15. **Compare the lesson of this poem with that of "The Bugle Song"; with that of "If."**

"The Bugle Song" speaks of our deeds that "grow forever and ever;" "If" speaks of inheriting the earth through our good deeds; "The Chambered Nautilus" speaks of building "stately mansions" through our deeds.

16. **Find in the glossary the meaning of: siren, irised, rent, crypt, lustrous, Triton.**

17. **Pronounce: coral, wont.**

A DEFINITION OF A GENTLEMAN, P. 324

Note to the teacher: These questions are reflective in nature and will have varying responses. Use them as discussion starters rather than seeking specific answers.

1. **What undesirable qualities does Cardinal Newman mention that you have perhaps discovered in yourself—or in others—and that you have determined to make war against?**
2. **What useful hints have you learned for making and preserving friendships, and for the treatment of enemies?**
3. **Memorize and apply Tennyson's lines about manners: "For manners are not idle, but the fruit of loyal nature and of noble mind."**
4. **Have you observed in your school social affairs that everyone has a good time when all the boys and girls "have eyes on all the company," instead of separating into cliques?**
5. **What does this selection add to your idea of service?**
6. **Why is this selection a fitting summary of the poems that precede it in this group?**
7. **Find in the glossary the meaning of: initiative, retort, insinuate, indolent, resigned, candor.**
8. **Pronounce: affronted, irreparable, misconceive, province.**

A Suggested Problem

Make a list of five suggestions learned from Cardinal Newman which you resolve to put into practice, choosing the ones that apply especially to you; keep the list before you and check up on yourself. (Like means were used by Washington and Franklin to improve their conduct.)

ABRAHAM LINCOLN WALKS AT MIDNIGHT, P. 326

1. **Abraham Lincoln typifies the life and yearnings of the common people, and for this reason he has appealed to the poets who help interpret life for us; mention some other poets who have made Lincoln the subject of poems.**

   See question 7 in this selection for a short poem on Lincoln by Arthur Guitarman. Also, Edward Sims Van Zile's poem, "Close Up the Ranks!" in this Reader could be a reference to Abraham Lincoln. Poems about Lincoln that can be found in *The Elson Reader, Book Seven* include Walt Whitman's, "O Captain! My Captain" and Richard Henry Stoddard's "Abraham Lincoln."

2. **Why does this poet feel that Lincoln cannot "sleep upon the hill"?**

   "He is among us—as in times before!...His head is bowed. He thinks on men and kings...The sins of all the war-lords burn his heart"

3. **What will bring rest to him again?**

   "He cannot rest until a spirit-dawn shall come."

4. **What is being done today to bring about the "spirit-dawn"?**

   Encourage students to discuss actions in their communities and/or country that enable the "spirit-dawn" to come.

5. **What answer would you like to make to the poet's question?**

   Answers will vary.

6. **What lines do you like especially well?**

   Answers will vary.

7. **Another modern poet, Arthur Guitarman, in "He Leads Us Still," has also expressed the idea that Lincoln's spirit lives today. The poem closes—**

   "He leads us still' O'er chasms yet unspanned
   Our pathway lies, the work is but begun.
   But we shall do our part and leave our land
   The mightier for noble battles won.
   Here truth must triumph, honor must prevail;
   The nation Lincoln died for cannot fail."

8. **Find in the glossary the meaning of: portentous, state, scouring, main, Cornland, Alp, travail.**

Close Up the Ranks!, p. 328

1. What thought in "Close Up the Ranks!" is similar to that expressed in "Abraham Lincoln Walks at Midnight" and in "He Leads Us Still"?

This poem states "Let us vow to do our leader's will! Close up the ranks." In "Abraham Lincoln Walks at Midnight," we read "the league of sober folk, the Worker's Earth, bringing long peace to Cornland, Alp and Sea." In "He Leads Us Still," we read, "We shall do our part and leave our land the mightier for noble battles won."

2. What ideals that Roosevelt stood for are expressed in this poem?

Roosevelt, in "The Heritage of Noble Lives," honors the "sad, patient, kindly Lincoln, who for years toiled and suffered for the people." He praises Lincoln for his noble leadership and character. In the same way, this poem expresses appreciation for Lincoln's service and strength in leading our nation.

3. What is the significance of the title?

"Close Up the Ranks" challenges readers to join together and together "vow to do our leader's will! Close up the ranks! Our Captain is not dead! His soul shall live, and by his soul we're led."

4. Lines 4-8, page 329, utter a warning against certain types of men who spread "seed" that will result in "a harvest of despair." What types of such men does Roosevelt warn us against in "The Heritage of Noble Lives," on page 308?

Roosevelt warns us of the unscrupulous speculator, the oppressive capitalist, the agitator, the corrupt man, and the morally or mentally deficient political leader.

5. Find in the glossary the meaning of: crusade, clarion.

Magazine Reading

In the *Review of Reviews* for July 1919, there is a collection of poems written on the death of Theodore Roosevelt, among them "Great-Heart," by Kipling, who was an admirer of Roosevelt. Be prepared to read to the class the poem in this collection that appeals most strongly to you.

Extended Activity:

The well-known authors of the poems in this section span the entire nineteenth century and have greatly affected American readers, as well as readers around the world. After students have read the poems in this section, have them design a timeline of the authors recording their dates of birth and death sequentially, along with information regarding their impact on literature. To assist the students in recording their data, have them refer to the chart regarding authors in "Part I, Birds" of this Guide. Completing such a chart for these authors would help students to see clearly the historical overlaps and the important contributions these authors have made.

NAME______________________________CLASS__________DATE____

CLOSE UP THE RANKS!, p. 328

The well-known authors of the poems in this section span the entire nineteenth century and have greatly impacted American readers, as well as readers around the world. After you have read the poems in this section, design a timeline of the authors recording their dates of birth and death sequentially, along with information regarding their impact on literature.

NAME____________________ **CLASS**________ **DATE**_____

Story	***Find in the glossary the meaning of:***
Reader p. 259	**zephyr**__________
	arena__________
	belie__________
	Jupiter__________
	venerable__________
	Adonis__________
Reader p. 263	**voiceless**__________
	lay__________
	degenerate__________
	fettered__________
Reader p. 267	**grenadier**__________
	impetuous__________
	spectral__________
	tranquil__________
	emerge__________
Reader p. 272	**arched**__________
	embattled__________
	votive__________
Reader p. 275	**meter**__________
	aureole__________
	Gael__________
Reader p. 281	**eradicated**__________
	ignominiously__________
	copious__________
	apprise__________
	covertly__________
	insidiously__________
	palladium__________
	alienate__________
	local__________
	efficacious__________
	acquiescence__________
	maxim__________
	hypothesis__________
	usurpation__________
	subvert__________
	felicity__________
	impostures__________
Reader p. 286	**conception**__________

void______________________________
stable______________________________
Reader p. 289 pedant______________________________
clouted______________________________
Reader p. 291 conceived______________________________
proposition______________________________
hallow______________________________
detract______________________________
measure______________________________
Reader p. 293 significant______________________________
democracy______________________________
aristocracy______________________________
fealty______________________________
catholic______________________________
consummation______________________________
depict______________________________
familiars______________________________
communing______________________________
vestal______________________________
transmute______________________________
Reader p. 298 dimpling______________________________
provincial______________________________
unbartered______________________________
allegiance______________________________
Reader p. 301 materialistic______________________________
sordid______________________________
corruption______________________________
stodgy______________________________
mandate______________________________
Reader p. 306 worthies______________________________
sunder______________________________
material______________________________
jangling______________________________
prevalent______________________________
unscrupulous______________________________
sectional______________________________
consciousness______________________________
Reader p. 310 beguile______________________________
bereavement______________________________
Reader p. 311 prying______________________________
enkindleth______________________________
sheik______________________________
Reader p. 315 impostor______________________________

knave________________________________

Reader p. 317 **blanched**________________________________

very________________________________

dread________________________________

Reader p. 321 **siren**________________________________

irised________________________________

rent________________________________

crypt________________________________

lustrous________________________________

Triton________________________________

Reader p. 324 **initiative**________________________________

retort________________________________

insinuate________________________________

indolent________________________________

resigned________________________________

candor________________________________

Reader p. 326 **portentous**________________________________

state________________________________

scouring________________________________

main________________________________

Cornland________________________________

Alp________________________________

travail________________________________

Reader p. 328 **crusade**________________________________

clarion________________________________

Pronounce:

recesses, sinews, dearth, bacchanal, barrack, alder, rendezvous,. Rouge Bouquet, stalwart, address, artifice, essay, precedent, inveterate, amicable, solicitude, ally, benignity, pretense, redress, haunts, dominant, validity, benignant, reassurance, permeating, sovereign, abhor, exaltation, individualistic, dauntless, incalculable, demagogue, adjutant, sacrifice, guinea, marquis, Joaquin, coral, wont, affronted, irreparable, misconceive, province.

Part IV:
Literature and Life in the Homeland

In This Section—

Objectives—

By completing "Part IV," the following objectives will be met.

1. The student will use effective reading strategies to construct meaning and identify the purpose of a text including:
    a. using illustrations
    b. defining unfamiliar words
    c. scanning for details
    d. retelling and summarizing
2. The student will determine the main idea or essential message and identify relevant supporting details and facts of a text.
3. The student will read and organize facts from the text and other sources to make a report, outline, and perform an authentic task.
4. The student will prepare for writing by focusing on the topic and organizing supporting details in a logical sequence.
5. The student will draft and revise writing.
6. The student will produce final documents that have been edited for correct spelling, punctuation, and grammar.
7. The student will write for a variety of audiences and purposes.
8. The student will write in a variety of genres including narrative and poetic.
9. The student will use reference materials (dictionaries, encyclopedias, maps, charts, and the Internet).
10. The student will use speaking strategies effectively such as eye contact, gestures, and visuals that engage the audience through poetry recitation.
11. The student will identify the development of plot and how conflicts are resolved in a story.
12. The student will identify and understand similarities and differences among the characters, settings, and events presented in various texts.
13. The student will identify the author's purpose and point of view.
14. The student will identify and use literary terminology such as alliteration and simile.
15. The student will respond critically to fiction, nonfiction, and poetry.
16. The student will respond to a text by explaining how the motives of the characters or events compare with those in his or her own life.
17. The student will use context clues to understand words and ideas.
18. The student will predict events that may occur in the text and explain the reasoning behind the prediction.
19. The student will understand the qualities necessary for people to become good citizens and apply those qualities to his or her personal life.
20. The student will understand the qualities necessary to develop good character and apply those qualities to his or her personal life.

American Scenes and Legends

Song of the Chattahoochee, p. 339

1. **Who is represented as talking in this poem?**

   The waters of the Chattahoochee River are supposedly talking in this poem.

2. **Find a line in the first stanza that tells the purpose of the river.**

   Line 3 tells the purpose of the river: "I hurry amain to reach the plain...With a lover's pain to attain the plain."

3. **Find a line in the last stanza that tells why the river holds to this purpose.**

   Line 29: "I am fain to water the plain...The dry fields burn and the mills are to turn, And a myriad flowers mortally yearn."

4. **What temptations to loiter does the second stanza mention?**

   The rushes, the water-weeds, the laurel, the ferns and grass, the dewberry, and the little reeds all called for the water to stay and delay his trip to the plain.

   The third?

   On the hills the various trees—hickory, poplar, chestnut, oak, walnut, and pine—all urged the water to "pass not so cold, these manifold deep shades of the hills."

   The fourth?

   The white quartz, brook stone, the jewels and crystals of ruby, garnet, and amethyst, all lured the river with their "lights of streaming stone."

5. **Find lines in the last stanza which show that the river was not turned aside from its duty by anything it met.**

   "But oh! not the hills of Habersham, And oh! not the valleys of Hall Avail."

6. **Find the lines which show that the river expected to give itself in service to others when it reached the plain.**

   "Downward the voices of Duty call—Downward, to toil and be mixed with the main."

7. **Do you feel that the poet is drawing a parallel between the Chattahoochee and life? Which method do you prefer—to let the reader make his own application to life, as in this poem, or to have the poet make it for him, as in Bryant's "To a Waterfowl"?**

Answers will vary. Encourage students to support their answers using the poem for support.

8. **If the poet, in the second stanza, may have had in mind the small delights that make for contentment in life, what may he have had in mind in the third stanza? In the fourth?**

Encourage students to discuss the poet's intentions regarding the symbolism of the towering trees in the third stanza and the glittering stones in the fourth stanza.

9. **Find examples of alliteration.**

The poet fills his poem with alliteration. Some possible answers include: hills of Habersham; run the rapid; flee from folly; pain to attain the plain; willful water-weeds; laving laurel; ferns and fondling; dewberry dipped for to work delay; Here in the hills of Habersham; High o'er the hills of Habersham; veiling the valleys; crystals clear or a-cloud; lures with the lights.

10. **What do you notice in the structure of the third and the eighth lines of the first stanza?**

The third and eighth lines include internal rhyme, words that rhyme within a line of poetry. They are as follows: "I hurry amain to reach the plain." "With a lover's pain to attain the plain."

11. **Find other lines in the poem which have the same rhyme scheme.**

The following lines include internal rhyme: stanza two, lines 3 and 8; stanza three, lines 3 and 8; stanza four, line 3; stanza five, lines 3, 6, and 8.

12. **Find in the glossary the meaning of: amain, thrall, laving, manifold, lures, avail.**

Class Reading

Bring to class and read Tennyson's "The Brook." Information and an excerpt from the poem may be found on the Internet at www.cs.rice.edu/~ssiyer/minstrels/poems. There is a collection of Tennyson's poetry entitled *The Brook*, which includes this poem.

Library Reading

"Little Rivers," van Dyke.

Snow-Bound, p. 342

SUMMARY

Whittier describes life in a snow-bound house as the blizzard rages outside. With colorful imagery he describes each of the residents, the stories they tell to pass the time, and their impact on his life. He invites the reader to dream with him of bygone days and to "pause to view these Flemish pictures of old days."

1. **Into what parts may this poem be divided?**

   A general outline may include:

   I. The coming of the storm
   II. The shut-ins
      A. Father
      B. Mother
      C. Uncle
      D. Aunt
      E. Older sister
      F. Little sister
      G. Teacher
      H. Guest
   III. Storm's End
   IV. Reflections on Winter Joys

2. **How does the description of the sun "that brief December day" prepare you for what is to follow?**

   The poet describes the sun as "cheerless over hills of gray, and, darkly circled, gave at noon a sadder light than waning noon." It sets the stage for the coming storm when all light was shut out by blinding, white snow.

3. **Of what was the appearance of the sun a "mute prophecy"?**

   It was a "mute prophecy" of "a portent seeming less than threat."

4. **What is the difference between a portent and a threat?**

   A portent, as noted in the glossary, is a sign of some future event. A threat suggests the concept of harm or danger.

5. **What told the coming of the storm?**

   The sun "sank from sight before it set" bringing with it "A chill no coat...could quite shut out, a hard dull bitterness of cold."

6. **What does the poet mention as being the "nightly chores" at his home?**

   The "nightly chores" included bringing in wood, cleaning stalls, and feeding the animals.

7. **What does the word "meanwhile" tell you as to the time at which they did these chores?**

   The waning sun darkened and the wind howled; "Meanwhile, we did our nightly chores."

8. **Find the lines that tell of the beginning of the snowstorm.**

Stanza three, lines 1-6 describe the storm's onset.

9. **In what connection is the word "swarm" commonly used? What picture does it give you of the snowflakes?**

"Swarm" is often connected with teeming bees, so thick they blacken the air with their mass movement. Used here, it gives the reader an image of storming, swirling, teeming snowflakes that blot out the light.

10. **How does the addition of the word "whirl-dance" change the picture you had made?**

"Whirl-dance" gives the reader the impression of lightness, gaiety, and laughter.

11. **What other words does the poet use to describe the crossing and recrossing of the snow?**

The author describes the snow "as zigzag wavering to and fro."

12. **Find two lines that tell the changes the snow made in the appearance of familiar objects.**

Students may identify any of the images in stanza three, line 10 to the end of the stanza. They include the strange new shapes of clothesline poles, sty and corncrib, garden-wall, wood pile, road, bridle-post, and well-curb.

13. **Why was the making of a path a necessity?**

They had to make a path to the barn to take care of the animals.

14. **Where is the story of Aladdin told? What were his lamp's "supernal powers"?**

The story of Aladdin is one of a collection of tales known as the *Arabian Nights*. With his lamp's "supernal powers," Aladdin conquered the evil magician and won the hand of the princess. The story can be found in *The Elson Readers, Book Five.*

15. **How does the poet make us feel the solitude of the farmhouse?**

In stanza 5 the poet describes the "solitude made more intense by dreary-voiced elements" of shrieking wind, moaning tree boughs, and "ghostly finger-tips of sleet" that shut out all "human life and thought outside."

16. **Try to give in your own words the picture of the moonlight on the snow.**

Students should draw from the images in stanza 7 that describes the moonlight on the snow.

17. **Try to give in your own words the picture of the hearth.**

The hearth is described in stanza 8.

18. **Of whom did the circle gathered around the fire consist?**

The circle consisted of the speaker and his brother and sire (stanza 9), his mother (stanza 11), his uncle (stanza 13) and aunt (stanza 14), the elder sister (stanza 15), the youngest sister (stanza 16), the "master of the school district" (stanza 17), and a guest (stanza 18).

19. **Select the lines that please you most in each description.**
Answers will vary.

20. **How did the members of the family amuse themselves?**
Stanza 10: "We sped the time with stories old; Wrought puzzles out, and riddles told; Or stammered from our schoolbook lore."

21. **Who told the stories?**
Father, Mother, the uncle, and the schoolmaster told stories.

22. **Of what did their library consist?**
The poet mentions "The Chief of Gambia's Golden Shore" (stanza 10), "Sewel's ancient tome," "Chalkley's Journal" (stanza 12), and the Almanac. Stanza 25 mentions they had a "little store of books and pamphlets, scarce a score; One harmless novel...and poetry."

23. **Who are meant by the "heathen Nine"?**
The glossary defines the "heathen Nine" as the "nine Muses of Greek mythology, patrons of the fine arts."

24. **Can you explain how Ellwood's Muse may be called a stranger to the "heathen Nine"?**
Ellwood's Muse refers to the Quaker Thomas Ellwood's "epic poem of the life of David" (see glossary). The "meek, drab-skirted Muse" of Ellwood would hardly be familiar with the "heathen Nine," patrons of the fine arts.

25. **What put the household again in touch with the outside world?**
Stanza 25: "At last the floundering carrier bore the village paper to our door."

26. **Of what did they read in the paper?**
"Its corner for the rustic Muse, Its monthly gauge of snow and rain, Its record, mingling in a breath The wedding bell and dirge of death; Jest, anecdote, and lovelorn tale, The latest culprit sent to jail; Its hue and cry of stolen and lost, Its vendue sales and goods at cost."

27. **What was printed in the "corner for the rustic Muse"?**
The glossary defines the "corner for the rustic Muse" as a "column of contributed poetry."

28. **What is meant by the "hue and cry"?**
"Hue and cry" is defined in the glossary as the "loud outcry with which lawbreakers were anciently pursued."

29. **Find lines that tell the effect of the news upon the snow-bound family.**
Stanza 25: "We felt the stir of hall and street, The pulse of life that round us beat; The chill embargo of the snow Was melted in the

genial glow; Wide swung again our ice-locked door, And all the world was ours once more!"

30. What is the voice that bids the dreamer leave his dreams?

Stanza 26: The "Angel of the backward look" is to "Shut down and clasp the heavy lids" of memory; reality calls the dreamer back to "larger hopes and graver fears."

31. What is meant by "Truce of God"?

The "Truce of God" was "an attempt of the Church in the middle ages to lessen the evils of private warfare" (see glossary).

32. Why does the poet compare the pictures he has shown with Flemish pictures?

The poet's pictures of winter storms and childhood memories, like Rembrandt's Flemish works, "treated simple subjects lovingly and in detail" (see glossary).

33. Memorize the lines you like particularly well.

34. Which scenes described in this poem can you picture most clearly?

Answers will vary.

35. What were you told in "Literature and Life" on pages 19 and 20 about literature as a source of learning the facts of life?

Literature "means the expression of the facts of life, or of the interpretation of life, or of the beauty of life, in language of such enduring charm that men treasure it and will not let it die."

How does this poem give you a clearer idea of "the facts of life" on a New England farm than you could gain from your history or geography or from an encyclopedia?

The poet uses sensory "language of such enduring charm" that the reader personally relives the experience, unlike the unemotional, factual information often presented in text books.

36. What did you read in the "Introduction" on pages 335 and 336 about literature as a "form of history"?

"Literature is a form of the history of a race and of a definite period of time. Men do certain things, make and unmake governments or win prosperity for their nations. The record of their achievements and failures is set down in history....Literature reveals the soul of a people. It shows what were the ideals of justice, brotherhood, love, religion, government, in any period."

What ideals of justice, brotherhood, industry, and thrift does this poem show were characteristic of the simple folk in this region?

Encourage students to find examples in the story that they believe represent these ideals.

37. Find in the glossary the meaning of: idyl, waning, portent, querulous, spherule, sweep, buskins, clean-winged.

38. Pronounce: stanchion, harem, silhouette, mirage, cavalcade.

Class Reading

Select some scene or incident in the poem for special preparation. Study the passage, using all the helps available until you can visualize the scene and enable your classmates to get a vivid picture from your reading.

Library Reading

The Life of a Pioneer, Shaw; *A Son of the Middle Border,* Garland.

Suggestions for Theme Topics

1. Contrast a modern farmhouse with which you are familiar with the Whittier house pictured in the poem.
2. Contrast the opportunities for education in rural districts in Whittier's boyhood days with those of the present time.
3. Discuss the influence that the schoolmaster might exert on such a household as Whittier describes, illustrating from Whittier's own life.
4. Modes of cooperation in country life in early days, and the necessity for it.
5. The most interesting person about the Whittier fireside.
6. An account of the work of Gilbert White in the English village of Selborne (See *The Natural History of Selborne,* White).
7. Rural customs in old New England, as "village dance," etc.

A Suggested Problem

In the "Introduction" on page 338 you were told that the selections in this unit are only examples of glimpses into American life, and that the better you understand American life, the better citizen you will be.

Prepare a program for a class period devoted to Little Pictures of Varied American Life. Members of the class who have lived for a time, or traveled, in some distant part of the country may give three minute talks about life in these communities (illustrated, if possible, by pictures). Pupils who cannot contribute any first-hand experiences, may gain material for their discussion from books similar to those listed above, under the topic "Library Reading."

RIP VAN WINKLE, P. 366

SUMMARY

Rip Van Winkle is the story of a village ne'er-do-well who, with his dog, escapes his nagging wife by taking a trip into the woods. While there, he is lured by the ghost of an earlier settler to a mountain cove where he takes a draught of the liquor making its rounds among the crew. He falls asleep to awaken twenty years later to a very different world. During his slumber, the American Revolution has occurred and the colonists are now free from Britain's control. He is a stranger in his own village until he can explain his long absence.

1. **Where is the scene of this story laid?**
   This story takes place in New York along the Hudson River at the foot of the "Kaatskill Mountains."
2. **What is the time?**
   The story begins when the colonies were still under British rule.
3. **Into what three parts does the story naturally divide?**
   The story can be divided into village life before Rip's long sleep, his mountain encounter with the ghosts of Hendrick Hudson and the Half Moon crew, and Rip's life after his long sleep.
4. **Describe the hero of the story.**
   Rip was a happy-go-lucky, ne'er-do-well villager. The village women doted on him, the neighbors respected him, and the village children clambered on him. However, he had "an insuperable aversion to all kinds of profitable labor" and allowed his own business to go unattended, so he was endlessly nagged by his quarrelsome wife.
5. **Where were the idle men of the village in the habit of meeting?**
   They met "on a bench before a small inn, designated by a rubicund portrait of His Majesty George the Third."
6. **How were these meetings frequently broken up?**
   "From even this stronghold the unlucky Rip was at length routed by his termagant wife, who would suddenly break in upon the tranquility of the assemblage, and call the members all to naught."
7. **Where did Rip Van Winkle go to escape from his home?**
   "His only alternative, to escape from the labor of the farm and clamor of his wife, was to take gun in hand and stroll away into the woods." There with his dog, Wolf, he would take comfort in the silence of the mountains.
8. **Describe in your own words what he saw from his resting place high up in the mountain.**
   From his spot high in the mountains he could see the lowlands before him with the Hudson winding its way through the valley.

On the other side of the mountain, he could see "a deep mountain glen, wild, lonely, and shagged," dimmed by the shadows of the high hills.

9. **What was the time of day?**

It was late afternoon as the sun was setting.

10. **How does the mention of the shadows and solitude prepare you for what is to follow?**

The images Irving uses are designed to place in the reader a dark foreboding: impending cliffs, setting sun, long blue shadows, heavy sigh, encountering the terrors.

11. **What does Wolf's behavior when Rip's name is called lead you to expect?**

"Wolf bristled up his back, and giving a low growl, skulked to his master's side, looking fearfully down into the glen." The reader expects danger ahead when even the dog is wary.

12. **Why were you surprised at the appearance of the person who called to Rip?**

Answers may vary but may reflect the concept that since the setting elicited dark, eerie feelings, the reader may have expected the person to be ghostly in appearance. As it was, the person was properly, though somewhat oddly, clothed.

13. **Why did the author picture the players in old Dutch dress? What trick did the stranger play on Rip?**

Rip's village was settled by Dutch immigrants. The Dutch dress reminded Rip of the Flemish paintings brought over from Holland when the village was settled. Rip himself may have had Dutch ancestors; therefore, he may have been acquainted with their appearance and less hesitant to join them. The stranger motioned Rip to serve the contents of the jug to the crew. Eventually, Rip's curiosity overcame him, and he tasted the drink himself, concluding that it had the "flavor of excellent Hollands." He went back for repeated drinks and, finally, overcome with weariness, slept for twenty years.

14. **Describe Rip's awakening.**

When he woke up, he reached for his gun but found only rusted, broken remains where he had left his gun. When he called for Wolf, he got no response. Thinking the crew had tricked him, he set out to find the party and request the return of his dog and gun.

15. **What difficulties did he meet in trying to return home by the way he had ascended the mountain?**

The gully he'd climbed up was now a rolling mountain stream, his former path was now overgrown with brambles and weeds, and the ravine was now a roaring waterfall.

16. What strange sights did he see when he entered the village?

He knew none of the villagers on the street, nor did he recognize their clothing. They stared at him as he stared at them, and when he stroked his chin, he found his beard had grown a foot long. Strange children laughed at him, unfamiliar dogs barked at him, strange new houses and names over doors met him at every turn.

17. How was the sign on the inn changed?

King George's "red coat was changed for one of blue and buff, a sword was held in the hand instead of a scepter, the head was decorated with a cocked hat, and underneath was painted in large characters, General Washington."

18. What does this tell you?

During his twenty years of slumber, the colonists had fought and won the Revolutionary War. King George was no longer their king.

19. What questions did the "tavern politicians" ask Rip?

They asked him on which side he voted, whether he was Federal or Democrat, and why he came to elections bringing a gun accompanied by a mob. Did he intend to start a riot?

20. How did Rip make himself known to the villagers?

After inquiring about his former friends only to learn they had either died or left the village, he finally cried out, "Does nobody here know Rip Van Winkle?" When they pointed out his son and daughter, he grabbed his daughter in his arms and declared he was her long-lost father.

21. What legend corroborated Rip's story of the strange men on the mountain?

Peter, the oldest inhabitant of the village, corroborated Rip's story by recalling "that the great Hendrick Hudson, the first discoverer of the river and country," returned to the mountains every twenty years to keep an eye on the place. Peter's own father had seen the crew in their Dutch dress playing ninepins and had heard the thunder of their rolling balls in the mountains.

22. How is the interest of the story increased by the particular period which the author chose for Rip's sleep?

That particular period in history was the single event that most changed American life. When Rip returned after the Revolutionary War, he would certainly have noticed drastic changes from the colonial life he'd lived prior to his slumber.

23. How much do the appearance and character of Rip's daughter add to the pleasure given by the story?

His daughter stirred old images of his wife. Her "air" and "tone of voice" "awakened a train of recollection in his mind." Seeing her and being reminded of his wife, Rip finally was able to make himself known to the village.

24. What do you think of the description of Rip's son? Why is this description given?

Rip's son is described as "a precise counterpart of himself as he went up the mountain; apparently as lazy, and certainly as ragged." Rip is able to see himself as he appeared to the villagers in his pre-slumber days.

25. Make a list of passages that are particularly humorous.

Answers will vary.

26. In addition to amusing you with its humor, this selection has given you glimpses into early life in New York. Mention some features of this early life that interested you.

Answers will vary.

27. Find in the glossary the meaning of: described, obsequious, patrimonial, alacrity, amphitheater, visage, impenetrable, connubial, austere, corroborated, evinced.

28. Pronounce: termagant, insuperable, patriarch, vehemently, august, alternative, unfrequented, gesture, disputatious, phlegm, refugee, draught.

Class Reading

Make a list of descriptions to be read aloud in class.

Outline for Testing Silent Reading

Make an outline to guide you in telling the story.

Library Reading

Other stories from *The Sketch Book.*

Extended Activity:

Brainstorm with the students what the world might look like if they went to sleep and woke up in twenty years. Have them write a narrative, describing what led them to sleep for twenty years and how the world was changed when they awoke.

NAME______________________________ **CLASS**__________ **DATE**____

RIP VAN WINKLE, P. 366

Brainstorm what the world might look like if you went to sleep and woke up in twenty years. Write a narrative, describing what led you to sleep for twenty years and how the world was changed when you awoke.

EVANGELINE: A TALE OF ACADIE, P. 384

SUMMARY

Longfellow's "Evangeline" tells the story of the forced departure of the French colonists from Nova Scotia during the 1700s (see "Historical Note" in the Reader). It tells the sad story of two lovers torn apart by the move. Evangeline spends years searching the colonies for her lover, Gabriel. She finally becomes a nun and nurses sick and dying patients suffering from an epidemic. While making her rounds, she recognizes the dying face of Gabriel, cradles his aged head in her arms, and kisses him good-bye.

1. **Into what parts is the poem divided?**
   The poem is divided into three parts: Prelude, Part the First, and Part the Second.
2. **With what does Part the First deal? Part the Second?**
   Part the First deals with life in the Acadian land; Part the Second deals with the lives of the Acadians after they have fled their ravished homes to survive in America.
3. **What purpose does the Prelude serve?**
   The Prelude sets the stage for a very old tale as seen by the "forest primeval" that has taken over the village and homes of the ancient Acadians.
4. **What may have given rise to the comparison of the trees to harpers?**
   The "murmuring pines and the hemlocks" may have been a symbol of the harpers playing a mournful dirge for the lost villagers.
5. **What tells us that the mood of the ocean is in sympathy with the melancholy of the forest?**
   The "deep-voiced neighboring ocean" responded to "the wail of the forest."
6. **To what are the lives of the farmers compared?**
   The lives of the farmers "glided on like rivers that water the woodlands."
7. **On whom does the poet call to listen to his story?**
   "Ye who believe in affection that hopes, and endures, and is patient,
   Ye who believe in the beauty and strength of women's devotion,
   List to the mournful tradition still sung by the pines of the forest."

Part the First

(I)

1. **What does Longfellow mean when he says that vast meadows gave the village its name?**
   The Grand-Pre is French for great prairie (see glossary). The vast meadows were home to flocks without number, "spreading afar and unfenced o'er the plain."

2. **In what sense was the richest in Acadie poor?**
The Acadians lived together in love, free from fear and envy; "neither locks had they to their doors, nor bars to their windows."

3. **Find lines that describe Evangeline's father.**
Page 387, lines 5-7 describe her father. He was strong, stately, healthy, and hale, with hair as white as snow and cheeks "as brown as oak-leaves."

4. **Find lines that describe Evangeline.**
Page 387, lines 8-24 describe Evangeline. At seventeen she was fair to behold with black eyes, brown hair, sweet breath and a "celestial brightness" on her face.

5. **How has the "craft of the smith" been regarded from earliest times? How can you account for this?**
The "craft of the smith" was "held in repute by the people" since the beginning of time, "throughout all ages and nations." It was the "craft of the smith" that helped to build civilization, industry, and trade.

(II)

6. **What do we call that "beautiful season" which the Acadians called the "Summer of All-Saints"?**
We call that time Indian Summer when "arrayed in its robes of russet and scarlet and yellow...each glittering tree of the forest flashed like the plane-tree."

7. **What pictures make up the evening scene?**
The poet describes the evening star, the cattle heading home from the fields, and the shepherds herding their flocks followed by a faithful watchdog.

(III)

8. **How was the betrothal celebrated?**
Page 398, line 10: The notary wrote the date and age of the bridal couple, "naming the dower of the bride in flocks of sheep and cattle…Then from his leathern pouch the farmer threw on the table Three times the old man's fee in solid pieces of silver; And the notary rising, and blessing the bride and bridegroom, Lifted aloft the tankard of ale and drank to their welfare."

9. **What forebodings were expressed?**
English ships of war had anchored off the coast, and no one knew their intent. The men of the village had been called to meet in the church the following day. As Evangeline prepares for a night of sleep, "a feeling of sadness passes o'er her soul."

(IV)

10. **What proclamation was made at the church?**
Page 402, line 15: "Namely, that all your lands, and dwellings, and cattle of all kinds Forfeited be to the crown; and that

you yourselves from this province Be transported to other lands....Prisoners now I declare you, for such is His Majesty's pleasure!"

11. **How was it received by the Acadians?**
Page 403, line 1: "Silent a moment they stood in speechless wonder, and then rose Louder and louder a wail of sorrow and anger; And, by one impulse moved, they madly rushed to the doorway." But they found themselves prisoners in their own church, restrained by the soldiers. The news spread through the village, and women and children "wandered, wailing, from house to house."

12. **How did Evangeline try to help the women and children?**
Page 405, line 8: "Then, all forgetful of self, she wandered into the village, Cheering with looks and words the disconsolate hearts of the women."

(V)

13. **What happened when the time came for entering the boats?**
Page 408, line 7: "And in the confusion Wives were torn from their husbands, and mothers, too late, saw their children left on the land, extending their arms, with wildest entreaties." With escape cut off by sentinels, the Acadians camped for the night.

14. **What was done to the homes that the Acadians had left?**
Page 410, line 12: "Columns of shining smoke arose, and flashes of flame" leapt from thatched roof to thatched roof, devouring their houses, destroying their village, driving away their livestock. "Speechless at first they stood, then cried aloud in their anguish, 'We shall behold no more our homes in the village of Grand-Pre.'"

15. **What caused the death of Evangeline's father?**
Shock and sorrow killed her father. "Lo! from his seat he had fallen, and stretched abroad on the seashore Motionless lay his form, from which the soul had departed."

16. **Find in the glossary the meaning of: (I) ethereal, mutation, (II) regent, glebe, notary, (III) irascible, congealed, (IV) jocund, vibrant, dissonant, convened, solstice, imprecations, (V) refluent, kelp, unperturbed, gleeds, oblivious.**

17. **Pronounce: prelude, (I) hearth, heirloom, exquisite, (III) warier, (v) sonorous, clement, mien, contrition.**

Part the Second

(I)

1. **Where did the Acadians land?**

Students will read in the "Historical Notes" that the Acadians landed on American shores and were scattered throughout the colonies.

2. **What did the exiles do in the strange country?**

"They wandered from city to city, From the cold lakes of the North to sultry Southern savannas, From the bleak shores of the sea to the lands where the Father of Waters Siezes the hills in his hands, and drags then down to the ocean."

3. **Find the words with which the priest comforted Evangeline.**

The priest's words are found on page 414, lines 12-20.

4. **How does the poet say he will follow Evangeline's footsteps?**

Page 415, line 3-9: He would follow her footsteps "as a traveler follows a streamlet's course through the valley."

(II)

5. **Who accompanied Evangeline and the priest on their journey down the Mississippi?**

Acadian boatmen, exiles from a "shipwrecked nation," and men, women and children in search of their families traveled down the river together.

6. **What thought sustained Evangeline on this voyage?**

Page 417, line 3: "But Evangeline's heart, was sustained by a vision that faintly Floated before her eyes, and beckoned her on through the moonlight. It was the thought of her brain that assumed the shape of a phantom. Through those shadowy aisles had Gabriel wandered before her, And every stroke of the oar now brought him nearer and nearer."

7. **What vision came to her?**

Page 419, line 12: "O Father Felician! Something says in my heart that near me Gabriel wanders."

(III)

8. **Describe the meeting with Basil.**

Page 422, line 12-20. "There in the arbor of roses with endless question and answer Gave they vent to their hearts, and renewed their friendly embraces, Laughing and weeping by turns, or sitting silent and thoughtful."

9. **Find lines in which Basil contrasts his new home with the old.**

Page 424, line 15 - page 425, line 5 tell about his contrasts.

10. **Why was it that Evangeline's party failed to see Gabriel's boat?**

Hidden under willow bows, Evangeline's party was asleep when Gabriel's boat glided by them in the night.

(IV)

11. Where did Evangeline seek for Gabriel as the years passed?

She searched for him "at the base of the Ozark Mountains," until she came to a Jesuit Mission where she stayed in hopes that Gabriel would return after his hunting expedition.

12. How did her appearance change as time went on?

Page 434, line 29 to page 435, line 5: "Fair was she and young when in hope began the long journey; Faded was she and old when in disappointment it ended."

(V)

13. What had her life of sorrow taught her?

Page 436, line 9: "Patience and abnegation of self, and devotion to others, This was the lesson a life of trial and sorrow had taught her."

14. What did her loving heart lead her to do?

Page 436, line 13: "Other hope had she none, not wish in life, but to follow, Meekly with reverent steps, the sacred feet of her Savior. Thus many years she lived as a Sister of Mercy."

15. Where did her work as a Sister of Mercy take her?

Page 436, line 16: Her work took her to the "Lonely and wretched roofs in the crowded lanes of the city, Where distress and want concealed themselves from the sunlight, Where disease and sorrow in garrets languished neglected."

16. How had the priest's words come true?

Refer to question 3 for the priest's words on page 414. "Therefore accomplish thy labor of love, till the heart is made godlike, Purified, strengthened, perfected, and rendered more worthy of heaven!" As a Sister of Mercy, Evangeline "entered the chambers of sickness" and those who "Looked up into her face, and thought, indeed, to behold there Gleams of celestial light encircle her forehead with splendor."

17. Contrast the conduct of Evangeline in the time of pestilence with that of Prince Prospero in Poe's story "The Masque of the Red Death."

When faced with a pestilence, Prince Prospero (Part II) gathered his friends and "retired to the deep seclusion of one of his castellated abbeys." He refused to help those in need.

Evangeline, on the other hand, went to the dying and "Noiselessly moved about the assiduous, careful attendants, Moistening the feverish lip and the aching brow, and in silence Closing the sightless eyes of the dead."

18. What helped Evangeline to recognize Gabriel?

Page 438, line 26: "But, as he lay in the morning light, his face for a moment Seemed to assume once more the forms of its earlier manhood."

19. What reasons for thankfulness did she have?

Pagc 439, line 23: "All was ended now, the hope and the fear, and the sorrow, All the aching of heart, the restless, unsatisfied longing, All the dull, deep pain, and constant anguish of patience!"

20. What words of the good priest may have come to her mind at this time?

The good priest had several words of comfort for Evangeline. Students should justify their responses with appropriate lines. One possible response may be found on page 419, line 25: "There the long-wandering bride shall be given again to her bridegroom."

21. This is a tale of devotion showing the beauty and holiness of affection "that hopes and endures and is patient"; it also teaches certain facts about early American history. Which of these values do you think the poct wished to impress upon us?

Answers will vary.

22. The poem has the "twofold province" about which you read in the "Introduction" on pages 336; can you show that this is true?

"Literature, then, has a twofold province: one that has nothing to do with space and time; the other presenting a form of a history of a people." While this story relates the history of the scattering of the Acadians, it tells also about love, patience, and endurance that transcend space and time.

23. This poem consists of a series of descriptions, each forming a beautiful picture; make a list of these scenes, and place a star before those that you can see most distinctly

24. What did you learn from the "Introduction" on page 336 about the value of literature as a supplement to your history?

"Literature reveals the soul of a people. It shows what were the ideals of justice, brotherhood, love, religion, government, in any period."

How has this poem added to your understanding of the wild, unsettled regions of early America?

Answers will vary.

25. If you have seen Evangeline in motion pictures tell how the film story differed from the poem story.

26. Find in the glossary the meaning of: (I) inarticulate, shards, devious, (II) multitudinous, (III) hilarious, accordant, inundate, oracular, (IV) incantation, cloisters, mendicant, (V) abnegation, diffused, assiduous.

27. Pronounce: (II) tenebrous, demoniac, buoy, (IV) implacable, taciturn, subtle, (V) presaged.

Library Reading.

The Last of the Mohicans, Cooper.

Suggestions for Theme Topics

Contrast the advantages of living in your home region with living in some other section of our country, as Basil contrasted the advantages of Louisiana over Canada.

A Suggested Problem

Dramatize selected scenes from this poem; or prepare a program for a "Longfellow Day."

Extended Activity:

1. Allusion in literature is a reference to a well-known character, place, or event in history. To understand the point the writer is making, the reader must be familiar with the character, place, or event.

Throughout this work, Longfellow alludes to many biblical events, characters, and places. Have students identify the biblical illusions and research their connection to the story.

The allusions mentioned include: Page 388, lines 14-15: Peter and the cock Matthew 26:69-75; page 390, line 21: Jacob and the angel Genesis 32: 22-32; page 400, line 4: Ishmael and Hagar Genesis 21: 8-21; Page 404, line 3-10: Crucified Christ Luke 23:26-43; page 404, line 15: Elijah ascending to heaven 2 Kings 2:11-12; page 405, line 13: The prophet descending from Sinai Exodus 34:29-30; page 409, line 11: Paul on Melita's shore Acts 27: 27-Acts 28:10; page 418, line 16: Jacob's ladder Genesis 28:10-17; page 426, line 24: Hand that wrote "Upharsin" Daniel 5 KJV; page 427, line 16: Prodigal son Luke 15:11-32; page 427, line 17: Foolish virgin Matthew 25:1-13; page 429, line 2: Ishmael's children Genesis 25: 12-18; page 432, line 1: Mary and Jesus Matthew 1: 18-25; page 437, line 12: The poor you always have with you Mark 14:7; page 439, line 2: Hebrews with blood sprinkled on its portals Exodus 12: 1-13.

2. Characterization refers to the writer's methods of developing the characters in the story. The writer develops the character by describing his or her appearance, thoughts, and actions, as well as the thoughts and reactions of other characters in the story about the main character.

Longfellow uses a variety of strategies to develop the character of Evangeline. Have the students complete the chart by finding and listing examples of each technique that show her character. (*See next page.*)

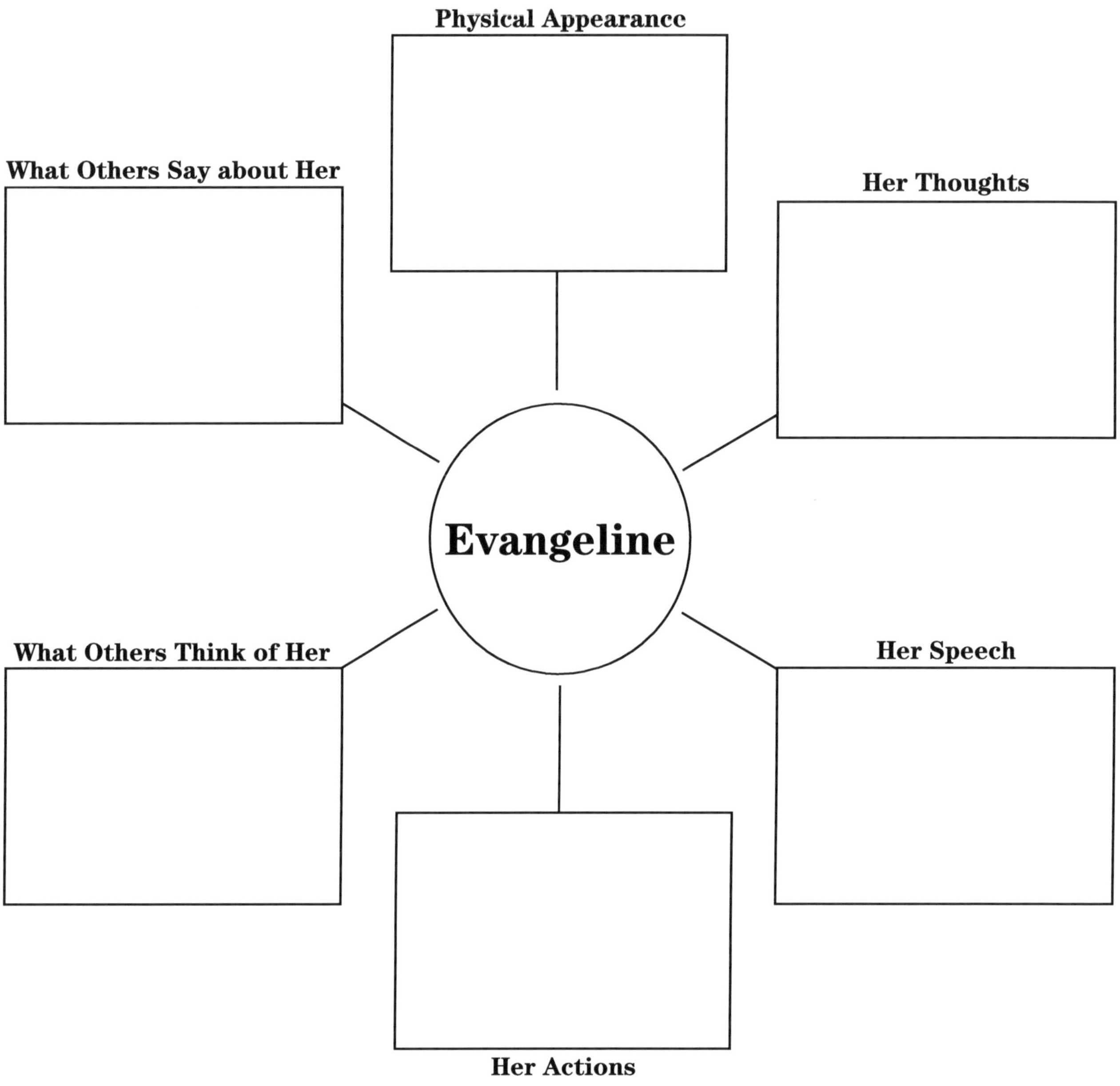
Physical Appearance
What Others Say about Her
Her Thoughts
Evangeline
What Others Think of Her
Her Speech
Her Actions

NAME______________________________ **CLASS**__________ **DATE**____

EVANGELINE, p. 384

1. **Allusion in literature is a reference to a well-known character, place, or event in history. To understand the point the writer is making, the reader must be familiar with the character, place, or event.**

   Throughout this work, Longfellow alludes to many biblical events, characters, and places. Identify the biblical illusions and research their connection to the story.

2. Characterization refers to the writer's methods of developing the characters in the story. The writer develops the character by describing his or her appearance, thoughts, and actions, as well as the thoughts and reactions of other characters in the story about the main character.

Longfellow uses a variety of strategies to develop the character of Evangeline. Complete the chart by finding and listing examples of each technique that show her character.

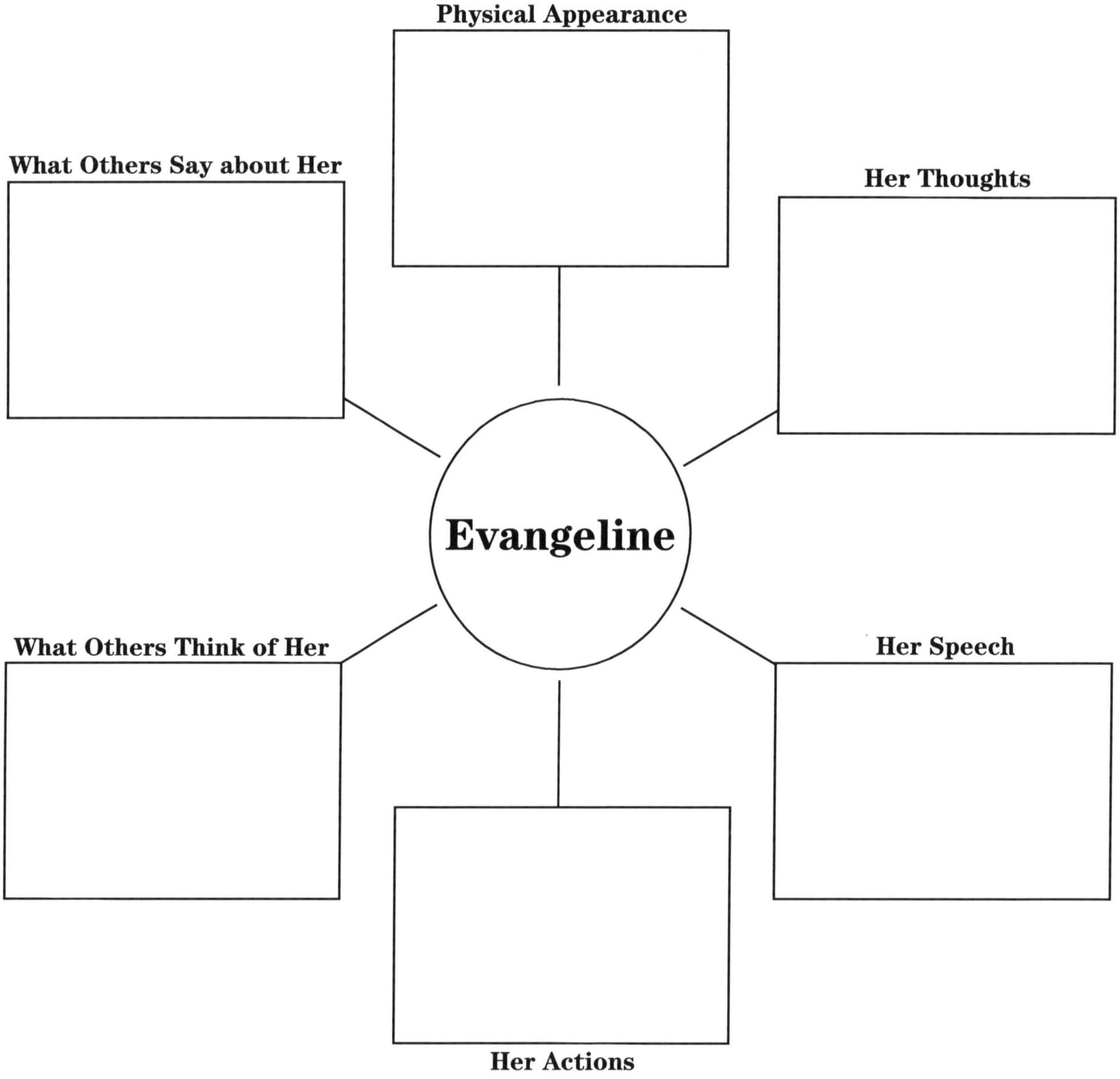

THE GRAY CHAMPION, P. 443

SUMMARY

As New England groaned under the tyranny of the king, the people took to the streets to protest the heavy hand of his governor. Trying to quell the disturbances, the governor amassed his men and attempted to put down the disturbance with a show of force. During a showdown in the streets, the Gray Champion stepped forward and faced down the enemy, bringing peace to the village and an end to their terror.

1. **Note that part of the story which pictures the conditions of New England under Andros.**

   The conditions of New England are described in the first paragraph.

2. **What were the wrongs under which the people suffered?**

   "A governor and council holding office from the king, and wholly independent of the country; laws made and taxes levied without concurrence of the people, immediate or by their representatives; the rights of private citizens violated, and the titles of all landed property declared void; the voice of complaint stifled by restrictions on the press; and, finally, disaffection overawed by the first band of mercenary troops that ever marched on our free soil."

3. **Did they submit willingly?**

   No, they were "kept in sullen submission."

4. **What rumor gave them hope of a return of "civil and religious rights"?**

   "At length a rumor reached our shores that the Prince of Orange had ventured on an enterprise the success of which would be the triumph of civil and religious rights and the salvation of New England."

5. **How did this rumor affect the governor and his councilors?**

   They "resolved to avert (an uprising) by an imposing display of strength, and perhaps to confirm their despotism by yet harsher measures."

6. **Why was the Guard assembled?**

   The Governor's Guard assembled to reinforce the governor's presence and "strike terror, by a parade of military force."

7. **What effect on the people had its appearance at this time?**

   Some feared they were to be massacred; others shouted to their countrymen to stand firm against the governor.

8. **What does Hawthorne call this scene in the street?**

   "The whole scene was a picture of the condition of New England, and its moral."

9. **What does he say is its "moral"?**
   Its moral is "the deformity of any government that does not grow out of the nature of things and the character of the people."
10. **Who came to have the advantage, the governor and his soldiers, or the people?**
    The people came to have the advantage. The governor and his soldiers retreated.
11. **Find all that accounts for the Champion and his sudden appearance.**
    The people cried out to the "Lord of Hosts" to "provide a champion" for them. "This ejaculation was loudly uttered, and served as a herald's cry, to introduce a remarkable personage." To their amazement the "Lord of Hosts" seemed to answer their cries when "Suddenly, there was seen the figure of an ancient man, who seemed to have emerged from among the people, and was walking by himself along the center of the street to confront the armed band."
12. **What great cause did he come to champion?**
    "I am here, Sir Governor, because the cry of an oppressed people hath disturbed me in my secret place; and beseeching this favor earnestly of the Lord, it was vouchsafed me to appear once again on earth in the good old cause of his saints."
13. **What cause were Andros and his soldiers supporting?**
    They were supporting the cause of England's King James.
14. **Who was victorious?**
    The Gray Champion was victorious; Sir Edmund Andros and his men retreated.
15. **Tell briefly the main incident.**
    The Gray Champion held his ground against the scornful, threatening soldiers, warning the governor that his power would be ended that very night and ordered the governor to turn back. As he warned, "Before another sunset, the governor and all that rode so proudly with him, were prisoners," and King James was dethroned.
16. **Give your opinion as to Hawthorne's purpose in writing this story.**
    Answers will vary.
17. **Read "The Short Story," page 106, and see if you can find the four parts of this story.**
    The four parts of the story are: an introduction, a main incident, a powerful climax, and a conclusion. The introduction described the dire living conditions of the New Englanders. The main incident occurred when Sir Edmund and his soldiers paraded in the streets to threaten and cower the people to submission.

They were met, however, by the imposing figure of the Gray Champion. The powerful climax occurred when the Gray Champion confronted the governor and warned him to retreat. The conclusion tells of the Champion's continued presence at the American battles that won our nation's freedom.

18. Show how this story, though based upon a legend, is the kind of literature mentioned in the "Introduction," page 337, that supplements your knowledge of history.

Stories such as this "help you to realize what were the hardships, the manner of life, the types of manhood and womanhood that produced the colonies." The story helps the reader to visualize the very real deprivations and injustices that finally led our nation to throw off the oppressive governments that ruled them.

19. In the "Introduction" to "Part III," on page 256, you read a discussion of the "Eternal Spirit of Freedom." What similar ideas did you gain from reading "The Gray Champion"?

The "Introduction" asserts that "firmly imbedded in the human heart is the conviction that men ought to be free, free to shape their lives according to their desires and their abilities and not according to the commands of emperor or king." "The Gray Champion" expresses the same idea. Students may identify additional similarities.

20. Find in the glossary the meaning of: concurrence, filial, extinct, confound, constituted, arch-enemy, sensible, blenched, abdicated, obelisk.

21. Pronounce: inquiry, apostolic, predecessor, truncheon, dotard.

Class Reading

Select passages to be read aloud in class.

Outline for Testing Silent Reading

Make an outline to guide you in telling the story.

Library Reading

The "Introduction" on page 338 tells you that the more selections you read like the ones given in this part of your book, the better you will understand America. Such reading may well include other stories from *Twice-Told Tales,* such as "The May-Pole of Merry Mount," "Legends of the Province House," "The Gentle Boy," "Sights from the Steeple," also *The Hoosier Schoolmaster,* Eggleston; *Northwestern Fights and Fighters,* Brady; The *Story of Tonty,* Catherwood; *Cadet Days,* King; *The Pilot,* Cooper.

Extended Activities:

The following activities can be used with any of the stories in this section.

1. Choose a character such as Rip or The Gray Champion and draw a portrait that captures the character's personality and physical traits.
2. Draw a comic book version of an episode taken from one of the stories. Include the action, characters, dialogue, and setting.
3. A diorama is a three-dimensional miniature scene in a box. Choose an episode from one of the stories to depict in a diorama scene.
4. Design a sculpture using papier-mâché or clay that reflects a character or event from the story.
5. Compose a song based on one of the stories. Choose a melody and rhythm to reflect the mood of that story.
6. Work with a group to create a drama from one of the scenes.
7. Find pictures from magazines and newspapers that remind you of one of the main characters or events in a story and create a collage that reflects that image.

NAME_______________________________CLASS__________DATE____

EXTENDED ACTIVITIES

The following activities can be used with any of the stories in this section.

1. **Choose a character such as Rip or The Gray Champion and draw a portrait that captures the character's personality and physical traits.**
2. **Draw a comic book version of an episode taken from one of the stories. Include the action, characters, dialogue, and setting.**
3. **A diorama is a three-dimensional miniature scene in a box. Choose an episode from one of the stories to depict in a diorama scene.**
4. **Design a sculpture using papier-mâché or clay that reflects a character or event from that story.**
5. **Compose a song based on one of the stories. Choose a melody and rhythm to reflect the mood of the story.**
6. **Work with a group to create a drama from one of the scenes.**
7. **Find pictures from magazines and newspapers that remind you of one of the main characters or events in a story and create a collage that reflects that image.**

American Literature of Lighter Vein

The Deacon's Masterpiece, p. 454

1. **What is a chaise?**
   The glossary defines a chaise as a "light carriage."
2. **Explain the allusion to Lisbon.**
   Lisbon, Portugal, experienced an earthquake in 1755 (see glossary).
3. **What is meant by "Braddock's army"?**
   "Braddock's army" included the "men under General Braddock, defeated by the French and Indians, 1755" (see glossary).
4. **Of what besides chaises is the statement in the second line of the third stanza true?**
   "There is always *somewhere* a weakest spot." Encourage students to brainstorm how this statement might be true in other areas of life.
5. **What did the deacon determine to do?**
   Stanza 4: "But the Deacon swore...He would build one shay to beat the taown...It would be so built that it couldn't break daown."
6. **Find the words that tell how the deacon thought this could be done.**
   Stanza 4: "'N' the way t' fix it, uz I maintain, is only jest T' make that place uz strong uz the rest."
7. **What woods were used in making the chaise?**
   He used oak, lancewood, ash, and white-wood.
8. **Find the lines in which the poet mentions the only things that keep their youth.**
   Stanza 8: "In fact, there's nothing that keeps its youth, So far as I know, but a tree and truth."
9. **What happened on the morning of the hundredth year of the "shay's" life?**
   The parson took a drive and the shay fell "in a heap or a mound, As if it had been to the mill and ground."
10. **Explain how the chaise went "to pieces all at once."**
    "First a shiver, and then a thrill. Then something decidedly like a spill...You see, of course, if you're not a dunce, How it went to pieces all at once."
11. **Have you ever heard of a carriage or coach that lasted one hundred years?**
    Answers will vary.

12. Which is it that is funny, the thought that the chaise lasted one hundred years, or the thought that it "went to pieces all at once"?

Answers will vary.

13. Did you ever hear of such a happening? Do you think the poet ever heard of such an occurrence?

Answers will vary.

14. Find lines in which the humor is furnished by the poet's manner of telling the incident.

The poet uses dialect and exaggeration to create humor in the poem. Have students identify the lines or phrases that they find humorous.

15. Pronounce: "ellum," "hahnsum," encore.

Class Reading

Bring to class and read the selection by Holmes that you think is his funniest.

A Suggested Problem

Make a program for a "Holmes Day" celebration in your school. Holmes was a member of the famous Harvard class of 1829, which held annual reunions as long as any of its members were able to attend. In 1889, at the sixtieth anniversary, ten of the fifty-nine classmates were still living. At these class reunions everyone looked to Holmes for the anniversary poem; some of these anniversary poems are; "Bill and Joe" (1851); "The Boys" (1859); "Lines" (1860); "The Smiling Listener" (1871); "The Archbishop of Gil Blas" (1879); and "After the Curfew" (1889). Some of the more interesting of these class poems, together with other selections by Holmes found or suggested in this book, will furnish material for an interesting program.

Suggestions for Theme Topics

1. Present-day "newspaper fun."
2. A proposed exhibit of humorous clippings from newspapers.
3. A plan for making a collection of the best cartoons for "Cartoon Day" in your school.

The Ballad of the Oysterman, p. 459

1. **This poem is a parody on the old ballads, that is, it mimics the style of these ballads in such a way as to make it absurd. In what respects does it resemble the early ballads you have read? In what ways does it differ?**

Ballads are narrative poems; they tell a story using rhyme and rhythm. Like this ballad, they are usually written in four-line stanzas with a variety of rhyme schemes such as AABB, ABAB, or ABCD. Have students identify this rhyme scheme and compare it to other ballads they may have read. Ballads often include a tragic ending, like this poem; however, unlike other ballads, this is a parody that pokes fun at the lovers' tragic ending.

2. **What is the story of Leander and the Hellespont?**

In the glossary students will read that Leander and Hellespont refer to an old Greek legend. Leander was "the lover of Hero, whom he swam the Hellespont (modern Dardanelles) to visit each night. One night her light, by which he was guided, went out and he perished. When Hero discovered his body on shore, she killed herself."

3. **What expression used by the Oysterman makes his resolve to swim across the river ludicrous, instead of heroic?**

"I guess I'll leave the skiff at home, for fear that folks should see." He was afraid to be seen kissing his love.

4. **To what does the poet compare the pale face of the girl with the hair falling around it?**

Her falling hair was compared to "seaweed on a clam."

5. **To what might he have compared it if he had wished to rouse your sympathy?**

Have students brainstorm more delicate, tragic comparisons for her falling hair.

Library Reading

"The Broomstick Train," "The September Gale," and prose selections by Holmes: "My Hunt After the Captain," "The Physiology of Walking," "The Three Johns" (from chapter III of *The Autocrat of the Breakfast-Table*).

New England Weather, p. 461

1. **What do you know to be true of the New England climate?**
According to Mark Twain, the one known fact about New England weather is that it is unpredictable.
What has the author done to this well-known fact to produce the humor of this selection?
He compares it to the stability of weather reports in other areas of the country, exaggerating its myriad changes that provide "hundreds of kinds of weather."
2. **Who is meant by "Old Probabilities"?**
"Old Probabilities" refers to the "chief office furnishing weather reports" (see glossary).
3. **In what way does the weather forecast for New England, as outlined by the author, differ from forecasts you read in the daily papers?**
Weather forecasts in the daily paper report only a narrow range of weather possibilities. Twain, on the other hand, describes New England forecasts with wild variations. "High and low barometer, swapping around from place to place; probable areas of rain, snow, hail, and drought, succeeded or preceded by earthquakes with thunder and lightening."
4. **Why does the author predict earthquakes for New England?**
New England is not an earthquake-prone area; he predicts earthquakes to contrast the wild variations of New England's weather patterns from the norm.
5. **In what part of the selection do you think the writer is in earnest?**
He is in earnest when he describes the ice storm.
6. **Find the lines that describe the effect of the sun on the ice-covered trees.**
Page 462, line 25: "The sun comes out and turns all those myriads of beads and drops to prisms that glow and burn and flash with all manner of colored fires; which change and change again, with inconceivable rapidity, from blue to red, from red to green, and green to gold."
7. **What does this description tell you about the author's powers of observation?**
Twain is a close observer of nature.
8. **For what does he say this beautiful sight atones?**
The sight of the sun on the ice atones for the unpredictable weather. "Your little faults and foibles count for nothing; you are the most enchanting weather in the world."

9. How does the author make his story humorous? Find particularly good examples of his humor.

He describes weather as a useful commodity that can be spared, hired out, sold, deposited, invested, and given to the poor. He describes wide-ranging forecasts that run the entire spectrum of possible weather patterns within a brief period of time. Encourage students to identify lines that they find humorous.

10. Find in the glossary the meaning of: centennial, vagaries.

Class Reading

Bring to class and read some humorous selections from recent issues of *Life,* or other magazines devoted to humor.

Library Reading

Huckleberry Finn, Mark Twain; *The Boy's Life of Mark Twain,* Paine.

The Ransom of Red Chief, p. 464

1. **Show that this is a typical short story.**
It includes the basic elements of a short story: introduction, main incident, climax, conclusion.
2. **What is the climax?**
The climax occurs in the letter from Mr. Dorset requesting $250 for Red Chief's return.
3. **Can you think of an outcome that would furnish greater surprise than the proposals contained in Dorset's letter?**
Answers will vary.
4. **Find examples of comic exaggeration.**
Students will find a variety of possible answers, among them Bill's statement, "In ten minutes I shall cross the Central, Southern, and Middle Western States, and be legging it trippingly for the Canadian border."
5. **What other selection by this author have you read?**
Answers will vary. O. Henry wrote "The Gift of the Magi" found in *The Elson Readers, Book Seven.*
6. **What did you learn in the "Introduction," pages 335 and 338, about the value to America of the spirit of laughter and good humor?**
Laughter is "one of our national traits that has played no small part in our success as a people. For the conquest of this vast continent has been a task demanding ceaseless toil, and it has been the spirit of laughter and good humor that has helped Americans to keep life sweet, despite its tenseness."
What evidence do you find in newspapers and magazines that humor plays a prominent part in American thought today?
Americans enjoy a variety of humorous writings including comic strips and political cartoons that find humor in American life.
7. **Find in the glossary the meaning of: apparition, diatribe, welterweight, incontinently, surreptitiously, renegade, counter-proposition.**
8. **Pronounce: bas-relief, reconnoiter, contiguous, somnolent, casually, palatable.**

Class Reading

Make a list of passages containing good examples of humor, to be read aloud in class.

Outline for Testing Silent Reading.

Make an outline to guide you in telling the story.

Library Reading

Other stories from *Whirligigs.*

Newspaper Reading

Bring to class and read the best example of a humorous short story you can find in a newspaper or a magazine.

Extended Activity:

O. Henry's story is filled with irony, the contrast between what is expected and what really occurs. Irony can be verbal: through a spoken word or phrase; situational: when a situation has an opposite outcome; or dramatic: when the reader knows information about the scene that the character does not know.

Have students complete the chart by identifying the ironic twists in the story.

Expectation	Irony
The prospect for an easy kidnapping looked good.	It turned out to be a disaster.
Ebenezer would melt down for a ransom of $2000.	He asked to be paid $250 to take his son back.
They thought the boy would want a bag of candy and a nice ride.	The boy hit him with a rock.
The boy would be afraid of the kidnappers.	They were afraid of him.
They thought he would want to return home.	He begged not to be taken home.
They thought his parents would dote on him.	Parents were hesitant to take him back.
The village would be beating the bushes searching for the boy.	All was quiet in the village.
Bill hobbled into camp thinking he'd sent the boy home.	The boy was following him back to camp.
Everyone would be glad to see the boy come home again.	The neighbors would harm the kidnappers for returning the boy.

NAME______________________________CLASS__________DATE_____

THE RANSOM OF RED CHIEF, P. 464

O. Henry's story is filled with irony, the contrast between what is expected and what really occurs. Irony can be verbal: through a spoken word or phrase; situational: when a situation has an opposite outcome; or dramatic: when the reader knows information about the scene that the character does not know.

Complete the chart by identifying the ironic twists in the story.

Expectation	Irony
The prospect for an easy kidnapping looked good.	
Ebenezer would melt down for a ransom of $2000.	
They thought the boy would want a bag of candy and a nice ride.	
The boy would be afraid of the kidnappers.	
They thought he would want to return home.	
They thought his parents would dote on him.	
The village would be beating the bushes searching for the boy.	
Bill hobbled into camp thinking he'd sent the boy home.	
Everyone would be glad to see the boy come home again.	

American Workers and Their Work

Work: A Song of Triumph, p. 477

1. **To what is work compared in the first stanza?**
Work is compared to might, ardor, urge, and delight.
2. **What is meant by the "stern command" that challenges "brain and heart and hand"?**
Work that "springs from the heart's desire" is the "stern command" that challenges "brain and heart and hand."
3. **What does work do to stupor and despair? What does work do for the dreamer?**
Work masters stupor and despair; work moves "the dreamer to do and dare."
4. **Read the third stanza so that you feel the swift pace of the horses to which your purpose, your mind, and your will are compared.**
5. **Who is the driver?**
Work is "the Power that drives behind, Guiding the purposes, taming the mind."
6. **What is meant by the expression "runaway wishes"?**
Work holds back the "runaway wishes," those dreams and desires that would sidetrack us from reaching our goal, "desires we should not give in to" (see glossary).
7. **How does work hold them back?**
Work reins "the will to one steady track, triumphing over disaster."
8. **What is meant by "reining the will"?**
The glossary refers to "reining the will" as "keeping all energies directed toward" our goal.
9. **What may the goad be which forces us on?**
The glossary defines a goad as "necessity which acts as a whip." Encourage students to identify the goad that drives them to succeed.
10. **To what is work compared in the first part of the fourth stanza?**
Work is compared to the "clamoring, hammering ring" of a blacksmith at work on his anvil.
11. **Who were the Titans?**
Titans were "the fabled giants who lived at the beginning of the world" (see glossary). They were gods of Greek mythology who represented the earth, sun, and sky.

12. Why are swamps drained?

Swamps are drained to make way for roads, homes, and commerce.

13. When is it necessary to blast hills?

Like swamps, hills are blasted to expand trade and housing.

14. The making of what great canals may be described as "rending a continent apart"?

The Panama Canal is recognized for literally "rending a continent apart," separating North and South America. The Erie Canal also united the Great Lakes with the Atlantic Ocean, expanding the ease of trade from East to West.

15. What other great achievements can you mention as the result of man's work?

Encourage students to identify great achievements in modern history as a result of man's work.

16. Why should everyone do his part of the world's work?

The world's work requires all our skills, whether we are dreamers, leaders, or skilled laborers.

17. In the "Introduction" on page 338 what is said to be the secret of our national prosperity?

"For the secret of our national prosperity is summed up in the ideal of faithful, honest labor."

What is said about the need for cooperation?

"The one supreme essential for success is a loyal spirit of cooperation among all who join to carry on the vast industries on which our national progress is founded."

Point out lines in this poem that express somewhat the same ideas.

Work moves "the dreamer to do and dare;" work is our response to "the dream of the Master heart."

18. Find in the glossary the meaning of: torpid, taming, goad.

Library Reading

"The Telephone Directory" and "The Power Plant," Braley (in *Songs of a Workaday World*); *Famous Leaders of Industry,* Wildman; *Heroes of Progress,* Morris; *Modern Americans,* Sanford and Owen; *The Silver Horde,* Beach; *Pictures of the Wonder of Work,* Pennell; the magazine *The World's Work;* "Biography of Angela Morgan," *The Review of Reviews* for April, 1919.

Pete of the Steel-Mills, p. 480

1. **Notice how the author makes the story seem real by vivid pictures; by the conversation of the men; by making clear the difficulty of the work, amidst the heat and the noise, through describing the effects they produce; find examples of these devices.**

Students will find many examples of vivid imagery like the following scenes. "The sweat in great drops fell from his blistered face, ran in tiny rivulets from his arms and hands, and splashed on the iron floor. He trembled, he gasped for breath, and I thought he was going to sink down from pure exhaustion..." "To be aroused by a screaming whistle above your head at two o'clock in the morning; to seize a shovel and run to the open door of a white-hot furnace and there in its blistering heat to shovel in heavy ore...until every stitch of clothing on your body is soaked with perspiration; to stagger with pulses thumping, and drop down upon a bench, only to be ordered out into a nipping winter air..."

2. **What do you admire most in Pete's conduct?**

Answers will vary. Pete's cheerful attitude in the face of daunting work and an angry boss make him admirable. He does not allow his lack of education to stop him from doing a job well.

3. **What do you learn from this story about the work in the steel mills?**

The steel mills, the backbone of American commerce, required excruciatingly hard work, vigilant diligence and rugged determination from its workers. Without them, we could not have achieved the development of the New World at such a rapid pace.

4. **Make a list of humorous passages.**

Answers will vary. Students may mention the contrast in the worker and the chemist's answers to why manganese was put into steel, the author's description of his body aches when he awoke the second day of work and Pete's frustration at his lack of education as humorous passages.

5. **Does the language of the workers seem suited to the speakers?**

The language of the workers seems to fit with Pete's evaluation of himself: "Can't write, can't figger, can't talk—don't know nothin'!"

6. **What did Mike mean when he advised the author "to learn to spell"?**

Page 485, line 8: "Now, ye're on a twelve-hour turn here, and ye ain't expected to work like a fool. Ye want to learn to spell.

(Mike wasn't referring to my orthographic shortcomings.)" Mike was referring to the author's ability to pace himself and work "smarter" rather than faster.

7. **Find the lines on page 484 where the author speaks humorously about the poet's idea of work.**

   Lines 8-11: "Uh-huh! But you'll get over it. 'Bout tomorrow mornin', when your clock goes rattlety-bang and you look to see what's up and find it's five o'clock, you"ll not be thinkin' it so interestin', oh no!"

   Do you think the author would seriously doubt the truth of Angela Morgan's poem "Work: A Song of Triumph"?

   The author would probably agree with Morgan's poem since he was a diligent worker.

8. **How is the heroism of toil shown in this story?**

   Heroic toil is toil that takes pleasure in one's work, no matter how difficult or long. This story shows the pleasure, as well as the pain, connected to toil and how one man, working steadily, faithfully, and honestly, found satisfaction in his work.

9. **What were you told in "Literature and Life," pages 17 and 18, about literature as a source of learning the "facts of life"?**

   The "facts of life" found in literature include the ideals of democracy, pictures of life in early America, and glimpses of romance found in toil.

   How does this story give you a clearer idea of the "facts of life" in a great steel mill than you could gain from your geography or from an encyclopedia?

   This author paints vivid pictures of laughter and toil, pain and friendship that a textbook would not include.

10. **Find in the glossary the meaning of: alloys, ductility, malleability, elucidation, fused, bonus.**
11. **Pronounce: orthographic, laboratory, harass, admirable, ignoramus, genuine, debris, column.**

Outline for Testing Silent Reading

Tell the story, following this outline:

(a) Outside the steel mills: winter was coming, jobs were scarce, a war was occurring, and life was desperate in the village

(b) The open hearth with its long line of furnaces: the furnaces belched tongues of fire while men, stripped to the waist and bathed in sweat, pried and jabbed at the burning steel, testing and removing it to cool.

(c) The workers: the "small man," Pete and his favorite jest, Mike and his advice; the "small man" waited anxiously with Hall outside the steel mill, envying Hall's promise of a job. He'd been trying to get a job for two weeks without success and believed it was because he was "kind o' small for most of the work in there." Pete, the "open-hearth" man, was a good-natured, fast and dependable worker who took Hall under his wing and showed him the skill of getting heat "from a roof;" His favorite line was "Ought never to have left the farm, ought we? Eh, Buddy?" Mike, was the "maid of all work" who introduced Hall to the mill and taught him how to survive in the heat and horror. He advised Hall to steer clear of Pete since the boss disliked Pete and anyone who consorted with Pete. He also advised Hall to "learn to spell"—pace his work and not "work like a fool."

(d) Night work: Roused by screaming whistles, the night workers slaved in front of the white-hot furnace which threw off a blistering heat; dripping in sweat the workers shoveled heavy ore in to the blaze and then went directly into the bitter winter night to check the gas valve. It was excruciating labor, but as the "small man" so aptly put it, "You got to do it if you're goin' to work in the mills."

(e) Pete and the boss: the boss hated Pete, moving him from job to job to try to get Pete fired. At length they came to blows, the boss was fired, and Pete took his job.

(f) Pete as foreman: he was intimidated by the enormity of his job and his lack of education, but he didn't let that stop him. He took on the responsibilities of foreman with the same diligence as he had shown on the floor.

(g) Pete's education: determined to succeed, Pete spent every spare moment poring over books, hiring a private tutor to help him learn to read and write.

(h) The accident: A giant crane, lifting its eighty-ton load of liquid steel, snapped a cable, pouring the white hot metal on a pool of water; a tremendous explosion followed in which Pete lost his life.

Library Reading

Steel Preferred, Hall

Newspaper Reading

Bring to class and read the most interesting account you can find in a newspaper or magazine, telling about conditions of work in some industry such as mining, fishery, etc.

A Suggested Problem

Find out by a personal visit all you can about the way some industry or business is carried on (for example, some local store, or your father's business) and report to the class. Illustrate your talk, if possible, by pictures or blackboard drawings.

THE THINKER, P. 494

1. **What is the theme of the poem?**
Behind every worker is the dreamer, the thinker, the mastermind, and together they make "the dream come true!"
2. **What is the relation of the planner to the worker?**
The planner and the worker together "give the work a soul!"
3. **What confidence does the poet express in the worker? In the "Dreamer"?**
The worker is the "eye that scans" the machinery, "watching through stress and strain;" his is the "strength of the sweating toiler, Greatly in these we trust." The "Dreamer" is the one "Who's making the dream come true!"
4. **What does the poet mean when he says that the brain is back of the brawn?**
The brawn is the "physical strength" (see glossary) provided by the worker; the brain "is the Mind behind the worker" that guides the work.
5. **Show that the poem is a plea for the cooperation that is discussed in the "Introduction" on page 336.**
The "Introduction" mentions the "dreamer of great projects, the complicated planning and organizing of the leader, the skillful labor of the doer" as essential components for success. This poem delineates the connection between dreamer and doer, as well. One cannot succeed without the other.

Class Reading

Read the poem aloud to bring out the meaning and the rhythm; bring to class and read other poems from *Songs of a Workaday World* that particularly interest you.

The Way to Wealth, p. 495

1. **What question led to this speech by Father Abraham?**
"Pray, Father Abraham, what think you of the times? Will not these heavy taxes quite ruin the country? How shall we ever be able to pay them? What would you advise us to do?"
2. **What taxes besides government taxes does he say we pay?**
We pay taxes for idleness, pride, and folly.
3. **How much does idleness tax people?**
"We are taxed twice as much by our idleness."
4. **What is better than wishing for better times?**
Better than wishing is working. "We can make these times better if we bestir ourselves. 'Industry need not wish, and he that lives upon hopes will die fasting.'"
5. **Against what practices do these maxims warn us?**
They warn us against idle dreaming and wasteful spending.
6. **What habits or virtues do they advise us to acquire?**
"Industry, and frugality, and prudence" are the virtues we should seek.
7. **Can you explain how Benjamin Franklin helped his country by publishing these maxims?**
He encouraged early Americans to practice the disciplines of "industry, and frugality, and prudence," which made our country great.
8. **With which of the maxims are you familiar? What ones will you learn today? Which one will help most?**
Answers will vary.
9. **What was done to encourage thrift during the World Wars?**
Thrift was encouraged by planting Victory Gardens, rationing basic foods and fuel, and purchasing Liberty bonds and thrift stamps.
10. **Find in the glossary the meaning of: abatement, sloth, diligence, ape, superfluities, veracity, doctrine, harangue, ascribed, gleanings.**

Library Reading

Autobiography, Franklin.

Suggestions for Theme Topics

1. What I know about thrift stamps.
2. Other thrift measures in use during the World Wars.

A MESSAGE TO GARCIA, P. 500

Note to the teacher: These questions are designed for discussion rather than specific answers; a wide variety of responses are possible.

1. **Discuss whether or not, in your opinion, the author is too hard on "help."**
2. **Why do you think the New York Central Railway distributed copies among its employees?**
3. **What resolve might you well make after reading "A Message to Garcia"?**
4. **Are you one of the "Rowans" in your school?**
5. **How does Rowan's devotion differ from that of the hero in the "Incident of the French Camp"?**

   Rowan "took the letter, sealed it up in an oilskin pouch, strapped it over his heart, in four days landed by night off the coast of Cuba from an open boat, disappeared into the jungle, and in three weeks came out on the other side of the island, having traversed a hostile country on foot, and delivered his letter to Garcia." The hero in the "Incident of the French Camp" took his message on horseback, riding a shorter distance, delivered his news, and died smiling at the feet of his hero.
6. **Which is of more value to a country, devotion to a cause or to a leader?**
7. **What other story on efficiency in work have you read?**
8. **Point out sentences in this selection that show the author's belief in the importance of the cooperation discussed in the "Introduction" on page 338.**
9. **Find in the glossary the meaning of: insurgents, traversed, vertebrae, appalled, imbecility, memorandum, accountant, maudlin, denizens, missive.**
10. **Pronounce: horizon, encyclopedia, rapacious.**

Class Reading

Make a list of passages to be read aloud in class.

Questions for Testing Silent Reading

Make a list of questions to bring out the main thought of the story.

Magazine Reading

Make a report in class on the most interesting article, on efficiency and faithfulness to duty, that you have read in *The American Magazine, The World's Work,* or in any other periodical.

The Building of the Ship, p. 506

1. **What two stories run side by side in this poem?**
The building of a ship for the sea and the molding of a youth for the "sea of life" run side by side in this poem.
2. **Who is represented as speaking lines 1 to 4 on page 504? To whom are these words addressed?**
The merchant is asking the shipbuilder to build him a seaworthy ship.
3. **What is the story of the "Great Harry?"**
The glossary identifies the "Great Harry" as the "first warship of the British navy, built in 1488."
4. **What trees are mentioned as furnishing timber for the vessel?**
"Timber of chestnut, and elm, and oak, And scattered here and there, with these, The knarred and crooked cedar knees" were used to build the vessel.
5. **What comparison do the long level shadows of the early morning bring to the mind of the poet?**
They are compared to "A youth, against an anchor leaning, Listened, to catch (the Master's) slightest meaning."
6. **What is the significance of having Maine cedar and Georgia pine help to build a vessel that is to be called the Union?**
Maine cedar and Georgia pine signify a Union made up of both Northern and Southern states, each contributing to the whole.
7. **Find the lines in which the poet first compares the master's daughter to a ship.**
Page 509, line 24: "Like a beauteous barge was she, Still at rest on the sandy beach, Just beyond the billows reach."
8. **To what does the poet compare the rudder of the ship?**
Page 512, line 6: "Lay the rudder on the sand, That, like a thought, should have control Over the movement of the whole."
To what does he compare the anchor?
Page 512, line 9: "And near it the anchor, whose giant hand Would reach down and grapple with the land."
To what does he compare the pines that were felled to make the mast?
Page 513, line 11: "Those captive kings so straight and tall, To be shorn of their streaming hair."
9. **Find lines that describe the flag at the masthead.**
Page 513, line 23: "White, blue, and red, A flag unrolls the Stripes and Stars."
10. **What two brides does the poet show us?**

The poet shows the ship as a bride leaping "into the ocean's arms," and he shows the daughter as a bride meeting her bridegroom.

11. **Find lines in which he addresses the ship that has been launched.**

Page 517, line 4: "Sail forth into the sea, O ship! Through wind and wave right onward steer!"

12. **Find lines addressed to the girl who has become the wife of the shipbuilder.**

Page 517, line 8: "Sail forth into the sea of life, O gentle, loving, trusting wife, And safe from all adversity Upon the bosom of that sea Thy comings and thy goings be!"

13. **Find the lines addressed to the "Ship of State."**

Page 517, line 17: "Thou, too, sail on, O ship of State! Sail on, O Union, strong and great!"

14. **What lines on page 508 suggest the need of cooperation?**

Page 508, line 6: "There's not a ship that sails the ocean, But every climate, every soil, Must bring its tribute, great or small, And help to build the wooden wall!"

Compare the thought in lines 20 to 22, page 517, with what Webster says in the last paragraph of "The American Experiment."

Lines 20-22: "With all the hopes of future years, Is hanging breathless on thy fate!" Webster similarly states, "The spirit of human liberty and of free government, nurtured and grown into strength and beauty in America, has stretched its course into the midst of the nations. Like an emanation from Heaven, it has gone forth, and it will not return void."

15. **How many of the terms used by the poet in describing the building of the ship are familiar to you?**

Answers will vary.

16. **Where or how did you learn the ones you know? How did Longfellow learn so much about ships?**

Longfellow must have been a keen observer of ships and spent time talking with the master builders.

17. **Perhaps these lines from his poem, "My Lost Youth," will help you to understand how it was possible for Longfellow to write so understandingly and lovingly about a ship: "I remember the black wharves and the slips. And the sea-tides tossing free, And Spanish sailors with bearded lips, And the beauty and the mystery of the ships, And the magic of the sea."**

18. **Point out lines in the poem that express some of the same ideas about work that you read in the "Introduction" on page 338.**

The "Introduction" mentions the "loyal spirit of cooperation among all who join to carry on the vast industries on which our national progress is founded." Encourage students to find lines that reflect the cooperation needed to produce a great ship or a mature life.

19. **A cantata for this poem, prepared by Henry C. Lahee, was published by Oliver Ditson Company, Boston.**
20. **Find in the glossary the meaning of: argosy, behest, Naiad, sark.**
21. **Pronounce: stanch, miniature.**

Suggestions for Theme Topics

1. What I know about shipbuilding in America during the World Wars.
2. Some advantages that come to a country that has a large fleet of merchant ships.

Library Reading

Our Industrial Victory, Schwab; "Ships for the Seven Seas," Grave (in the *National Geographic Magazine,* September, 1918); "Cargoes," Masefield (in *Collected Poems*).

Name______________________________ **Class**__________ **Date**______

Story	***Find in the glossary the meaning of:***
Reader p. 339	**amain**__________
	thrall__________
	laving__________
	manifold__________
	ures__________
	avail__________
Reader p. 342	**idyl**__________
	waning__________
	portent__________
	querulous__________
	spherule__________
	sweep__________
	buskins__________
	clean-winged__________
Reader p. 366	**described**__________
	obsequious__________
	patrimonial__________
	alacrity__________
	amphitheater__________
	visage__________
	impenetrable__________
	connubial__________
	austere__________
	corroborated__________
	evinced__________
Reader p. 384	**ethereal**__________
	mutation__________
	regent__________
	glebe__________
	notary__________
	irascible__________
	congealed__________
	jocund__________
	vibrant__________
	dissonant__________
	convened__________
	solstice__________
	imprecations__________
	refluent__________

kelp___
unperturbed
gleeds
oblivious
inarticulate
shards
devious
multitudinous
hilarious
accordant
inundate
oracular
incantation
cloisters
mendicant
abnegation
diffused
assiduous
Reader p. 443 **concurrence**
filial
extinct
confound
constituted
arch-enemy
sensible
blenched
abdicated
obelisk
Reader p. 461 **centennial**
vagaries
Reader p. 464 **apparition**
diatribe
welterweight
incontinently
surreptitiously
renegade
counter-proposition
Reader p. 477 **torpid**
taming
goad
Reader p. 480 **alloys**
ductility
malleability

elucidation

fused

bonus

Reader p. 495 abatement

sloth

diligence

ape

superfluities

veracity

doctrine

harangue

ascribed

gleanings

Reader p. 500 insurgents

traversed

vertebrae

appalled

imbecility

memorandum

accountant

maudlin

denizens

missive

Reader p. 506 argosy

behest

Naiad

sark

Pronounce:

stanchion, harem, silhouette, mirage, cavalcade, termagant, insuperable, patriarch, vehemently, august, alternative, unfrequented, gesture, disputatious, phlegm, refugee, draught, prelude, hearth, heirloom, exquisite, warier, sonorous, clement, mien, contrition, tenebrous, demoniac, buoy, implacable, taciturn, subtle, presaged, inquiry, apostolic, predecessor, truncheon, dotard, "ellum," "hahnsum," encore, bas-relief, reconnoiter, contiguous, somnolent, casually, palatable, orthographic, laboratory, harass, admirable, ignoramus, genuine, debris, column, horizon, encyclopedia, rapacious, stanch, miniature.

Appendix I
Instructional Aids

> The first section of this appendix, "Silent and Oral Reading," appears in the original *Elson Readers, Book Seven* and offers the teacher and/or parent a useful method of assisting the student(s) in attaining the objectives in this guide. The remaining aids have been written specially for this guide by the authors as additional resources for the teacher and parent.

Silent and Oral Reading

Silent Reading. This book includes abundant material for both silent and oral reading. Some stories and poems must be read thoughtfully in order to gain the author's full meaning; such reading cannot be done rapidly. In other selections the meaning can be grasped easily, and the reading can be rapid; in such cases we read mainly for the central thought, for the story element.

You read silently more often than you read aloud to others; you should, therefore, train yourself in rapid silent reading, concentrating your mind on the thought of the selection. You will soon discover that as you give closer attention to a story you will not only understand it better, but you will also remember more of it. In previous grades your training in silent reading has enabled you to gather facts from individual paragraphs and to hold in mind the thread of the narrative in shorter selections. But you are to extend this power steadily until you can gather facts and follow the unfolding plot in selections of considerable length. A number of stories in this book are long enough to train you to read with intelligence a newspaper, a magazine article, or a book. And this is precisely the ability you most need, not only in preparing lessons in history and other school subjects, but in all your reading throughout life. As you train yourself to grasp swiftly and accurately the meaning of a page, you increase your capacity to enjoy books—one of the most pleasurable things in life. Theodore Roosevelt trained himself to be such a rapid reader that he was able to grasp the central thought of a page almost as quickly as he could turn the leaves of the book.

In preparing lessons in geography and history and in the use of geographical and historical stories, you have a splendid opportunity to increase your ability to gather facts quickly from the printed page. These informational studies, however, do not take the place of the reading lesson in literature. They merely offer additional opportunity for you to increase your ability in rapid silent reading.

Notice that the rapid silent readers in your class generally gain and retain from their reading more facts than the slow readers do. Notice, too, that you read more rapidly when you are looking for the answer to some particular question or looking for a certain passage than you do when you read merely to follow the thread of the story. Moving your lips or pointing to the words with your finger retards your speed. In the selections in this book suggested for silent reading you may test your ability at thought-getting in any of the following ways:

1. By using a list of questions covering the most important ideas of the selection (see "Questions for Testing Silent Reading," p. 40).
2. By telling the story from a given outline (see "Outline for Testing Silent Reading," p. 44).
3. By making a list of questions yourself, allowing some classmate to use them to test his or her ability at thought-getting, while you make similar use of his or her questions.
4. By telling the story from an outline that you have made. Telling the substance of the story from your own outline is an excellent kind of test because you test not only your understanding of the story, but also your memory and your power to express the thought of what you have read.

In all your reading, both at home and at school, you should read as rapidly as you can, but not so fast that you fail to get the thought. In preparing your lessons on selections in this book, test yourself by seeing how many of the questions, under "Discussion," that develop the most important thoughts of the story, you can answer after one reading. You may have to read parts of the story more than once in order to gain the full meaning. If, from time to time, you record your reading speed and your thought-getting ability, comparing your standing with that of your classmates and with the standard for seventh-grade pupils, you will be able to see whether or not you are making satisfactory progress. The standard for seventh-grade boys and girls is 250 words per minute, with the ability to reproduce after one reading 50% of the ideas in a 400-word passage.

The following form will suggest a way to record the results of your test:

INDIVIDUAL RECORD

Date	Titles	Speed		Comprehension
		No. of minutes required to read story	No. words per minute	Ten points for each of ten test questions*
	Hunting the Grizzly Bear Total No. Words, 1957			
	The Great Stone Face... Total No. Words, 7475			

*Questions to be selected by the teacher.

CLASS RECORD

Date	Speed			Comprehension			
	No. words per minute			Ten points for each of ten test questions			
	Lowest	Highest	Median	Lowest	Highest	Median	

Oral Reading. In the prose selections suggested for silent reading, you will wish to read aloud certain passages because of their beauty, their dramatic quality, or the forceful way in which the author has expressed his thoughts. In these selections, "Class Readings" are listed for this purpose. Sometimes these readings are intended for individual pupils; sometimes, particularly in dialogue, they are intended for groups. "Class Readings" include also supplementary poems and stories suggested for oral presentation.

In general, all poetry should be read aloud, for much of the beauty of poetry lies in its rhythm. The voice, with its infinite possibilities of change, is an important factor in interpreting a poem. As you listen to your teacher or some other good reader, you will appreciate how much pleasure one who has learned the art of reading is able to give others. Oral reading trains the ear of the listener to become sensitive to a pleasing voice, to correct pronunciation, and to distinct articulation. The sympathetic reading of many of the poems in this book will reveal to you the beauty of the language that we speak and by which we express our thoughts. Longfellow says, "Of equal honor with him who writes a grand poem is he who reads it grandly."

Outline for Oral Presentations

The following rubric is a general guideline to consider when critiquing student oral presentations. As the teacher, you may want to assign a point value to each of the items which you consider to be pertinent to the assignment.

General Guidelines

	Points Possible	Points Earned
Completed on time		
Fulfilled the guidelines of the assignment		
Message: **Clear and pertinent**		
Appealing and detailed		
Research: **Current and varied**		
Properly cited		
Technology: **Used technical materials, (i.e., computer, puppets, tools appropriately)**		
Used art materials (i.e. wood, paint, paper creatively)		
Presentation: **Good posture**		
Eye contact with the audience		
Voice control, volume, rate, and expression		
Body language shows enthusiasm		

Presentation Checklist

The following checklist is designed to assist the student in gathering materials and information for an oral presentation. The student should be encouraged to complete the proposal and review it with the teacher to insure a well-organized presentation.

Proposal

Topic on which I'll speak

____

Supporting facts I plan to use

____

____

____

____

Supporting anecdotes or stories to interest my listeners

____

____

____

____

Visual aids to enhance my speech

____

____

Musical background to accompany my speech

____

____

Technological equipment I will need

____

____

What do I want my listeners to learn from this presentation

____

____

My conclusion

____

The Stages of the Writing Process

Throughout the Reader, students are encouraged to write essays on a variety of topics for a variety of audiences and purposes. The following general guideline for the stages of the writing process will assist the student in producing a meaningful, well-organized, well-crafted essay. The writing process includes four stages: prewrite, draft, edit/revise, final copy.

Prewrite Planning Guide:

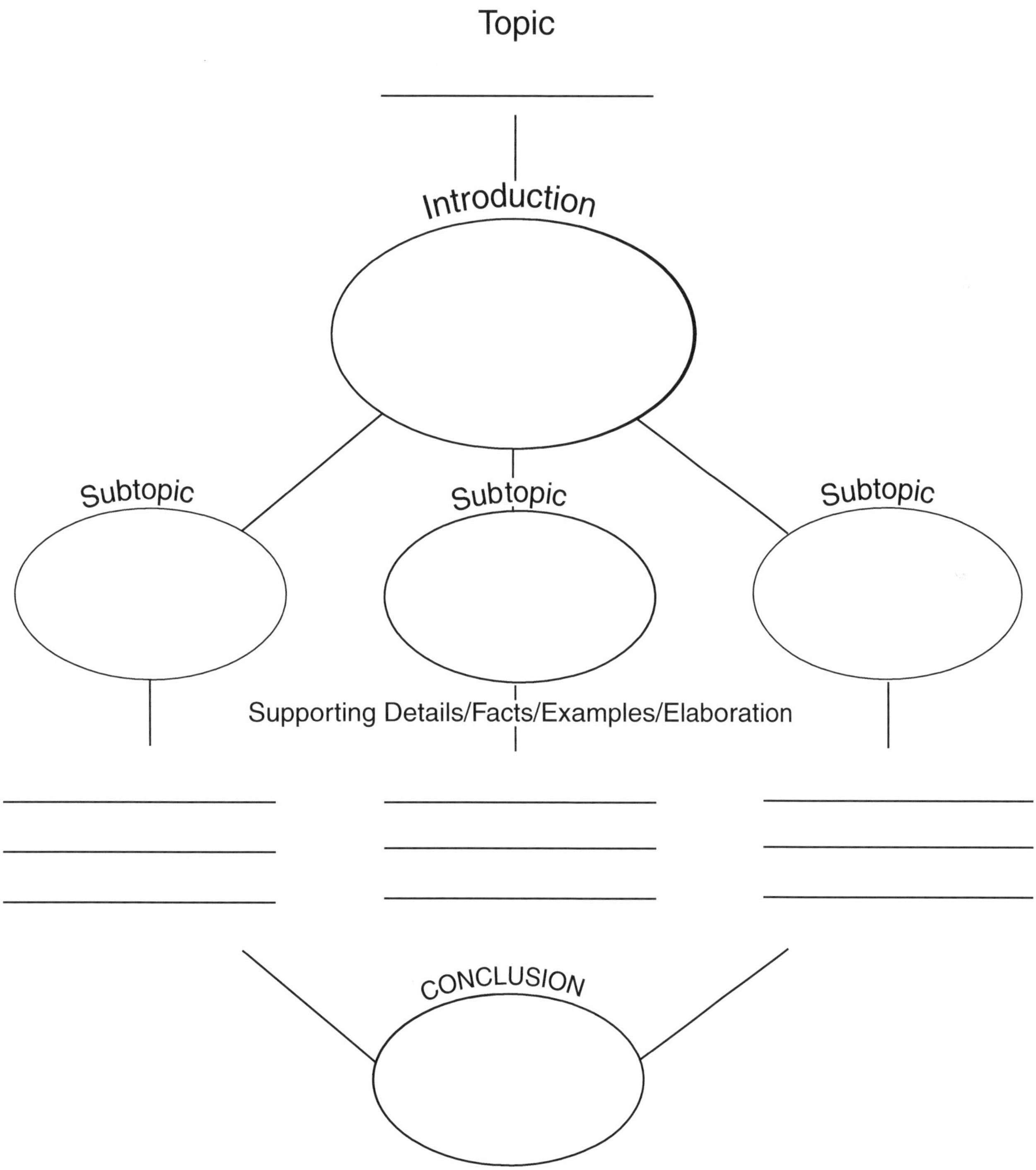

1. Introduction:

I. Students should develop their paper with the following elements:

A. Introduction:

a. Hook sentence—This sentence "hooks" the interest of the reader. A hook sentence can be a quote, a question, an interesting fact, or anecdote.

b. Thesis sentence—This sentence must include the subject about which the paper is written and an opinion. For example: Those living near the Mississippi River need to be prepared for floods. NOT: I'm going to write about floods along the Mississippi River.

c. Map sentence—This sentence lists the three main points of the body of the paper.

2. Body:

Develop the main reasons, one paragraph for each reason, using vivid sensory details. As appropriate use statistics, quotations, stories, and examples to support the reason. Use transitions appropriately at the beginning and within each body paragraph.

TREEES paragraphs

Topic
Reason
  Elaboration
Example
  Elaboration
Summary

3. Conclusion:

Restate the thesis and summarize your main reasons. Challenge the reader with a closing thought, action, or recommendation. In the conclusion, do not use exact words or phrases from the introduction.

Edit/Revise:

Review the essay to make sure it is organized with vivid details and examples that support the thesis, the tone is appropriate for the audience, and word choice is precise and lively. Sentences should be complete and varied in length and structure. Grammar should be appropriate, and spelling and punctuation are generally correct.

Final Draft:

Rewrite the essay to include the revisions made in the editing stage.

Evaluation Rubric (Checklist):

At right.

	Points Possible	Points Earned
Planning:		
Draft:		
Revision/ Editing:		
Final Copy: **Conventions** spelling, punctuation, grammar		
Supporting Details		
Neatness		
Introduction		
Conclusion		
Organization		

Appendix II

World War One had ended just a few years before the original *Elson Readers* appeared. This event was fresh in the mind of Americans and profoundly changed the way they looked at themelves and their role in the world. This changed outlook is reflected in *The Elson Readers,* in both the literature that was included and in the study questions. This brief description of that great event is provided as both a source of background information and a starting point for parents, teachers, and students to begin discussions on this turning point in American history.

A Brief Description of World War One

by Andy Jameson

World War One (also known as the Great War) lasted for four years—from 1914 to the end of 1918. The war was fought between Germany and its allies (Austria-Hungary of the Hapsburg Empire and Turkey of the Ottoman Empire) known as the Central Powers (or the Triple Alliance), and Great Britain, France, Russia, Italy, Japan, and, from 1917, the United States called the Allies. Germany was forced to fight the war on two fronts: the Western Front against the Allies and the Eastern Front against Russia. It was the first international conflict in which the United States participated.

The leading causes of the war were the alliance system of the late nineteenth century, which divided European states into two contending camps; the German victory over France in the Franco-German War (1870-71); the unification of Germany under Chancellor Otto von Bismarck and its rapid industrialization; the nationalist and ethnic agitation in the Balkans; and the fact that by 1900, European states were engaged in an escalating arms race and building vast military and naval forces in peacetime. The alliance system was symptomatic of the tension in European society between the growth of an international economy—the competition for goods and markets—and the political outlook of European states based on their own narrow national interests.

Bismarck set out to build a German empire based on the nationalistic premise that Germany also deserved a "place in the sun"—which meant an international political, economic, and military position like that of the British Empire. In Europe, the Germans claimed that they were being encircled by France and Russia. The entrance of Germany into the world scene exacerbated the intense rivalry for power and colonial markets in Africa, the Near East, and the Far East, as well as control of the seas. When the Germans decided to build a navy in 1891, they began the Anglo-German naval race.

The "race for empire" led to crises in Morocco, where Germany sent a gunboat to protect German interests, and in the Balkans, where Germany supported its Austrian ally against the national liberation movements which threatened the integrity of the Austro-Hungarian Empire. The three Balkan Wars (1912-1913), which were a prelude to World War One, also involved the Turks, whose Ottoman Empire had been disintegrating under the liberation movements of the Greeks and the southern Slavic peoples (Serbs, Croats, Bulgarians), and the Russians, who intervened in the Balkans as the "big Slavic" protectors of the Orthodox Christians—thus posing a threat to the Central Powers.

It was the nationalist movements in the Balkans that provided the "spark" that began World War One. On June 29, 1914, the heir to the Hapsburg Empire, Archduke Franz Ferdinand, was assassinated in Sarajevo (the capital of Bosnia). The Germans supported their Austrian ally, while the French supported the Russians. Protected by their navy, the British tried to maintain their policy of "splendid isolation," but the threat to the British naval forces in the North Sea from the German fleet, and with the French coast of the Channel open to German naval attack, the British were forced to protect their sea lanes and defend their French ally. When the Russians refused a German demand to stop their mobilization on the eastern border, Germany declared war (August 1, 1914), and France followed with its declaration (August 3). And when the Germans launched their Schlieffen Plan—a military strategy which involved a rapid thrust through Belgium to crush the French forces (in violation of the treaty which guaranteed the neutrality of Belgium)—Great Britain also declared war on Germany (August 4).

To supply their Russian ally, the British and French launched a disastrous naval attack on Turkey via the Dardanelles (1915), but the campaign was called off when the Allies lost 143,000 killed or wounded in the Gallipoli campaign.

On the Eastern Front, the early Russian offensive of 1914, which had driven into German territories in Prussia, Poland, and Galicia, was stopped and driven back by the Austro-German offensive of 1915.

By 1916, the war of maneuver on the Western Front ground to a halt, and it became a war of position and attrition—the massive armies were deadlocked in trench warfare. The machine gun—a new weapon—immobilized the troops that could advance only with staggering losses, while the tank, which was to become the antidote to the machine gun, and the airplane, the future antidote to the tank, were still in the experimental stages of development as weapons of war. The stalemate on the Western Front, however, ended when the Russians withdrew from, and the Americans entered, the war. The imperial Russian armies, plagued by poor military leadership and inadequate supplies, collapsed, and Czar Nicholas II was forced to abdicate from the internal pressure of the socialists (Marxists), especially from the leader of the Bolsheviks, the extreme faction of the Russian Marxists, V. I. Lenin (who formed the Communist party). When the czar abdicated, Lenin seized power in November, 1917, and the Bolsheviks signed the treaty of Brest-Litovsk with the Germans (December 3, 1917). At this point the war shifted to the Western Front, where the German High Command, under its Generals Hindenburg and Ludendorff, planned an offensive against the Allies. The Germans moved their army from the Russian front to the west via the railroad.

The German policy of unrestricted submarine warfare led United States President Woodrow Wilson to break off diplomatic relations with Germany, and when the British ship Lusitania was sunk with American passengers on board, and American ships were lost to U-boat action, he asked Congress for a declaration of war "to make the world safe for democracy"(April 2, 1917). But it would be one year before the American military force and industrial production were prepared for war, and American soldiers arrived on the Western Front. With conscription administered by a Selective Service system, the armed services built a force of over four million. The government undertook the massive task of converting producers in the lumber, steel, automobile, and other industries to war production. Shipping tonnage increased from one million to ten million tons. The war effort encouraged citizens to conserve food (sugar was rationed and meatless Tuesdays were introduced) and fuel (daylight-saving time was adopted to save coal), and to purchase government Liberty bonds—the Treasury Department staged rallies at which Hollywood stars appeared to promote bond sales. At the same time, farmers were induced to grow more crops, and the production of civilian goods was cut (75,000 tons of tin were diverted to military production from children's toys and 8,000 tons of steel from the manufacture of women's corsets to munitions). The United States also provided loans to the Allies, which they used to purchase food and supplies.

While American military and economic power were geared up, the French and British suffered great losses in holding the line on the Western Front. When asked about an allied offensive, French General Pétain said, "I am waiting for the Americans and the tanks." In June, 1918, American troops under the command of General John J. Pershing, engaged the Germans at the Battles of Château-Thierry, Belleau Wood, and the Argonne, as 250,000 Americans were landing in France each month. Faced with this allied buildup, the German command realized that Germany could not win the war, and the government of Kaiser Wilhelm II began peace negotiations. By the time the armistice was signed (November 11, 1918), there were two million American soldiers in France and another million were heading for Europe. The Allies suffered ten million killed and twenty million casualties in the war, and the United States lost 115,000 dead and 315,000 casualties. While the allied losses far surpassed those of the Americans, it was the specter and the reality of American military and economic power that were decisive in ending the war.

In military history, World War One is notable for the brutal conditions under which the war was fought and for the incompetent leadership of the commanders—and the effect on the morale and discipline of the troops. The idea that soldiers were "manipulated from above" subject to the traditional military concept of obedience based on punishment resulted in revision of the military code of conduct.

Among the legacies of the war, which affected the course of the twentieth century, were the creation of the League of Nations (an international consortium), the rise of totalitarianism, and the imperial partition of the Near East (which resulted in the future states of Iraq, Syria, and Jordan).

Glossary

a as in mat	ə as in banana	ä as in father	Ø as in side
e as in bed	ər as in further	aů as in loud	ŋ as in sing
i as in tip	ā as in day	ē as in need	ō as in snow
ȯ as in saw	ȯi as in coin	ü as in rule	u̇ as in pull
	^{ə} as in eaten	th as in heather	

A

a bate ment (ə-bāt-mənt) decrease
ab by ('a-bē) monastery; castle
ab di cat ed ('ab-di-kā-təd) given up the throne
ab hor (əb-'hȯr) hate
ab ject ('ab-jekt) humble
ab ne ga tion (ab-ni-'gā-shən) giving up all thought
aboard, laid went onto
Abraham...Ishmael...Hagar ('ā-brə-ham; 'ish-mā-əl; 'hā-gär) *see* Genesis XXI:9-20
Abrahams pictures of Abraham
a breast (ə-'brest) side by side
ab sti nence ('ab-stə-nənts) going without
ab stract ing (ab-'strak-tiŋ) sneaking
A by dos (ə-'bØ-dəs)
a byss (ə-'bis) immeasurable space; deep gulf; sea
A ca di a (ə-'kā-dē-ə) former name of Nova Scotia
A ca die (ä-kä-'dē) see Acadia
ac ced ed (ak-'sē-dəd) agreed
ac cor dant (ə-'kȯr-d^{ə}nt) harmonious
accountant one who makes financial statements
ac me ('ak-mē) perfection
ac qui es cence (a-kwē-'e-s^{ə}nts) agreement
ad a mant ('a-də-mənt) hardest stone
A day es ('ä-dā-ēz)
ad dled ('a-d^{ə}ld) confused
ad dress (ə-'dres) formal speech
ad her ent (ad-'hir-ənt) supporter
Ad ju tant ('a-jə-tənt) officer through whom the Commander receives communications and gives orders

ad mi ra ble (ˈad-mə-rə-bəl) praiseworthy
Adonis dandy. Adonis, in mythology, was a beautiful youth beloved by the goddess Venus
ad vent (ˈad-vent) beginning
ad ver sary (ˈad-vər-ser-ē) foe; opponent
ad verse currents streams that flow different ways
ad ver si ty (ad-ˈvər-sə-tē) misfortune
ad vo ca cy (ˈad-və-kə-sē) behalf
ae ri al (ˈar-ē-əl) airy
Aer shot (ˈär-skȯt) town in Belgium
af fa bil i ty (a-fə-ˈbi-lə-tē) friendliness
af front (ə-ˈfrənt) insult
affronted offended
aft (ˈaft) toward the stern
ag gres sor (ə-ˈgre-sər) enemy
a ghast (ə-ˈgast) horrified
ag i tat ed (ˈa-jə-tā-təd) blown; excited
a gog (ə-ˈgäg) eager
Ai denn (ˈā-dən) paradise
Aix (ˈāks) city in France
alac ri ty (ə-ˈla-krə-tē) willingness
al der (ȯl-dər) tree which grows in moist ground
A li Ba ba (a-lē; ˈbä-bə)
alien (ˈā-lē-ən) foreigner
alien ate (ˈā-lē-ə-nāt) separate
Al la hu (ˈä-lə-hü) Allah
al le giance (ə-ˈlē-jənts) loyalty
al lit er a tion (ə-li-tə-ˈrā-shən) repetition of the same letter or sound at the beginning of successive words
al loys (ˈa-lȯiz) combinations of metals
all per va sive (pər-ˈvā-siv) universal
al lu sion (ə-ˈlü-zhən) reference
al ly (ə-ˈlØ) friend; aid
al mond (ˈäl-mənd)
alms house (ˈälmz-hau̇s) poorhouse
al oe (ˈa-lō) plant which blossoms when it is one hundred years old
alp mountains in general
al ter na tive (ȯl-ˈtər-nə-tiv) choice
a lu mi num (ə-ˈlü-mə-nəm) very lightweight metal, silver-colored
a main (ə-ˈmān) at full speed
am a ranth (ˈa-mə-ranth) an imaginary flower which never fades

am bro si al (am-'brō-zhəl) beautiful
ami a ble ('ā-mē-ə-bəl) lovely
am i ca ble ('a-mi-kə-bəl) friendly; peaceful
Am o noo suck (am-ō-'nü-sək)
a mor phas (ə-'mȯr-fəs) the amorpha, a flowering plant
a move or two "the ways of the world"
am phi the ater ('amp-fə-thē-ə-tər) a circular building with seats gradually higher toward the back; in the large central open space, called the arena, the Romans had their gladiatorial contests
A mun ('ä-mün) one of the Egyptian gods, represented as a ram with curling horns
anat o my (ə-'na-tə-mē) study of the human body
an cho rite monk ('aŋ-kə-rØt) one bound by a vow to live in solitude
anew (ə-'nü) again
Angel of the backward look angel that records our lives
An ge lus ('an-jə-ləs) bell calling the people to evening prayer
Anglo-Saxon divinity of Spring Eoster, worshiped by the Early English as the goddess who brought back life to the earth
an ni hi la tion (ə-nØ-ə-'lā-shən) total destruction
an nulled the charters (ə-'nəld) taken away the legal writing which allowed certain rights
a non (ə-'nän) soon; immediately
a non y mous (ə-'nä-nə-məs) nameless
answer to his inward thought correspond to his idea of what he wished to be
an tag o nis tic (an-ta-gə-'nis-tik) strongly opposed
an ti dote ('an-ti-dōt) a remedy to counteract the effects of something taken, or applied, by mistake
ape ('āp) imitate
Ap ol lo ni us (a-pə-'lō-nē-əs) ancient Roman philosopher who lived at the time of Christ and was said to be able to converse with birds and animals
ap o plec tic op u lence (a-pə-'plek-tik; 'ä-pyə-lənts) overflowing riches
ap os tol ic (a-pə-'stä-lik) spiritual
ap palled (ə-'pȯld) horrified
ap pa ri tion (a-pə-'ri-shən) ghost
ap pel la tion (a-pə-'lā-shən) name
ap praised (ə-'prāzd) priced
ap pre hen sion (a-pri-'hen-shən) fear
ap pren tice (ə-'pren-təs) helper who is learning the business; apprenticed, taught a trade while working; 'prentice, young man learning his trade
ap prise (ə-'prØz) inform

ap pro ba tion (a-prə-'bā-shən) approval
apt ly ('apt-lē) fittingly
Ar ab ('ar-əb) Arabian
ar a besque (ar-ə-'besk) in geometric design
arched made an arch over
arch-enemy worst enemy
a re na (ə-'rē-nə) *see* amphitheater
Ar go nauts ('är-gə-nöts) sailors on the Argo who went in search of the Golden Fleece. *see* a mythology
ar go sy ('är-gə-sē) airy; imaginary vessel made of sunbeams
Ariel-airy ease ('ar-ē-əl) with the light movements of Ariel, a spirit of the air, in Shakespeare's *The Tempest*
ar is toc ra cy (ar-ə-'stä-krə-sē) more fortunate classes in society which have riches, power, education, etc.
a ro ma (ə-'rō-mə) fragrance
ar o mat ic (ar-ə-'ma-tik) fragrant; strong scented
artful coquettish; artful dog, mind, a clever fellow, you may be sure
articles of dep re da tion (de-prə-'dā-shən) agreement to kidnap
ar ti cu la tion (är-ti-kyə-'lā-shən) careful sounding of consonants
ar ti fice ('är-tə-fəs) unnatural covering; trick
as cribed to me (ə-'skrØbd) said was mine
a skance (ə-'skants) sideways
as pho del ('as-fə-dəl) in Greek mythology, a flower associated with the underworld and the dead
as pi ra tions (as-pə-'rā-shənz) ambitions
as pire (ə-'spØr) fly upward; hope to reach
as si du i ty (a-sə-'dü-ə-tē) industry
as sid u ous (ə-'sij-wəs) devoted
as sign (ə-'sØn) representative
as suage (ə-'swāj) relieve
as sump tions (ə-'səmp-shənz) boldness
Atchaf a laya (ə-cha-fə-'lØ-ə) bayou which is an outlet of the Red and the Mississippi rivers
at his famous best as fast as it was possible for him
attained the extremity walked through to the opposite side
attunes his pipe anew begins singing again
au gust (ȯ-'gəst) dignified
au re ole ('ȯr-ē-ōl) circle of light around the head, i.e., a halo
aus tere (ȯ-'stir) severe; **austerity** severity
avail (ə-'vāl) have power to hold me back; help
av a lanche ('a-və-lanch) ice, snow, or land sliding down a mountainside.

av a rice ('a-və-rəs) greediness
av a tar ('a-və-tär) symbol
A ve Ma ri a (ä-vā-mə-'rē-ə)
aye and a non ('∅; ə-'nän) constantly
az ure ('a-zhər) clear blue

B

Babylonish jargon (ba-bə-'lō-nish; 'jär-gən) confusion; Genesis XI:1-10
bac cha nal ('ba-kə-n°l) a drunken merry-maker; Bacchanals, the followers of Bacchus, the god of wine
bac chan tes (bə-'kants) riotous merry-makers
bale ful ('bāl-fəl) gloomy
bal let dancer ('ba-lā) toe-dancer
balm something delightful or soothing
balm in Gil e ad ('gi-lē-əd) relief from pain, in heaven
Bap tiste
bar prevent
bar bar ic (bär-'bar-ik) vivid and striking (as used by primitive peoples)
bard professional poet and singer
barge ('bärj) small, graceful sailboat
bar rack ('bar-ək) of the soldier's lodgings
Basin of Mi nas ('mi-nəs) Eastern arm of Bay of Fundy
bas re lief ('bä-ri-'lēf) standing out from the rest of his face
bast ed been ('bās-təd) had water poured over them as a roast has
bat tal ions (bə-'tal-yənz) crowds
bay reddish-brown horse
bay ou ('b∅-ü) inlet from the Gulf of Mexico, lake, or large river, sometimes sluggish; of Plaquemine, town in Louisiana
beam widest part
Beau Sejour (bō; sā-'zhür) town in Acadia, attacked by the British in 1745
Beautiful River Ohio River
be dight (bi-'d∅t) decorated
Bedlam ('bed-ləm) insane asylum in London
beetling jutting out into the street
be guile (bi-'g∅l) spend; deceive; beguile you from, make you forget; beguiling, coaxing
be hest (bi-'hest) command
be lie, did (bi-'l∅) acted in a manner opposite to
Belle Fontaine (bel-ə-fän-'tān)
Bel loy en San terre (bel-'wä-än-sȯn-'tär)

Bel shaz zars (bel-'sha-zərz) pictures of Belshazzar, last king of Babylon
belted half the horizon extended half-way along the skyline
Ben e dic i te (ben-ā-'dēs-i-tā) bless you
be nev o lence (bə-'nev-lənts) kindness; organ of, heart
be nig nant (bi-'nig-nənt) kind
be nig ni ty (bi-'nig-nə-tē) kindness
be parties to assist in telling
be reave ment (bi-'rēv-mənt) sorrow
be tro thal (bi-'trō-thəl) engagement
bid defiance to contagion live without fear of the disease
big no ni a (big-'nō-nē-ə) a kind of tropical vine which bears flowers
big ot ry ('bi-gə-trē) narrow mindedness
birds of passage birds going south for the winter
bishop wine and fruit juices
bi zarre (bə-'zär) unusual
blanched ('blancht) grew pale; pale; whitened
blank verse poetry with rhythm but no rhyme
blas phe mous ('blas-fə-məs) indecent
blenched ('blencht) hesitated
Blom i don ('bläm-i-dən) a mountain
blooms, leafless the blossoms come before the leaves in the spring
bluff headland high, steep bank
Board of Trade the committee having charge of commerce
"bob" slang for shilling
bodiced zone waist encircled with a wide girdle
bole ('bōl) trunk
bonnet and plume tam o'shanter with a large feather for decoration
bo nus ('bō-nəs) extra pay
boon ('bün) favor
bootless idle
border region between England and Scotland
bor ough ('bər-ō) village
Bourbon scepter the rule of the Bourbons, a French family, members of which became tyrannical rulers in France, Spain, and Italy
bow ('bau̇) front part of a ship
Bow doin ('bō-dᵊn) in Brunswick, Maine
bows ('bōwz) U-shaped pieces about the necks of oxen, fastened to the yoke brace, pair
brackish ('bra-kish) salt-water
Braddock's army men under General Braddock, defeated by the French and Indians, 1755

Brains of Labor genius of invention, organization, etc., which is the great force back of all labor
brake thicket
brant ('brant) kind of wild duck
brawn ('brȯn) roasted meat; physical strength
bra zier ('brā-zhər) pan for burning coals
breach opening
breeches ('brē-chəz)
brewing on a large scale cooking in large quantities with clouds of steam
brig ands ('bri-gandz) highwaymen
Brig id ('bri-jəd) Saint Brigid, patroness of Ireland (453-523)
broad-girthed large and fat
brooch ('brōch) pin
brood ing ('brü-diŋ) thoughtful
buck dashing young fellow
bucking leaping
buffcoat close, leather coat
buffer protection to lessen the shock
buffoon (bə-'fün) clown
Bunker Hill a famous battle of the early Revolutionary days (June 17, 1775)
buoy ('bü-ē) object kept afloat on the water to mark something below the surface
bur gess ('bər-jəs) citizen
burlesque (bər-'lesk) caricature
burning Sappho ('sa-fō) Greek lyric poetess of intense feeling (600 B.C.)
bus kins ('bəs-kənz) high boots
but all except their sun, is set the greatness they have been famous for is now gone
butte ('byüt) hill
but ting ('bə-tiŋ) pushing
butts ('bəts) handle ends
by common consent unanimously

C

cables ropes and chains
cadence ('kād-ᵊns) rhythm
Cains and Abels pictures of Cain and Abel, sons of Adam and Eve; See Genesis IV
caldron ('kȯl-drən) kettle

calender one who presses cloth between rollers to glaze it
Cal i ban ('ka-lə-ban) an ugly creature, half man, half monster, in Shakespeare's *The Tempest*
cal li o pe (kə-'l∅-ə-pē) a musical instrument with steam whistles
Camden Town a suburb of London
"came down" handsomely did a generous thing (a pun)
can de la brum (kan-də-'lä-brəm) large ornamental branched candlestick
can dor ('kan-dər) frankness
can is ters ('ka-nə-stərz) cases for coffee and tea
Can no bie Lee ('kan-ə-bē) rising ground in southern Scotland
cant ('kant) hypocritical preaching
can ta ta (kən-'tä-tə) musical accompaniment
ca pa cious (kə-'pā-shəs) roomy; broad
ca pi tal ('ka-pə-tᵊl) attractive
ca pi ta list ('ka-pə-tᵊl-ist) a possessor and controller of money
cap sule ('kap-səl) small cylindrical-shaped case
car a coled ('kar-ə-kōld) turned
cardinal a high officer in the Catholic church
ca reer ing (ka-'ri-riŋ) running
car ri on ('kar-ē-ən) dead body
Car thu sian (kär-'thü-zhən) one of the order of monks whose rigid vows compel almost absolute silence
Ca sa Gui di ('kä-sə; 'gwē-dē)
case ment ('kās-mənt) window opening on hinges from one side
cas tel la ted ('kas-tə-lā-təd) built like a castle, with towers and ramparts
castes ('kasts) different ranks of society
cas u al ly ('kazh-wə-lē) carelessly
catch a round
cath o lic ('kath-lik) universal
caus tic ('kȯs-tik) sharp
cau ter ized ('kȯ-tə-r∅zd) burned to prevent infection
cav al cade (ka-vəl-'kād) horseback procession
Ca wein (kā-'w∅n)
Ce dra ('sē-drə) a river
celebrated herd in the poem *see* Wordsworth's poem "March"
ce les tial (sə-'les-chəl) divine
cen ser ('sen-sər) vessel for perfumes or to burn incense in
Cen ten ni al (sen-'te-nē-əl) 100th anniversary of 1776; centennial birthday, 100th anniversary
certain flight straight, sure path
ces sa tion (se-'sā-shən) stopping

C'est toi, c'est toi, Marcel! Mon frere comme je suis heureuse ('sā 'twä mär-'sel mō 'frer 'kem 'zhə 'swē zər-'rüz)
chafed ocean-side ('chāft) wave-washed shore
chaf finch ('cha-finch) common European song bird
chaise ('shāz) light carriage; chaise and pair, carriage and two horses
Chal de an plain (kal-'dē-ən) wide, uncultivated stretches of land in Chaldea, an ancient country of Asia
cha lised ('cha-ləst) cup shaped
Chalk ley's journal ('chȯk-lēz) the incident was retold from the *Journal of Thomas Chalkley* (1675-1741), a traveling Quaker preacher
chambered cell roomlike part of the shell
chan cel ('chan-səl) the part of the church reserved for the ministers or priests
change ling ('chānj-liŋ) child supposed to have been changed, by fairies, for another
'Change, upon in the Royal Exchange, the center of London commerce
chap let ('chap-lət) rosary
character standing
chargeable burdensome
charger horse
Charles the Voluptuous (və-'ləp-chə-wəs) Charles II of England (1630-1685), who cared only for pleasure
char wo man ('chär-wu̇-mən) woman hired by the day to clean
chasm ('ka-zᵊm) deep break in the earth
chaunt ('chȯnt) song of praise
cheapens his array makes his plumage look dull and faded
Cheapside street in London
Cher so nese ('kər-sə-nēz) Eastern Greece
chi val rous ('shi-vəl-rəs) valiant
Chris ti na, Fort (kris-'tē-nə)
chro nic ('krä-nik) habitual
chro ni cle ('krä-ni-kəl) living record
chub a kind of fish
ci de vant ('sē-də-'vän) former
cir cuit ('sər-kət) journeys from hour to hour
civil and religious both of citizenship and of the church
claim his toll ('tōl) seize his share, and kill for food
clap boards ('kla-bōrdz) extra boards to keep out rain, shingles
cla ret ('klar-ət) purplish red
clar i on ('klar-ē-ən) clear and loud, like a trumpet
clean-winged swept clean with a turkey's wing

clem ent (ˈkle-mənt) indulgent
clois ter (ˈklȯi-stər) covered outdoor passage lined with columns
clout ed (ˈklau̇-təd) patched
Co che cho (kō-ˈchē-kō)
coil chain; trouble
col lab o rat ed (kə-ˈla-bə-rā-təd) wrote together
col league (ˈkä-lēg) associate
col on nades (kä-lē-ˈnādz) series of columns of trees
Columbian Plains in Western Canada
Columkill Saint Columba, an Irish missionary to Scotland in the sixth century
col umn (ˈkä-ləm) pillar
Co man ches (kə-ˈman-chēz) warlike Indian tribe
come ly (ˈkəm-lē) good-looking
comforter long, knitted scarf
commonplace likenesses
communing (kə-ˈmyü-niŋ) having personal relations
com pact (käm-ˈpakt) crowded together
com pass (ˈkäm-pəs) range
compassed controlled
compass flower plant with leaves which indicate the points of the compass
com pen sate (ˈkäm-pən-sāt) make up
com pe tence (ˈkäm-pə-təns) wealth
com pe tent (ˈkäm-pə-tənt) good
composed at rest
com pound (ˈkäm-pau̇nd) mixture
com pre hen sive (käm-pri-ˈhend-siv) extensive; comprehensive ocean, vast extent
con ceived (kən-ˈsēvd) begun
con cep tion (kən-ˈsep-shən) design; idea
con cur rence (kən-ˈkər-əns) agreement
con curs with their movements (kən-ˈkərz) assists in their undertakings
con demn (kən-ˈdem) criticize
con de scen sion (kän-di-ˈsen-chən) friendliness as though they were equals
con duce (kən-ˈdüs) lead
con du cive (kən-ˈdü-siv) helpful
con fis ca ted (ˈkän-fə-skā-təd) seized
con fla gra tion (ˈkän-flə-ˈgrā-shən) fire
con found (kən-ˈfau̇nd) confuse
con gealed (kən-ˈjēld) hardened; congealed into, shown in
con i cal (ˈkä-ni-kəl) cone shaped

con jec ture (kən-ˈjek-chər) infer; think
con nu bi al (kə-ˈnü-bē-əl) matrimonial
con scious ness (ˈkän-chəs-nəs) knowledge
con se cra tion (ˈkän-sə-ˈkrā-shən) giving up in a noble manner
constituted lawful—here, English
con sum ma tion (kän-sə-ˈmā-shən) bringing to a perfect close
contemplation of theorists (ˈthē-ə-rists) attention of those who merely think about it and do not put their ideas into practice
con tem po ra ry (kən-ˈtem-pə-rer-ē) of the present day
con tig u ous (kən-ˈti-gyə-wəs) adjoining
con tri tion (kən-ˈtri-shən) repentance
con tro ver sy (ˈkän-trə-vər-sē) dispute
con vened (kən-ˈvēnd) called together
conventional standards of greatness the way the majority of people decide whether a man is great or not
con vert (kän-ˈvərt) change
co op er at ion (kō-ä-pə-ˈrā-shən) help
cope (ˈkōp) canopy
co pi ous (ˈkō-pē-əs) many
copper wash-boiler; kettle
cor al reefs (ˈkȯr-əl) skeletons of certain small sea animals have been deposited through the ages and form islands
Corner for the Rustic Muse column of contributed poetry
Cornland farmland, in general
cor po ra tion (kȯr-pə-ˈrā-shən) legislative body
cor ral (kə-ˈral) an enclosure for confining animals
Cor reg gi o (kə-ˈre-jē-ō) Italian artist
cor rob o ra ted (kə-ˈrä-bə-rā-təd) admitted the truth of
corrupt spoiled; dishonest; corrupted, changed from good to bad; corruption, dishonesty
corse let (ˈkȯr-slət) armor
Cos ta Ri ca's everglades (kȯs-tä-ˈrē-kə) swamps of Costa Rica, a republic in Central America
Cotton Mather American clergyman (1663-1728)
couch ant (ˈkau̇-chənt) squatting
cou lee (ˈkü-lē) bed of a dried-up stream
coun ter feit (ˈkau̇nt-ər-fit) pretend
counterplots schemes to defeat him
counter-proposition proposal in answer to your own
cou reurs des bois (kü-ˈrər-dā-bwä) French or French and Indian hunters and traders of western North America, especially Canada

court i er ('kōr-tē-ər) attendant on a king, queen, or prince
cov ert ly ('kō-vərt-lē) secretly
cov et ous ('kə-və-təs) greedy
coy o te ('k∅-ō-tē) prairie wolf
crane iron hook for supporting kettles over a fire; machine for handling great weights
crank top heavy, a fault of ships of that time
cran nied ('kra-nēd) having crevices
cra vat (krə-'vat) necktie
crav en ('krā-vən) coward
craw crop
cre den tials (kri-'den-chəlz) letters of recommendation
cred i tor ('kre-di-tər) the one to whom you owe money
cre du li ty (kri-'dü-lə-tē) willingness to believe
creed of caste belief that one must remain in the class into which one was born
Creeks ('krēks) Indians who went from Georgia beyond the Mississippi in 1826
Cre ole ('krē-ōl) person of Spanish or French descent brought up in a colonial possession
cring ing ('krin-jiŋ) shrinking
croup ('krüp) back of the horse
crown English coin, ordinarily worth about $1.20 [1921]
cru sade (krü-'sād) fight for American ideals
crypt ('kript) hiding place
crys tal line ('kris-tə-lən) uncloudy
Cuban business Spanish-American war, 1898, to free Cuba from Spanish misrule
cumberless free
cum brous ('kəm-brəs) clumsy
cunning-warded carefully guarded
cu po la ('kyü-pə-lə) peaked structure
cur few ('kər-fyü) a bell signalling people to retire to their homes
cut lass ('kət-ləs) short, heavy sword
cy press tree ('s∅-prəs) tree used as a symbol of mourning

D

daft foolish
das tard ('das-tərd) coward
daunt ed ('dȯn-təd) scared

daunt less ('dȯnt-ləs) brave
daws ('dȯz) jackdaws, birds noted for stealing
deal forms benches made of pine
dearth ('dərth) want
de bris (də-'brē) ruins; rubbish
de cant er (di-'kan-tər) glass bottle
de ceased (di-'sēst) dead
dec i sive (di-'s∅-siv) clear
de co ra of mere fashion (dā-'kȯ-rə) the style of the times
de co rum (dē-'kōr-əm) idea of what was proper; dignity
decrepitude (di-'kre-pə-tüd) feebleness
de cry (di-'kr∅) undervalue
def er ence ('de-fə-rəns) respect
de fi ance (di-'f∅-əns) challenge
de file (di-'f∅l) narrow pass
deflowered opened out; killed
deformity (di-'fȯr-mə-tē) wrong form
deftly cleverly
de gen er ate (di-'jen-ə-rāt) sink dishonored
deg ra da tion (də-gra-'dā-shən) gradual process of becoming worse
deigned ('dānd) kindly consented
delegated power ('de-li-gā-təd) power of one to act or vote for others, with their permission
de li ri ous (di-'lir-ē-əs) wildly happy
De los ('dē-läs) island southeast of Greece
dem a gogue ('de-mə-gäg) leader who has the confidence of the people but who has not their welfare at heart
de mean or (di-'mē-nər) bearing
De me tri us (di-'mē-trē-əs)
dem o cra cy (di-'mä-krə-sē) a government by the people
de mo ni ac (di-'mō-nē-ak) wicked
den i zens ('de-nə-zənz) workers
de pend ed (di-'pen-dəd) hung
de pict (di-'pikt) picture
de ploy ing (di-'plȯi-iŋ) enlarging
de pop u la ted (dē-'pä-pyə-lā-təd) deprived of inhabitants
de rived (di-'r∅vd) received; born
de scried (di-'skr∅d) made out
desert ('de-zərt) lonely; sandy waste
desert's highest born the proudest and most intelligent of the desert animals
destined end ('des-tənd) end nature intended for him

de tract (di-'trakt) take away (their honor)
de vice (di-'vØs) trick
de vi ous ('di-vē-əs) winding; restless
dev o tee (de-və-'tē) very religious person
dew drop ('dü-dräp)
dexterously ('dek-strə-əs-lē) skillfully
di a tribe ('dØ-ə-trØb) article of abuse
dif fuse (di-'fyüz) spread; diffused, given to many instead of to only one; diffusion, spreading
dight ('dØt) decked
di lap i dat ed (də-'la-pə-dā-təd) old and worn-out looking
diligence perseverance
dim i nu tion (di-mə-'nü-shən) lessening
dimpling valleys fertile, rolling ground
dip candle
dirge ('dərg) funeral song
dirges of his Hope death songs of his last hope
dis af fec tion (di-sə-'fek-shən) hostility
dis ci plined intellect ('di-sə-plənd) well-trained mind
dis con cert (dis-kən-'sərt) confusion
dis coun te nanc ing (dis-'kaün-tᵊn-ən(t)-siŋ) discouraging
dis course ('dis-kōrs) speech
dis cred i ted (dis-'krə-də-təd) disbelieved
dis gorged (dis-'gȯrjd) threw out
dis mant ling (dis-'mant-liŋ) removing its guns, and then selling
dis mem ber ed (dis-'mem-bərd) separate
dis pelled (di-'speld) driven away
dis perse (di-'spərs) send away
dis pu ta tious (dis-pyü-'tā-shəs) argumentative
dis si pat ed, been ('di-sə-pā-təd) disappeared
dis sol u tion (di-sə-'lü-shən) complete breaking down
dis so nant ('di-sə-nənt) discordant
distant unsociable
ditto image
di vers ('dØ-vərs) many; different
di ver si fied (də-'vər-sə-fØd) various
divert (də-'vərt) turn; diverted, amused
di vine (də-'vØn) foretell; guess
doc ile to the helm ('dä-səl) easily steered
doc trine ('däk-trən) lesson
doff remove

dog days hottest part of the summer
dog ged ('dȯ-gəd) stubborn
domestic trib u la tion (tri-byə-'lā-shən) matrimonial troubles
domestic tyranny ('tir-ə-nē) an enemy to democracy in our country
dom i cile ('dä-mə-sØl) home; here, wagon
dom i nant ('dä-mə-nənt) impressive
Don Juan ('dän-hwän)
dot age ('dō-tij) foolish affection
dot ard ('dō-tərd) old idiot
doub let ('dəb-lət) close-fitting coat
dow er ('daů-ər) treasure; gift, wealth, or property which a bride brings to her husband; dowering, supporting; dowerless, without any money or property to bring to her husband
draught ('draft) drink
draught-board ('draft) checker board
dread ('dred) dreadful
drought ('draůt) dryness
Druids of eld ancient order of Celts who held trees sacred
Dryad ('drØ-ad) wood nymph
du bi ous ('dü-bē-əs) uncertain
duc til i ty (dək-'ti-lə-tē) imparts "makes it so it'll roll"
Duf feld ('də-felt) town in Belgium
dug out ('dəg-aůt) cave where the soldiers lived
du ly ('dü-lē) conscientiously
Du val (dü-'väl)

E

Earthquake day *see* Lisbon
Ec cen tric (ik-'sen-trik) peculiar
ec sta sy ('ek-stə-sē) happy outburst; great joy
Eden never lost, charm which love
ed i fice ('e-də-fəs) a house
ef fi ca cious (e-fə-'kā-shəs) efficient
ef fi ca cy ('e-fi-kə-se) power
eg lan tine ('e-glən-tØn) the sweetbrier
e go tism ('ē-gə-ti-zəm) conceit
e jac u la tion (i-ja-kyə-'lā-shən) exclamation
eke ('ēk) also
elements noise of the wind, etc.
elfin fairy

e lic i ted (i-ˈli-sə-təd) drew the information
"el lum" dialect for elm
Ellwood, Thomas Quaker author of an epic poem of the life of David
elm-tree (ˈelm)
e lu ci da tion (i-lü-sə-ˈdā-shən) explanation
Elysian Fields (i-ˈli-zhən) the Greeks' name for paradise; they believed the soul would be forced to wander about through eternity unless the body was buried
em a na tion (e-mə-ˈna-shən) gift
em bar go (im-ˈbär-gō) obstruction
embattled armed
em bel lish ments (im-ˈbe-lish-mənts) decorations
em bod i ment (im-ˈbä-di-mənt) example
em bra sure (im-ˈbrā-zhər) wall opening
e merge (i-ˈmərj) appear
em i nence (ˈe-mə-nəns) height
e mit ted (ē-ˈmi-təd) uttered
em pow er ed (im-ˈpau̇-ərd) given the power
en am eled (i-ˈna-məld) glossy
en am ored (i-ˈna-mərd) much in love
en com pass (in-ˈkem-pəs) surround
en core (ˈän-kōr) besides
en cy clo pe di a (in-s∅-klə-ˈpē-dē-ə) book of information for reference
ends will change future will be different
en gross es you (in-ˈgrō-səs) occupies all your thought and time
en join (in-ˈjȯin) require; enjoined, commanded
en kind leth (in-ˈkin-də-ləth) inspires
en voy (ˈen-vȯi) representative
envy the vice of republics in a country where all people are politically equal, some are likely to dislike those who have more money or intelligence then they
e rad i cat ed (i-ˈra-də-kā-təd) removed
Erze roum (erz-ˈrüm) a division of Turkey
Esq., esquire title of courtesy
es say (ˈe-sā) attempt
es say (e-ˈsā) to try
es sence (ˈe-sᵊns) soul
eternal summer summer all the year round
e the re al (i-ˈthir-ē-əl) spiritual
ethereal minstrel celestial singer
eu lo gy (ˈyü-lə-jē) oration of praise

even (ˈē-vᵊn) evening
ever-during constant
e vinced (i-ˈvinst) clearly showed
ev o lu tions (e-və-ˈlü-shənz) dancing
ewe-necked (ˈyü) with a hollowed-out, thin neck
ex al ta tion (eg-zȯl-ˈtā-shən) glorifying; intense emotion
ex cheq uer (ˈeks-che-kər) purse
ex e cra ble (ˈek-si-krə-bəl) shocking
ex e cu tor (ig-ˈze-kyə-tər) person appointed to carry out the provisions of a will
ex em pli fy (ig-ˈzem-plə-fØ) illustrate
Ex pe di tion a ry (ek-spə-ˈdi-shə-ner-ē) sent from one country to another
ex pos tu la tions (ik-späs-chə-ˈlā-shənz) protests
ex qui site (ek-ˈskwi-zət) perfect
extent of its compass length of range, from high notes to low
ex tinct (ik-ˈstiŋkt) dead
ex trav a gance (ik-ˈstra-vi-gənts) absurdity
ex trem i ty (ik-ˈstre-mə-tē) farthest part; worst place he could think of
ex u ber ant fertility (ig-ˈzü-bə-rənt) great richness
ex ul ta tion (ek-səl-ˈtā-shən) delight

F

Fabre (ˈfäbrᵊ)
fabric of social order organization of humanity
facetious (fə-ˈsē-shəs) agreeable
fac ile (ˈfa-səl) easy
fac il i ty (fə-ˈsi-lə-tē) readiness
fac tion (ˈfak-shən) party politics
fac tious (ˈfak-shəs) own selfish
fain (ˈfān) forced; gladly; fain for, eager to
Fal co Star len (ˈfal-kō; stär-lən)
familiar of men companion of people
familiars intimate friends
Fan euil Hall (ˈfan-yəl)
fan tas tic (fan-ˈtas-tik) extraordinary; queer
far thing (ˈfär-thiŋ) fourth of an English penny, half cent in our money [1921]
fastnesses strongholds
fatal sisters three Fates of Greek mythology, who were believed to decide the course of men's lives

Fa ta Mor ga na (fä-tə; mȯr-'gä-nə) a mirage, that is, an appearance which seems real but actually is not
fate of a nation future happiness of the land
Father of Waters Mississippi River
fath om ('fa-thəm) six feet
fay ('fā) fairy
fe al ty ('fēl-tē) loyalty
Federal or Democrat the names of the political parties of that time
feign ('fān) imitate; like to imagine
feint ('fānt) pretense; trick
Fe lic ian (fi-'li-shən)
fe lic i ty (fi-'li-sə-tē) happiness
fell marsh; fierce
fel loe ('fel-ō) wooden rim of a wheel
fer ment ('fər-ment) tumult
fer ret ('fer-ət) sharp—like a ferret's teeth
fete ('fāt) festival
fet lock ('fet-läk) the tuft of hair on a horse's foot
fet tered ('fe-tərd) bound with chains; fettered race, enslaved people
feu dal or military principle ('fyü-dᵊl) system which requires people to remain in the class in which they were born, or that which keeps them under their ruler's military power
fictitious (fik-'ti-shəs) artificial
filberts nuts
fil i al ('fi-lē-əl) of a son or daughter
filled the chains had fallen into the "chains" or rigging along the sides
Fi na le (fə-'na-lē) end; last part
finished talent natural ability developed to its highest point
firelock old-fashioned gun
fire-winged by martyrdom many early Quakers suffered death, by burning, because of their religious beliefs
fir ma ment ('fər-mə-mənt) heavens
five-and-sixpence five shillings and sixpence = $1.32 [1921]
flag-bird French flag, flying in the air
fla gon ('fla-gən) a large drinking vessel
flake ('flāk) bunch
flam ing ('flām-iŋ) set on fire by the enemy
flat heresy ('her-ə-sē) absolute disloyalty
flaunt ing ('flȯn-tiŋ) insolent
Flemish pictures pictures which treat simple subjects lovingly and in detail. Rembrandt's works are good examples of this school

Fleu rette (flü-'ret)
fluc tu ate ('flək-chə-wāt) changed
flue ('flü) pipe
foal ('fōl) colt
foc sle ('fōk-səl) forecastle, fore part of upper deck
foi ble ('fȯi-bəl) weakness
foil ('fȯil) outwit
folded ('fōl-dəd) put in their enclosure for the night
fo li age ('fō-lē-ij)
Fontaine-qui-bout (fän-'tān-ke-bü)
Foolish Virgin see Matthew XXV:1-13
for age ('fȯr-ij) food, usually for animals
for bear (fȯr-'bar) stop
forbearance patience
for bears (fȯr-'barz) ancestors
fore bod ing (fōr-'bō-diŋ) terrifying
forecloser man who forces his debtors to give up their property if they have no money
fore head ('for-həd)
for sworn (fȯr-'swōrn) forsaken
for that because
forwardness preparation
fouled the scuppers filled the holes used to let water run off the decks
fourscore eighty
fowler hunter
frail tenant the nautilus, a shellfish
Franks other European powers
fraught ('frȯt) burdened
fray ('frā) fight
fre quent ing ('frē-kwən-tiŋ) visiting often
from tent to tent from grave to grave
from zone to zone from north to south
fron tier (frən-'tir) farthest part of settled territory
front let ('frənt-lət) forehead
fru gal i ty (frü-'ga-lə-tē) thrift
fume ('fyüm) rage
funeral-pile the Romans burned their dead on wooden piles
furze ('ferz) evergreen shrubs
fused ('fyüzd) melted solidly together
fu tile ('fyü-tᵊl) powerless

G

Gael's blood ('gālz) fighting blood of the brave Irishmen of old
gain say (gān-'sā) contradict
gal lant ('ga-lənt) brave young lover
gal le on ('ga-lē-ən) ancient sailing vessel
gal liard ('gal-yərd) a dance by two
gal li-gas kins (ga-li-'gas-kənz) loose breeches
Gallipoli (ga-'li-pə-lē)
gallows air, with a as though he were about to be hung
Gam bi a ('gam-bē-ə) river in Africa. The quoted line is from "The African Chief" by Mrs. Sarah Wentworth Morton, in a school book of Whittier's
gam bol ('gam-bəl) prank; frisk about; party
garb ('gärb) clothing
Garcia (gär-'sē-ə)
garden-girt surrounded by gardens
gar goyle ('gär-gȯil) a queerly carved, ugly, stone animal head
gar ri son ('gar-ə-sən) body of troops; arms
gar ru lous ('gar-ə-ləs) talkative
Gas per eau ('gas-pər-ō)
Gate of Da mas cus (də-'mas-kəs) in "Bedreddin Hassin," from *The Arabian Nights*
Gates of Hercules Gibraltar
gaud y ('gȯ-dē) showy
gauge ('gāj) measure
gen i al (je-nyel) comfortable
ge nii ('jē-nē) supernatural being in *The Arabian Nights*
Gen i us ('jēn-yəs) spirit
gentlemen of the free-and-easy sort those who are not easily alarmed
gen u ine ('jen-yə-wən) real
ge o met ric signs (jē-ə-'me-trik) patterns in regular designs
Georg ius Se cun dus ('jōr-jəs; sē-'kən-dəs) George II, king of England (1727-1760), was born in Germany
Ger o ni mo (jə-'rä-nə-mō) a chief of the Apache Indians
ges ture ('jes-chər) movement
ghast ly wan ('gast-lē; wän) deathly pale
Ghent ('gent) a city in Belgium, one hundred miles from Aix
ghosts of shores the slightest trace of land
gigantic (j∅-'gan-tik) most; hardest
gills ('gilz) loose flap of red skin under beak
gird ed ('gər-dəd) bound

giveth grace unto every art makes all work delightful
glad i a tors (ˈgla-dē-a-tərz) those who fought with weapons for the amusement of the Roman public
glam our (ˈgla-mər) charm
glean ings (ˈglē-niŋz) collections
glebe (ˈglēb) ground
glee (ˈglē) song in parts
gleeds (ˈglēdz) burning coals
glistened at her noon she was still youthful in middle life
gloaming (ˈglō-miŋ) twilight
Glorious Revolution the people of England revolted against their king, James II, because he wished to rule without their aid
goad (ˈgōd) whip; necessity which acts as a whip
golden quest pursuit of wealth; the reference is to the story of Jason and the golden fleece
Go li ath (gə-ˈlØ-əth) the giant killed by David with a sling. See I Samuel XVII
Goody woman
Goth ic (ˈgä-thik) of Gothic architecture a beautiful and dignified style of medieval architecture distinguished especially by its pointed arches
gra da tion (grā-ˈdā-shən)blending of notes
gra na ry (ˈgrā-nə-rē) storehouse for grain
Grand-Pré (grän-ˈprā) French for *great prairie*
gra tis (ˈgra-təs) for nothing
Gray A zores (ˈā-zōrz) distant islands. The Azores are west of Spain in the Atlantic Ocean
Great Harry first warship of the British navy, built in 1488
great plot play taking place on "the great stage of the Nation's history"
gren a dier (grən-ə-ˈdir) a member of a special regiment or corps
grip ing (ˈgri-piŋ) painful
grist-mill mill for grinding grain
grizzled gray
groat (ˈgrōt) old English coin worth two cents in our money
grog (ˈgräg) mixture of liquor and water unsweetened
groom servant
gro tesque (grō-ˈtesk) very queer
guile (ˈgØl) deceit; guileless, innocent
guinea (ˈgi-nē) an English gold coin no longer in use worth about $5.11 [1921]
guise (ˈgØz) manner; appearance
gun da low (ˈgən-də-lō) variant of *gondola,* a flat-bottomed boat

H

ha bil i ments (hə-ˈbi-lə-mənts) clothing
hab i ta tion (ha-bə-ˈtā-shən) home
hag gard (ˈha-gərd) dreary; tired-out
"hahnsum" (ˈhan-səm) *handsome*, good looking
hake (ˈhāk) fish related to the cod
half a crown about sixty cents [1921]
half-a-quar tern of ig nit ed brandy (ˈkwȯr-tərn; ig-ˈnØ-təd) half a gill of brandy which had been lighted and burned for a few seconds
half-re cum bent (ri-ˈkəm-bənt) half-lying, half-sitting
hal low (ˈha-lō) make holy
hap less (ˈha-pləs) unfortunate
ha rangue (hə-ˈraŋ) speech; haranguing, giving a speech
har ass (hə-ˈras) annoy
ha rem (ˈhar-əm) here, hens. The wives of a Turk are called his harem
harmonious madness a burst of inspired poetry
har row (ˈhar-ō) agricultural implement to level plowed land
har ry (ˈhar-ē) attack; follow
haunts (ˈhȯntz) homes
haut boy (ˈhō-bȯi) a musical wind instrument
haz ard ing (ˈha-zər-diŋ) risking
hearth (ˈhärth) fireplaces
Heathen Nine nine Muses of Greek mythology, patrons of the fine arts
heath er (ˈhe-thər) small blossoming evergreen shrubs
he carries weight he is weighted down heavily as a handicap, as race horses sometimes are
heif er (ˈhe-fər) young cow
heir loom (ˈar-lüm) inherited gift
heir of his dex ter i ty (ˈar; dek-ˈster-ə-tē) one who would inherit one's skill
held in re pute (ri-ˈpyüt) considered honorable
Hel i con (ˈhe-lə-kän) a mountain in central Greece
helmsman man who steers
her e sy (ˈher-ə-sē) disloyalty
Her mes (ˈhər-mēz) famous Egyptian philosopher
Her mia (ˈhər-mi-ə)
Her na ni (ər-ˈnä-nē) an opera by Verdi, the Italian composer
high divide ridge of high ground between two drainage areas
hi la rious (hi-ˈlar-ē-əs) laughing and talking
hoar (ˈhōr) white with age

hoard ing (ˈhōr-diŋ) being saved
hob projection on a fireplace to warm things on
hobbling tying the legs so that the horses could not run away
Hollands strong, alcoholic drink
hol ster (ˈhōl-stər) pistol case
hom age (ˈä-mij) respect
ho ri zon (hə-ˈrØ-zᵊn) skyline; landscape: top
horny calloused
hostage from the future took gained what would help him in time to come
house of Stuart Scotch and English royal family to which Charles II, James II, and William III belonged
housings saddle cover and trimmings
hue and cry loud outcry with which law breakers were anciently pursued
humility (hyü-ˈmi-lə-tē) humbleness
Hy me ne al (hØ-mə-ˈnē-əl) for a wedding
hy pothe sis (hØ-ˈpä-thə-səs) supposition
hys sop (ˈhi-səp) sprinkler for holy water

I

id i om (ˈi-dē-əm) phrasing
i dyl (ˈi-dᵊl) poem of rustic life
idyl lic ease (Ø-ˈdi-lik) carefree life in the country
ig no ble (ig-ˈnō-bəl) undignified
ig no min i ous ly (ig-nə-ˈmi-nē-əs-lē) dishonored and disgraced
ig no ra mus (ig-nə-ˈrā-məs) an ignorant person
il lim it a ble (il-ˈli-mə-tə-bəl) boundless; absolute
il lus tri ous (i-ˈləs-trē-əs) remarkable
im be cil i ty (im-bə-ˈsi-lə-tē) stupidity
immortality life beyond the grave
imparted given
im pend ing (im-ˈpen-diŋ) overhanging
im pen e tra ble (im-ˈpe-nə-trə-bəl) dark which could not be seen through; which he could not get over
im per cep ti bly (im-pər-ˈsep-tə-blē) gradually
im pet u os i ty (im-pe-chə-ˈwä-sə-tē) impatience; impetuous, impatient
im pla ca ble (im-ˈpla-kə-bəl) unsatisfied
im por tu nate (im-ˈpȯr-chə-nət) insistent
im pos tor (im-ˈpäs-tər) pretender
im pos ture (im-ˈpäs-chər) trickery

im po tent (ˈim-pə-tənt) helpless
im pre ca tion (im-pri-ˈkā-shən) curse
im pro pri e ty (im-prə-ˈprØ-ə-tē) improper behavior
improvident (im-ˈprä-və-dənt) thoughtless of the future
im pro vi sa to ri (im-ˈprä-və-zə-ˈtōr-ē) those who compose and sing, or recite, short poems
in ad e quate to (i-ˈna-di-kwət) unable to meet
in ar tic u late (i-när-ˈti-kyə-lət) indistinct
in au di ble (i-ˈnȯ-də-bəl) which would not be heard
inborn certainty (ˈser-tᵊn-tē) perfect sureness
in cal cu la ble (in-ˈkal-kya-lə-bəl) priceless
in can ta tion (in-kan-ˈtā-shən) magic chant
in ca pac i ty (in-kə-ˈpa-sə-tē) inability
incessant constant (dropping of the sands in the hourglass)
in cle ment (in-ˈkle-mənt) severe
in co her ent (in-kō-ˈhir-ənt) which could not be understood
in con stan cy (in-ˈkän-stənt-sē) unfaithfulness
in con ti nent ly (in-ˈkänt-tᵊn-ənt-lē) uncontrollably
in cred i ble (in-ˈkre-də-bəl) unbelievable
in cred u lous (in-ˈkre-jə-ləs) doubtful
in dict ing (in-ˈdØ-tiŋ) using as a charge of arrest
indispensable (in-di-ˈspen-sə-bəl) absolutely necessary
in di vid u al is tic (in-də-vij-wə-ˈlis-tik) personal
in do lent (ˈin-də-lənt) even-tempered
in dom i ta ble (ˈin-dä-mə-tə-bəl) untamable
in ev i ta ble (i-ˈne-və-tə-bəl) unavoidable
in ex o ra ble (i-ˈnek-sə-rə-bəl) unrelenting
in ex pli ca ble (i-nik-ˈspli-kə-bəl) inexplainable
in fal li ble (in-ˈfa-lə-bəl) sure
in fa mous (ˈin-fə-məs) shameful
infernal atmosphere breeze from the lower regions; inferno, hot region
infractions (in-ˈfrak-shənz) breaks
in got (ˈin-gət) a bar of metal
in gress nor e gress (ˈin-grəs; ˈē-grəs) entrance nor departure
inimitable (i-ˈni-mə-tə-bəl) matchless
i ni ti a tive (i-ˈni-shə-tiv) leadership
in merry pin in a jolly mood
innocent of books whose knowledge had not come from reading
in quir y (in-ˈkwØr-ē) curiosity
in sid i ous ly (in-ˈsi-dē-əs-lē) treacherously
in sin u ate (in-ˈsin-yə-wāt) suggest

in stan ta ne ous (int-stən-'tā-nē-əs) immediate
in stinct (in-'stiŋkt) feeling
in su per a ble (in-'sü-pə-rə-bəl) incurable
in sur gents (in-'sər-jənts) rebels
in tan gi ble power (in-'tan-jə-bəl) a power not defined or necessarily legal, but very strong
in ter cedes (in-tər-'sēdz) pleads with
in ter course ('in-tər-kōrs) experience
in ter lude ('in-tər-lüd) short poem making a break in the longer one
in ter me di ate (in-tər-'mē-dē-ət) gradual
in ter ven tion (in-tər-'ven-shən) influence
in ti ma tion (in-tə-'mā-shən) suggestion
in tol er able (in-'tä-lə-rə-bəl) hardly to be stood
into the air's embrace straight over the open space
in tri cate ('in-tri-kət) many perplexing
in trigue (in-'trēg) plotting
in un date ('i-nən-dāt) flood; inundated, flooded
in vet er ate an tip i thies (in-'ve-tə-rət; an-'ti-pə-thēz) incurable; inveterate antipathies, long-standing hatreds
in vol un tar i ly (in-vä-lən-'ter-ə-lē) without thinking
inward light religious beliefs
i ras ci ble (i-'ra-sə-bəl) hot-tempered
i rised ('∅-rəst) colored
i ron-mon ger y ('∅-ərn 'mən-gə-rē) general name for all articles made of iron
ir rep a ra ble (i-'re-pə-rə-bəl) beyond repair; not to be prevented
ir re sist i ble (ir-i-'zis-tə-bəl) overpowering
ir res o lu tion (i-re-zə-'lü-shən) hesitation
Ish ma el's children ('ish-mā-əl) Indians who, like Ishmael, "lived in the wilderness" and were archers. *see* Genesis XXI:20
Islands of the Blest imaginary islands in the Atlantic where the favorites of the gods went after death
Is ling ton ('iz-liŋ-tən) a section of London
i so lat ed ('∅-sə-lā-təd) shut off

J

jack boots ('jak-büts) large knee-boots
Jacob, ladder of *see* Genesis XXVIII:12; Jacob of old, *see* Genesis XXXII
jad ed steers ('jā-dəd) exhausted oxen
jan gling ('jaŋ-gliŋ) quarreling

jer kin ('jər-kən) jacket
jes sa mine ('jes-mən) climbing shrub with fragrant yellow flowers; jasmine
Jes u it ('je-zü-ət) Catholic order of the Society of Jesus
Joaquin (wä-'kēn)
joc und ('jä-kənd) merry
Joe Miller an English comedian
John Rogers a religious martyr
Jolly Roger the black banner of pirates
journalist magazine or newspaper writer
jun to ('jən-tō) association
Jupiter chief of the gods

K

keel ('kel) ridge on bottom of a boat
keel son ('kel-sən) strengthening structure above the keel, which *see*
kelp ('kelp) seaweed
kenned ('kend) knew
khan ('kän) resting place for caravans
kindred points far-distant places that are alike
kine ('kØn) cows
King Herod king of Judea, who slew all children under two years of age. *see* Matthew II:16
kir tle ('kər-tᵊl) jacket and upper skirt attached to it
knave ('nāv) rascal
knees natural bends of wood selected to fit angles in frame of ship
knocker a more or less decorated metal door fixture which took the place of a doorbell
knolls ('nōlz) small round bills
Koor dis tan (kür-də-'stän) region formerly partly in Turkey and partly in Persia
Kur ro glou (kər-ə-'glü)
Ky rat ('kē-rät)

L

lab o ra to ry ('la-brə-tōr-ē) workroom for chemical experiments
lack a dai si cal (la-kə-'dā-zi-kəl) languid
laggard in love unworthy suitor
lagoon small shallow arm of a large body of water

La Illah illa Allah there is no God except Allah
La jeunesse (lä-zhü-ˈnəs)
lan guor (ˈlaŋ-gər) dullness
Lannes (ˈlän)
La oc o ön (lā-ˈä-kə-wän) Trojan priest of Apollo who with his two sons was killed by serpents coiling about them
laps ing (ˈlap-siŋ) gently splashing
Las car swarthy (ˈlas-kər) dark-skinned East Indian sailor
la tent (ˈlā-tᵊnt) hidden
Latin fraud Italian treachery. Greece knew she could not depend on Italy
laughed a pitiless laugh (ˈläft) was almost unbearably hot
lav ing (ˈlā-viŋ) dipping into the water
Law of Average, according to the there is as much chance that one will be right as there is that one will be wrong
lay (ˈlā) song
lea (ˈlē) meadow
lea guer (ˈlē-gər) camp of a besieging army
league, with (ˈlēg) with an understanding
Le an der (lē-ˈan-dər) in Greek legend, the lover of Hero, whom he swam the Hellespont (modern Dardanelles) to visit each night. One night her light, by which he was guided, went out, and he perished. When Hero discovered his body on shore, she killed herself
Le blanc (lə-ˈblȯnk)
Le Carillon de Dunkerque (ˈkar-ə-län; ˈdan-kərk) The Chimes of Dunkirk
ledgers account books
lee (ˈlē) the side protected from the wind; protection
le gend (ˈle-jənd) a story coming down from the past
le gion (ˈlē-jən) multitude; too many to count
Le tiche (ˈlə-tish)
Leuc tra (ˈlük-trə) where the Boeotians, to which people Spartacus's ancestors belonged, defeated the Spartans, another Greek people
Lexington and Concord the scene of the first bloodshed of the Revolution
like the Hebrew *see* Exodus XII:21,30
Li lin au (li-ˈlin-aủ)
lim pid (ˈlim-pəd) clear
linchpin pin to hold wheel on
linking fancy unto fancy imagining one thing after another
links torches
linnet small singing bird
Lis bon (ˈliz-bən) city of Portugal which had an earthquake in 1755
lis some (ˈli-səm) graceful

lists knightly contests
lithe ('lØth) graceful
littered ('li-tərd) spread down straw, hay, etc., as bedding for animals
little rel e van cy bore ('re-lə-vən-sē) had little to do with the matter asked about
li ve ry ('li-və-rē) citizens of London; uniform
livid ('li-ved) grayish; pale
local discriminations (dis-kri-mə-'nā-shənz) loyalty to one's state or city
Loch in var (lȯk-ən-'vär)
logical heirs rightful successors
lol ling ('lä-liŋ) lounging
loon large fish-eating bird
looping winding over
looted robbed
lore ('lōr) learning
Louisburg French fort on Cape Breton, captured by the English in 1745, in the war between France and England
Loup-garou (lü-gə-'rü) a person who has been changed into a wolf
loved her love a game with words beginning with letters of the alphabet
love-knot bow of ribbon as a token of love
low er ing ('laủ-ər-iŋ) gloomy
low-vaulted past outgrown habit of life
lu mi nous ('lü-mə-nəs) bright
lures made invited me
lu rid ('lür-əd) stern
lus trous ('ləs-trəs) shining
lyre ('lØr) harp-like musical instrument
Lys an der (lØ-'san-dər)

M

Mad a gas car (ma-də-'gas-kər) island off the east coast of Africa
magnesite and dolomite ('mag-nə-sØt; 'dō-lə-mØt) kinds of rock used in the making of steel
mail of Calvin's creed strict belief of John Calvin, French religious reformer
main ('mān) ocean
maize ('māz) corn
mal a dy ('ma-lə-dē) trouble
mal heureux (mal-hủ-'rü) French for *unhappy man*
mal le a bil i ty (ma-lē-ə-'bi-lə-tē) *see* ductility; malleable, yielding

Mal ta (mȯl-tə) British island in the Mediterranean Sea
Mammon's vilest dust money; Mammon is the god of riches
Mammoth large, elephant-like animal, which no longer exists
man date ('man-dāt) order
ma neu ver (mə-'nü-vər) plan to outwit the other player; act
man ga nese ('man-gə-nēz) hard, brittle, grayish white metal tinged with red
man i fold ('ma-nə-fōld) many
manslaughter killing a person
Mar a thon ('mar-ə-thän) a plain in Attica, Greece, where the Greeks won a great victory over the Persians
ma raud ers (ma-'rȯ-dərz) plundering bands
marge ('märj) poetic for *margin*
mar quis (mär-'kēz) a title of nobility
Marshal commander
mar tial ('mär-shəl) warlike
masquerade li cense was unlimited ('lØ-sənz) people had been allowed to wear any kind of costume they chose
matchlock an old-fashioned gun
material actual; worldly
ma te ri al is tic (mə-tir-ē-ə-'lis-tik) fonder of things than of ideals
mat in ('ma-tᵊn) morning song
ma tron ('mā-trən) married woman
ma ture (mə-'tu̇r) careful
maud lin ('mȯd-lən) silly and sentimental
max im ('mak-səm) principle
Mc Greg or (mə-'kgər-gər) Sir Gregor McGregor, who tried in 1822 to establish a colony in Costa Rica
measure lead have a dance
Mech eln ('me-keln) town in Belgium
medium means; medium of the plank, the captives of the pirates were blindfolded and compelled to walk off a plank into the sea
meet fitting
Melita ('me-lə-tə or me-'lē-tə) *see* shipwrecked Paul
mem o ran dum (me-mə-'ran-dəm) record; account; sketch
me mo ri al (mə-'mōr-ē-əl) Lincoln's birthplace, a log cabin near Hodgensville, Kentucky, was presented to the nation in 1916
Mem phre ma gog (mem-fri-'mā-gäg) lake in Vermont and Canada
men ace ('me-nəs) threat
men di cant ('men-di-kənt) begging
men in nations all the countries which were under Persian power

mental ap pa ri tion (a-pə-'ri-shən) Bill means mental **aberration** (a-bə-'rā-shən) confusion of mind
mer ce na ry troops ('mər-sᵊn-er-ē) soldiers paid to fight for a country not their own
merciless a creditor in his successor as cruel a man to owe money to in Scrooge's place
met a mor phosed (me-tə-'mȯr-fōzd) changed
me te or, hoary ('mē-tē-ər) strange white appearance in the sky—snow
meter ('mē-tər) about 3¼ feet
metes ('mēts) goals
mick le ('mi-kəl) great deal
Middlesex ('mi-dᵊl-seks) county in northeastern Massachusetts
mien ('mēn) manner
mi gra tion (m∅-'grā-shən) trip
Mil ti a des (mil-'t∅-ə-dēz) famous Athenian general and statesman
mimic flame reflected glow
mi mo sa (mə-'mō-sə) very sensitive tropical shrub
minded noticed
min i a ture ('mi-nē-ə-chu̇r) a small scale
minister messenger
mi rage (mə-'räzh) dream of the future
mired ('m∅rd) stuck fast
misanthropic (mi-sᵊn-'thrä-pik) gloomy looking
mis cel la ne ous tatters (mi-sə-'lā-nē-əs) many different kinds of rags
mis con ceive (mis-kən-'sēv) misunderstand
mis sal ('mi-səl) book of religious service of the Catholic church
mis sile ('mi-səl) weapon
missive ('mi-siv) letter
Mis so lon ghi ('mi-sə-loŋ-gē)
Missouri Bad Lands section of country that produces almost no vegetation
moat ('mōt) ditch of water around castle for protection
mob violence gaining what he wants by organized force—strikes, etc.
mo du la tions (mä-jə-'lā-shənz) tones
molten slag melted waste matter
mon a mi (mō-na-'mē) my friend
mon grel ('män-grəl) dog of mixed breed
mon o graph ('mä-nə-graf) written account of a single life
mo not o nous (mə-'nä-tᵊn-əs) unchanging; tiresome
moor ('mu̇r) stretch of waste land; sandy marsh
Mo ra vi an (mə-'rā-vē-ən) of the United Brethren

morning-star the brightest star of the morning
mo rose (mə-'rōs) ill-tempered; sullen
mortgage fancier ('mȯr-gij) one who takes pleasure in lending money as some enjoy pets
motley-braided ('mät-lē) made of rags of different colors
mounting the breach boldly rising to the occasion
Mo wis ('mō-wis)
Mo zart ('mōt-särt) Austrian composer and pianist (1756-1791)
mulled ('məld) sweetened and spiced
mulls meditates
mul ti tu di nous (məl-tə-'tüd-nəs) thousands of
mumbled chewed
mum mer ('mə-mər) masker
mu nif i (myu̇-'ni-fi) he was going to say munificence—generosity
must wander *see* Elysian Fields
mu ta tion (myü-'tā-shən) changes in the weather
mutual consideration joint thought
myr i ad ('mir-ē-əd) great number; numberless
Mystic river in Connecticut

N

Na iad ('nā-əd) water nymph
Natch i toch es (natch-ə-'tōch-ēz)
natural make own disposition
natural se quence ('sē-kwəns) logical order of events, cause followed by result
Nature's lyceum (l∅-'sē-əm) school of the outdoor world
Nebraska Platte River
neck or naught no matter what happened
ne gus ('nē-gəs) a beverage containing wine
ne pen the (nə-'pen-thē) a drink producing forgetfulness of pain
Ne ther by clan ('ne-thər-bē) Netherby was the name of the ancestor from whom they were descended
nethermost lowest
newt ('nüt) a small, lizard-like animal
night-encampment the cemetery
Night's Plutonian shore the borderland of Hades, ruled over by Pluto
night-wind of the Past, borne on the handed down in story
Ni lus ('n∅-ləs) Latin for *Nile*
nom i nal ('nä-mə-nᵊl) in name, not in actual practice

Nor folk Biffins (ˈnȯr-fək) apples from Norfolkshire, England

Norman cap cap worn in Normandy, which has square corners turned back from the face

no ta ry (ˈnō-tə-rē) a public officer who writes, or is witness to, legal papers

nothing loath no reluctance

Nu mid i an (nu̇-ˈmi-dē-ən) from Numidia, ancient country of North Africa

nup tials (ˈnəp-shəlz) marriage

nur tured (ˈnər-chərd) carefully tended

O

oath of allegiance solemn promise of loyalty

o bei sance (ō-ˈbē-səns) bow or other sign of respect

ob e lisk (ˈä-bə-lisk) four-sided tapering monument

O be ron (ˈō-bə-rän)

ob liq u ity of moral or mental vision (ō-ˈbli-kwə-tē) false ideas of right and wrong

ob liv i ous (ə-ˈbli-vē-əs) forgetting everything; oblivion, forgetfulness

ob scene (äb-ˈsēn) indecent

ob se qui ous (əb-ˈsē-kwē-əs) excessively humble

oc clud ed (ə-ˈklü-dəd) which it contains

oc cult (ə-ˈkəlt) mysterious

of credit and renown trusted and well known

of fal (ˈȯ-fəl) rubbish

offices services

of high mark extraordinary

Old Noll (ˈnol) Oliver Cromwell

Old Probabilities nickname for chief of office furnishing weather reports

O lym pus (ə-ˈlim-pəs) mountain in Greece, believed by the ancient Greeks to be the home of the gods

om i nous (ˈä-mə-nəs) threatening

one burden bore had one set expression

o paque (ō-ˈpāk) which could not be seen through

Op e lou sas (ȯ-pə-ˈlü-səs) Louisiana town

open-hearth one of the processes of making steel

oppressive burdened down

o rac u lar (ȯ-ˈra-kyə-lər) like an oracle. Oracles used to utter their prophecies from the depths of eaves

orbs (ˈȯrbz) eyes

Or fah ('ȯr-fə)
orthographic (ȯr-thə-'gra-fik) spelling
ost ler ('äs-lər) stableman
Ourcq ('ürk)
outgrown shell the body which the soul has freed itself from
out-Her o ded Herod ('her-ə-dəd) was worse than anyone could have imagined. The character of Herod in the old-time plays was always greatly exaggerated
O wy hee (ō-'wØ-hē) branch of the Snake River; the region is a mountainous and desert portion of Idaho

P

pa geant ('pā-jent) exhibition
painful Se wel's ancient tome ('sü-əlz) William Sewel's history of the Quakers and their sufferings
pal at a ble ('pa-lə-tə-bəl) agreeable tasting
pal imp sest ('pa-ləmp-sest) parchment which has been used several times, erased and rewritten
pall ('pōl) covering
pal la di um (pə-'lā-dē-əm) safeguard
Pal las ('pa-las) one of the names of Athena, goddess of wisdom
pal let ('pa-lət) poor, small bed
pal lid ('pa-ləd) pale colored; pale
pal met to (pal-'me-tō) palm tree
pal pa ble ('pal-pə-bəl) heavy and close
pan o ram ic (pa-ne-'ra-mik) with one scene after another in succession
par a pets ('par-ə-pəts) railings around the roof
pard like leopard like
Par lia ment ('pär-lə-mənt) law-making body in England corresponding to our Congress
parted seas the ocean, divided by the prow into two parts
parties people whose contract he was writing—a legal term
Pas ca gou la (pas-kə-'gü-lə) river in Mississippi
passion sin; evil ambition; anger
passionless uninterested
pa tri arch ('pā-trē-ärk) veteran
Patrick Saint Patrick, patron saint of Ireland
pat ri mo ni al (pa-trə-'mō-nē-əl) inherited from his father
pa tri ot ('pā-trē-ət) one who loves his or her country
pawn bro kers ('pȯn-brō-kərz) money lenders, where people may use per-

sonal property as security
ped a gogue ('pe-de-gäg) teacher
ped ant ('pe-dᵊnt) one who lays too much stress on book learning
pe des tri an (pə-'des-trē-ən) walking
peer ('pir) equal
pel li cle ('pe-li-kəl) tiny film of ice
pen ance ('pe-nəns) punishment
pen du lous ('pen-jə-ləs) hanging
pen du lous excrescence ('pen-jə-ləs; ik-'skre-ᵊns) wart hanging
pen i tent Peter ('pe-nə-tənt) *see* Matthew, XXVI:75-76
Penn the Apostle (ə-'pä-səl) William Penn, the great Quaker who founded Pennsylvania
penthouse overhanging; roof
pe remp to ry ('pə-remp-tə-rē) forceful
per force (pər-'fōrs) necessarily
per i he li on (per-ə-'hēl-yən) the spot nearest the horizon, so that it shows most plainly
per me a ting ('per-mē-ā-tiŋ) far reaching
per se ('pər-sā) in itself
per se vere (pər-sə-'vir) keep on
Persian's grave Marathon, where the Persians were defeated by the Greeks
per verse (pər-'vərs) wrongly
per ver sion (pər-'vər-zhən) disgrace
pestilent annoying
pet ri fac tion (pe-trə-'fak-shən) hardened stone (referring both to its actual material and its uninviting atmosphere)
Pe tru chi o's Kate (pə-'trü-ki-ōz) the scolding wife of Petruchio in Shakespeare's *The Taming of the Shrew*
phan tasm ('fan-ta-zəm) ghostliness
Pha raoh's daughters ('fer-ōz) pictures of Pharaoh's daughter, who found Moses in the bulrushes. *see* Exodus II:1-10
phe nom en on (fi-'nä-mə-nän) extraordinary occurrence
phil o mel ('fi-lə-mel) nightingale
phil o pro gen i tive ness (fi-lə-prō-'je-nə-tov-nəs) love for one's own children
phil o soph i cal principles, on (fə-'la-sə-fi-kəl) from sound reasoning; philosopher, thinker
phlegm ('flem) calmness
Phoe bus ('fē-bəs) Apollo, the god of the sun. He was supposed to have been born on the island of Delos
pilgrim traveler

pil laged ('pi-lidj) robbed
Pin dus-born A rax es ('pin-dəs; ə-'rak-sēz) now the Arta, a river famous in Greek mythology, which rises in the Pindus mountains
pin ion ('pin-yən) wing; pinioned, held
piping playing a tune
pi quan cy ('pē-kən-sē) smartness
pique ('pēk) spur
Pi sa's leaning miracle ('pē-zə) tower in Pisa, Italy, which leans to one side
Pis cat a qua (pi-'ska-tə-kwȯ) river forming the boundary line between Maine and New Hampshire
pith soundness
plac id ('pla-səd) peaceful looking
plain tive ('plān-tiv) pathetic
plaited mail very strong armor
plaiting ('plā-tiŋ) braiding
plane-tree the Persian adorned Xerxes, King of Persia, decorated a certain plane-tree (sycamore) that he admired, with silks and jewels
plash y ('pla-shē) wet
Plenty's horn large curving horn overflowing with fruits, etc., carried by Plenty, symbol of abundance
pli a ble ('plØ-ə-bəl) bendable
pli ant and mal le a ble ('plØ-ə-bəl; 'ma-lē-ə-bəl) easily handled and adaptable
plied ('plØd) worked at
plume ('plüm) pride
plundered mussed
poet laureate ('lȯr-ē-āt) office, with title of same name, given a poet by king of England. His duty is to write poems on historical events
poi lu (pwäl-'yü) French soldier
political unity one government for the entire country, North and South
polity ('pä-lə-tē) state
pol lu tion (pə-'lü-shən) something unclean
pom mel ('pə-məl) pound
pomp ('pämp) wealth
Poor Law law for the relief of the poor
Poor Richard the name Franklin assumed in *Poor Richard's Almanac*
pop ul ace ('pä-pyə-ləs) the common people
por tent ('pȯr-tent) sign
portentous (pȯr-'ten-təs) a thing full of meaning
porter ale; one who carries bundles
Port Royal town in Nova Scotia, now called Annapolis, captured by the

English in 1710
possessed of a demon under the control of an evil spirit
postboy driver
pos tern ('pōs-tərn) gate
posting down riding at full speed
po tent ('pō-tᵊnt) powerful
Poul ter ers shop ('pol-tər-ərz) where fowls are sold
pound British money, about five dollars [1921]
praetor ('prē-tər) public officer
prairie schooner ('skü-nər) canvas-covered wagon used for travel across the western plains
prec e dent (pri-'sē-dᵊnt) custom established by the action
pre cepts ('prē-septs) lessons
pre cincts ('prē-siŋkts) walls
pre cip i tate (pri-'si-pə-tət) very fast; precipitation, haste
pre cip i ta tion (pri-si-pə-'tā-shən) rash haste
pred e ces sor, his ('pre-də-sə-sər) governor who held office before him
pre dic a ment ('pri-di-kə-mənt) difficulty
pre dom i nant (pri-'dä-mə-nənt) in authority; predominance, authority
prel ac y and persecution ('pre-lə-sē) power of the church to rule and to punish
prel ude ('pre-lüd) introduction
pre ma ture ly (prē-mə-'tůr-lē) before expected
pre pos ter ous (pri-'päs-tə-rəs) absurd
pre saged ('pre-sijd) foretold
press newspaper or other publication
pre tense ('prē-tens) show
pretensions (pri-'ten-chənz) claims
prev a lent ('pre-və-lənt) common
prhyme ('prØm) best part of
Prhymer the first reader of the early colonists, much of its subject matter was religious
pri me val (prØ-'mē-vəl) that reminded one of the time when the world was new and uncivilized; primeval forest, forest whose trees have never been cut by man
prim ing ('prØ-miŋ) ammunition
Prince of Orange a Holland nobleman who became William III of England
prisms ('pri-zəmz) crystals
privacy of glorious light, etc. you are all alone, having flown too high for other birds to follow you
pro cliv i ties (prō-'kli-və-tēz) tendencies

procuring (prə-'kyu̇r-iŋ) management
Pro di gal Son ('prä-di-gəl) *see* St. Luke XV:11-32
prodigies ('prä-də-jēz) wonderful feats
pro di gious ly (prə-'di-jəs-lē) astonishingly
prof fer ('prä-fər) offer
pro fuse (prō-'fyüs) many; abundant
prone ('prōn) downcast
prop a gat ed in succession ('prä-pə-gā-təd) taken up by one after another
Prophet descending from Sinai ('sØ-nØ) Moses; see Exodus XXXIV
Prophet's rod *see* Exodus VII
proposition belief
pro pri e ty (prə-'prØ-ə-tē) decency
pros trate ('prä-strāt) powerless; prostrates principalities, overcomes tyranny
province proper uses; purpose
pro vin cial (prə-'vin-chəl) for one section alone
prying day ('prØ-iŋ) daylight that reveals everything
pseu do nym ('sü-dᵊn-im) pen name
purpling plain twilight landscape

Q

quaff ('kwäf) drink; quaffed off, drank
Queen of Leb an on ('lə-bə-nən) Lady Hester Stanhope, an eccentric Englishwoman with whom Harriet Livermore, "the half-welcome guest," lived for a time in Syria, where Lady Stanhope was leader of some half-civilized tribes. They both believed in the second coming of Christ in their lifetimes
Queens of She ba ('shē-bə) pictures of the Queen of Sheba, an ancient country in southern Arabia; *see* I Kings X
quer u lous ('kwer-ə-ləs) complaining
quidding tobacco chewing

R

rabble crowds of common people
radius region
rail make fun of
rak ish ('rā-kish) dashing
ral lied ('ra-lēd) joked
rank overgrown

ra pa cious (rə-ˈpā-shəs) greedy
ra pi er (ˈrā-pē-ər) sword
rapture burst of joyous song
Rat is bon (ˈrat-is-bon) a town in Germany
reach the dust-cloud overtake the long trail of dust left behind Kyrat
read the destiny for others see far enough ahead, as president of the United States, to judge what are the best courses to follow
re as sur ance (rē-ə-ˈshůr-əns) comfort
re ces ses (ˈrē-se-səs) far corners
re cip ro cat ed the sentiment (ri-ˈsi-prə-kā-təd) returned the feeling
rec la ma tion (re-klə-ˈmā-shən) reformation
recompensed (ˈre-kəm-penst) rewarded
rec on noi ter (rē-kə-ˈnȯi-tər) explore
re dress (ri-ˈdres) relief
red streamer sunrise glow
ref lu ent (ˈre-flü-ənt) receding, as the tide flows back to the sea
re frac to ries (ˈri-frak-tə-rēz) materials which form a glaze
refractory (ˈri-frak-tə-rē) unmanageable; obstinate
ref u gee (re-fyů-ˈjē) one who flees for safety; man in hiding because of his political beliefs
re fuse (ˈre-fyüs) cast off
re gent (ˈrē-jənt) one who takes the place of the rightful ruler—here, of the shepherd
regular firebrand of discontent person who always stirs up trouble wherever he goes
reigning the will to keeping all the energies directed toward
reign of the Henries last half of the sixteenth century. The Henries were French kings
re it er at ed (rē-ˈi-tə-rā-təd) repeated
re mon strat ed (ˈre-mən-strā-təd) protested
ren dez vous (ˈrän-di-vü) a meeting by appointment
ren e gade (ˈre-ni-gād) deserter
Re ne Le blanc (ˈrə-nā; lə-ˈblon)
rent broken
repeater small spring which makes a watch strike the time
re plet ed (ri-ˈple-təd) oversatisfied
re pute (ri-ˈpyüt) respect
re sid u a ry leg a tee (ri-ˈzi-jə-wer-ē; le-gə-ˈtē) heir to what is left after provisions of the will are carried out
re signed (rē-ˈsØnd) submissive
re sort (ri-ˈzȯrt) go; hiding

re source ('rē-sōrs) means of help
res pite ('res-pət) rest
re ten tive of (ri-'ten-tiv) similar to
retort quick reply, severe or witty, intended to quiet the person addressed
rev el ers ('re-və-lərz) merry-makers
rev els ('re-vəlz) frolics
re ver ber a tions (ri-vər-bə-'rā-shənz) echoes
rev er ie ('re-və-rē) daydream
revoke cancel; remove
Reyhan ('rā-ən)
rho do ra (rō-'dōr-ə) New England plant
ricks stacks protected from wet by some covering
rime short, white, stiff hair that suggested frost
ripened thought into action influenced others to carry out the good deeds they were thinking of
roan ('rōn) chestnut horse
Ro a noke ('rō-ə-nōk) river in Virginia and North Carolina
Robin Crusoe Robinson Crusoe, the hero of Defoe's famous story of that name. He had a slave named Friday and a parrot
ro bust ('rō-bəst) strong
roe ('rō) a kind of deer
roisterer ('rȯi-stər-ər) merry-maker
rood ('rüd) 40 square rods
Rouge Bouquet (rüzh; 'bü-kā)
roundheaded dignitary Puritan who revolted, under Oliver Cromwell, against Charles I in 1649. The Puritans wore their hair cut close as opposed to the royalists' long curls
Rou shan ('rü-shän)
royal commission king's order
rub i cund ('rü-bi-kənd) red faced
ruf fi an ('rə-fē-ən) rascal
rumor reached our shores the rumor that the Prince of Orange was to be put in power in place of James II
runaway wishes desires we should not give in to
running such a rig engaging in such a frolic
rural de i ties ('dē-ə-tēz) gods and goddesses of the farm
rus tic meal simple country meal
ruth less ly ('rüth-ləs-lē) pitilessly

S

sa ber (ˈsā-bər) sword
sac ri fice (ˈsa-krə-fØs) offering of unselfishness
sa ga cious (sə-ˈgā-shəs) wise
sages (ˈsā-jəz) wise people
Saint Dunstan English monk of the 10th century who was tempted at his forge by an evil spirit, whose nose he seized with his red-hot tongs
Saint Eu la le (sän; u-la-lē)
Sal a mis (ˈsa-lə-məs) ancient city of Cyprus
Salis bur y (ˈsȯlz-ber-ē) town in Massachusetts
Salm on (ˈsa-mən)
salts sailors
Sa mi an (ˈsā-mē-ən)
samp porridge made of Indian corn coarsely ground and browned
sampler piece of needlework which shows one's skill in sewing
sark (ˈsärk) drapery
sa ti ety (sə -ˈtØ-ə-tē) weariness
Sa to ry (ˈsä-tō-rē)
sa van na (sə-ˈva-nə) subtropical, treeless grassy plain
sa vor (ˈsā-vər) flavor; odor
scab bard (ˈska-bərd) case for sword
scarfed and bolted fitted together and screwed
scarred full of shell holes
schooner (ˈskü-nər) two-masted vessel, having fore-and-aft rig, the large sail being on the after mast; **schooner-rigged** (*see* above)
scourge (ˈskərj) curse
scouring searching
screw miser
Scriptural forms use of *thee, thou,* etc.
scrup ul ous in imputing motives to (ˈskrü-pyə-ləs) careful in suspecting
scru ti nize (ˈskrü-tᵊn-Øz) investigate
scut tled (ˈskə-tᵊld) filled with holes
sectional between two places, races, or classes
seed that's spread ideas which grow as they are spread
self-ac cu sa to ry (a-ˈkyü-zə-tōr-ē) blaming themselves
sensible aware; causing bodily injury
sep ul chers (ˈsə-pəl-kərs) gravelike piles
seraglio (sə-ˈral-yō) former official palace of the Turkish sultan
ser a phim (ˈser-ə-fim) angels
ses ter ces (ˈses-tər-sēz) the sesterce was a silver coin

Seventh Day there was on foot a movement to close on Sundays the public bake-shops, where the poor, whose houses contained fireplaces but no ovens, had much of their cooking (especially Sunday dinner) done at a small cost

shaft monument; steel bar

shagbark rough-barked, nut-bearing hickory tree

shah ('shä) ruler

shape and shadow life

shaped in a classic mold made to look like a Greek statue

shards sharp stones

share metal part of plow which cuts the ground

Shaw nee (shȯ-'nē) one of the tribe of Algonquins

shay for *chaise,* carriage

sheen shining; brilliance

sheer turn; absolute; straight up

Sheik ('shēk) Arab chief

Shelley, Percy Bysshe ('bish)

Ship of State the government

shipwrecked Paul the apostle Paul was shipwrecked off the coast of the island of Melita (now Malta) in the Mediterranean

shores supports

shorn of their streaming hair, be have their foliage cut off

shrapnel ('shrap-nᵊl) explosive shell

shrew ('shrü) a scold

shrine protection for a sacred relic. The little log house is placed within a granite shelter

shroud drapery; shrouds, ropes leading from the masthead

si dled ('si-dᵊld) moved sidewise

Sie na's saint (sē-'ə-näz) St. Catherine of Siena was noted for her sanctity and her wonderful visions

Si er ra (sē-'er-ə) range of mountains

significant full of meaning

sign of the Scorpion the Scorpion is a constellation which the sun enters about October 23

sil hou ette (si-lə-'wet) outline; shadow; silhouetted, outlined in black

sill timber on bottom of carriage

sylvan forest-covered; countrylike; sylvan glooms, forest darkness

silver sphere moon

sim i le ('si-mə-lē) comparison

sin ews ('sin-yüz) muscles; sinewy, strong

singular queer; unusual

singularity strangeness
si ren (ˈsi-rən) sea-nymph
"Sir Roger de Coverly" (ˈkə-vər-lē) a dance like the Virginia reel
skipper master of a vessel; here, teacher. *see* Chalkley
Sky ros (ˈskē-ròs)
slacker looser
sleek est (ˈslē-kəst) smoothest
slip platform on which ships are built
sloth (ˈslòth) laziness
Smithfield section of London where martyrs suffered death by burning
smithy blacksmith shop
Smyr na (ˈsmər-nə) town in Turkey
soar, but never roam rise, but always return
social the o rists (ˈthē-ə-rists) those who study people in their relations to one another
sol em nized (ˈsä-ləm-nØzd) honored
so lic i tude (sə-ˈli-sə-tüd) anxiety
solstice of summer (ˈsōl-stəs) one of the times when the sun is farthest from the equator—June 21
Sol way (ˈsäl-wā) Solway Firth, noted for its swift tides
som bre ro (səm-ˈbrer-ō) kind of broad-brimmed hat
som no lent (ˈsäm-nə-lənt) drowsy
son of the road one who lived out-of-doors; a highwayman
so no rous (sə-ˈnōr-əs) resounding
sor did (ˈsòr-dəd) unidealistic; selfish
sou brette (sü-ˈbret) frivolous young woman of the stage—here, a singer
soul's de bat a ble land (di-ˈbā-tə-bəl) province of right and wrong
sov er eign (ˈsä-vrən) important
sow the world with scatter over the earth
Spanish Main Caribbean Sea
spar (ˈspär) mast; mineral substance
Spartans (ˈspär-tᵊnz) a people of ancient Greece famous for their bravery and endurance
spe cies (ˈspē-shēz) kinds; type
spectral ghostly
sphere circle of activity
spher ule (ˈsfir-ül) little sphere-shaped particle
spon ta ne ous com bus tion (spän-ˈtā-nē-əs; kəm-ˈbəs-chən) fire caused by chemical action within a substance
spouse (ˈspaủs) wife
spume-flakes (ˈspyüm) froth

spurned Arabian plains rushed over the wide deserts of Arabia
spurs timbers which hold the ship
squab ('skwäb) short and fat
stable lasting
stagnant-blooded lazy
stal wart ('stȯl-wərt) strong and brave
stanch ('stȯnch) steadfast
stan chion ('stan-chən) of stalls
standard of values ideal to judge people's actions by
stars . . . cypress trees see cypress tree
state great importance
stature ('sta-chər) height
stave musical term, meaning staff. *A Christmas Carol* is therefore divided into staves rather than chapters
stays supports
stay spur stop using the spur; slow-up
St. Catherine St. Catherine was vowed to a single life; to braid her tresses is to remain unmarried
steeped in filled with; soaked
stem son ('stem-sən) piece of curved timber on the bow of a ship's frame
stern son-knee ('stərn-sən) end of a keelson, which *see*
St. Fran çois (san; frän-swä) St. Francis River, in Canada
stir rups ('stər-əps) foot supports hanging from saddle
St. Michael ('mi-kəl) in the Bible, the leader of the entire host of angels
stock wooden handle
stock and store supply of words
stodg y ('stä-jē) settled in their ways
Stony Point fort on the Hudson River captured by the British, and retaken by Americans in 1779
stop-gap temporary stoppage
strait waistcoat binding jacket for insane
stu ar ti a (stü-'är-shə) shrub with large single flowers
stubborn right abide, my acknowledge my power today
Stuy ve sant ('stØ-və-sənt)
subjugated he means *subjected*
submits its processes depends on for its development
sub sis tence (səb-'sis-təns) a living
substance wealth
sub tle ('sə-tᵊl) mysterious; subtly, mysteriously
sub vert (səb-'vərt) destroy
suf fuse (sə-'fyüs) overspread

suite ('swēt) number of adjoining rooms
Sultan's Groom a hunchback who sought the princess's hand. *see The Arabian Nights*
Summer of All-Saints Indian summer
sump tu ous ('səmp-shə-wəs) luxurious
sunder, in into parts
Su ni um ('sü-ni-üm) a rocky headland on the extreme south of Attica, now Cape Colonna
super superintendent
su perb (sủ-'pərb) beautifully formed
su per flu i ties (sü-pər-'flü-ə-tēz) things you do not need
su per nal ('sủ-'pər-nᵊl) heavenly
supernatural, the strange happenings
supplication entreaty
sur cease ('sər-sēs) forgetfulness
surge ('serj) waves
sur plus population ('sər-pləs) number of unnecessary people
sur rep ti tious ly (sər-əp-'ti-shəs-lē) in a stealthy manner
survival of the fittest selection and preservation of those who are the most able. This theory was worked out by Charles Darwin, nineteenth century scientist
sus cep ti ble (sə-'sep-tə-bəl) possible to be developed into
sustain its role ('rōl) act the part it was dressed to represent
su sur rus (sủ-'sər-əs) whispering
swain ('swān) young fellow
swales ('swālz) small valleys
swan-like, let me sing and die the swan was supposed to sing musically just before its death
swar ded ('swȯr-dəd) grassy
swarth y ('swȯr-thē) dark colored
swath ('swäth) line of grass already cut
sweep road; long pole attached to post, for lowering and raising a bucket
Sweet-water valley *see* Nebraska
swound ('swaủnd) swoon or faint
symbol of re gen er ate nature (ri-'je-nə-rāt) sign of newborn life
sym pho ny ('sim-fə-nē) music

T

tac it ly ('ta-sət-lē) silently
tac i turn ('ta-sə-tərn) silent

taffrail rail around a ship's stern, or poop
take a final stand make one last effort to exist
take six bars jump as high as he can
tallow-chandler maker of tallow candles
taming the mind controlling willfulness
tan gi ble ('tan-jə-bəl) real
tangled ram *see* Genesis XXI:1-13
tap quality
tap es tries ('ta-pə-strēz) heavy curtains and hangings
Tartar's lance long spear carried by Tartars, fierce horsemen of Asia
taw ny ('tȯ-nē) yellow; tawny mound, brown outline
Ta yg e tus (tā-'ij-ə-təs) mountain in Greece
teal ('tēl) river duck
Teche ('tesh) river in Louisiana
te di ous ('tē-dē-əs) long
tendril slender, coiling attachment to the stern
ten e brous ('te-nə-brəs) gloomy
Tents of Grace translation of the name given by the Moravians to their mission
termagant ('tər-mə-gənt) quarreling
ter res tri al (tə-'res-trē-əl) of the map of the world. The celestial globe shows heavenly bodies
terse ('tərs) brief
Ther mop y lae (thər-'mä-pə-lē) see "Historical Note," page 265
Theseus ('thē-süs)
the time-of-day whatever might happen during the day
thewed ('thüd) built
thill either of the two shafts between which a horse is hitched
thin atmosphere the higher up in the air, the thinner the air becomes
tholes supports to which the oars are fastened in rowing
thoroughbrace leather strap used as a spring
thrall ('thrȯl) in slavery
threadbare shabby
threading making his way carefully
thyme ('tØm) a fragrant plant
tier ('tir) layer
Time's burst of dawn beginning of the greatest period in history
Tit an ('tØ-tᵊn) see Titan-like
Ti ta ni a (tØ-'tān-ē-ə) queen of the fairies
Titan-like like the fabled giants, Titans, who lived at the beginning of the world
toc sin's a la rum ('täk-sənz; ə-'lär-əm) warning signal

to learn to spell learn to work and rest by turns
tol er a ble (ˈtä-lə-rə-bəl) moderate; tolerably, fairly
ton nage (ˈtə-nij) weight in tons
tor pid (ˈtȯr-pəd) stupid
torpor heavy sleep
Tory man on the king's side in the Revolution
Total Abstinence Principle rule of going without alcoholic liquor; here, having nothing to do with spirits
to the manner born who had been born to fill that very place in life
to the quick till they were sore
Tous les Bour geois de Chartres (tü-lā-ˈbür-zhwä-də-shärt) all the people of Charters
trainband captain captain of a company of trained citizen-soldiers
tram mels pen dent (ˈtra-məls; ˈpen-dənt) iron hooks to hang kettles over a fire
tran quil (ˈtraŋ-kwəl) calm; tranquillity, peace
transfigured beautifully changed in appearance; become a spiritual being
tran sient (ˈtran-sē-ənt) temporary
tran si tion very foreign (tran-ˈsi-shən) change in a trend of thought which was not customary
tran si to ry (ˈtran-sə-tōr-ē) brief
trans mute (trans-ˈmyüt) change
transports raptures
trav ail (trə-ˈvāl) work and suffering
tra versed (ˈtra-vərst) crossed
Treadmill a form of prison discipline
Treb i zond (ˈtre-bə-zänd) one of the former divisions of Turkey
trem u lous (ˈtrem-yə-ləs) shaky; tremulousness, fright
trice (ˈtrØs) instant
trim a condition
tri pod (ˈtrØ-päd) three-legged stand
Tripolitan (tri-ˈpä-lə-tᵊn) of Tripoli
Tri ton (ˈtrØ-tᵊn) a sea-god
Truce of God an attempt of the Church in the middle ages to lessen the evils of private warfare
trun cheon (ˈtrən-chən) staff of command
try the strength of gold test the real power of wealth
tucker front in her dress
tu mul tu ous (tu̇-ˈməl-chə-wəs) wild
tu nic (ˈtü-nik) long, loose garment
tur bu lent (ˈtər-byə-lənt) rushing

turnpike men keepers of the gate where a toll, or tax, had to be paid
twelfth-cakes cakes made for Twelfth Night, the 12th night after Christmas

U

u biq ui tous (yü-'bi-kwə-təs) who were everywhere at once
u na nim i ty (yü-nə-'ni-mə-tē) congeniality
unbartered not bought
unbeholden unseen
unbodied joy spirit of happiness
unconstrained de mea nor (di-'mē-nər) happy, informal conduct
unconventional different from most people
un couth (ən-'küth) rude; terrible
un del e te ri ous (ən-de-lə-'ti-rē-əs) harmless
undulating ('ən-jə-lā-tiŋ) rolling; undulations, waves
un fre quent ed (ən-frē-'kwen-təd) rarely visited
unhallowed (ən-'ha-lōd) unworthy
un im ped ed (ən-im-'pē-dəd) without hindrance
United States' security several of the states had just refused to be responsible for their bonds, thus weakening United States' credit abroad
un per turbed (ən-pər-'tərbd) untroubled
un pre med i tat ed art (ən-prē-'me-də-tā-təd) beautiful singing which comes so natural to you
unprofaned sacred
un scrup u lous (ən-'skrü-pyə-ləs) unprincipled
unseasonable allusions unsuitable remarks
unshadowed main the ocean which has nothing on it to cast a shadow
unstable unfixed; constantly changing
U phar sin (yü-'fär-sən) *see* Daniel V:1-3; The blazing comet reminds Evangeline of God's power as the handwriting on the wall reminded Belshazzar
up roar i ous (əp-'rōr-ē-əs) noisy and confused
u sur pa tion (yü-sər-'pā-shən) striking out entirely instead of by amending

V

va ga ries ('vā-gə-rēz) fickleness
Valentine...Orson characters in a legend of the time of Charlemagne
va lid i ty (və-'li-də-tē) truth
vanes ('vānz) weather vanes to show which way the wind was blowing
vans ('vanz) wings
various communions of our Christian faith different branches of the

Christian church
veered ('vird) turned
ve he ment ly ('vē-ə-mənt-lē) furiously
ven due ('ven-dü) auction
ve ner a ble ('ve-nə-rə-bəl) worthy old
vent express; expression
venturing boasting
veracity (və-'ra-sə-tē) truthfulness
Ver dun (vər-'dən) town in France
verge ('vərj) edge
ver i est ('ver-ē-əst) worst
ver nal ('vər-nᵊl) spring
ver te brae ('vər-tə-brā) plural of vertebra, a bone of the spinal column
very, the even the
ves tal ('ves-tᵊl) everlasting; the vestal virgins were young maidens who continually tended the sacred fires of Vesta, goddess of the hearth
ves tige ('ves-tij) trace
vestments robes
vi brant ('v∅-brənt) throbbing
victorious eagles the figure of an eagle was the Roman emblem. It was mounted on a tall staff and carried in front of the troops
vig il ('vi-jəl) watch; vigilant watchful
vin di cate their ancestry be loyal to the ideals of their forefathers
virago (və-'rä-gō) quarrelsome woman
virgins see vestal
vis age ('vi-zij) face
vision of life and death Roushan Beg alive, yet so near death
visitation visit
vis ta ('vis-tə) view; vistaed, arranged in two rows through which a view is seen
vit al ('v∅-tᵊl) powerful; vitality, power
vixen ('vik-sən) ill-tempered woman
voiceless shore shore on which the songs of liberty no longer are heard
void without having had any effect; illegal
voi là ('vwä-lä) there he is!
vol ley ('vä-lē) outburst
Vol tur nus (väl-'tůr-nō) a river, now spelled *Volturno*
vo lup tu ous (və-'ləp-chə-wəs) luxurious
vo tive stone ('vō-tiv) a monument sacred to them
vouchsafed (vaůch-'sāft) permitted
voy a geur (vȯi-ə-'zhər) one who transports goods to and from stations for

fur companies
vul ture ('vəl-chər) large, eaglelike, flesh-eating bird

W

waifs of things left by
wains ('wānz) wagons
Walk er slang term meaning "You don't mean it!"
Wa le way ('wä-lə-wā) branch of the Columbia river
wan ing ('wā-niŋ) passing; fading
wan ton ('wȯn-tᵊn) playful
Ward officer of the ward, one of the divisions of London
warded protected
wa ri er ('war-ē-ər) more cautious; warily, cautiously
water-gourd ('gōrd) pumpkinlike fruit hollowed out and dried to drink from
wayward self-willed
weary year months when I am an unimportant person
weeding-out process getting rid of inefficient employees
weld melt together so they could never be opened
welterweight medium weight
Westminster Abbey ('west-min-stər) famous church in London. It is the chief burial place of Great Britain's distinguished men and contains memorials to many noted foreigners
what odds what does it matter
what the knowing ones call "nuts" what people who know call the easiest thing in the world
where to have him how to annoy him
whims ('hwimz) notions
whippletree swinging bar to which part of a harness is fastened
White of Selborne's Gilbert White, who wrote *A Natural History of Selborne,* the district in England in which he was born
whitethroat European warbler
Wi ca co (wi-'kä-kō)
wielder user
wim pling ('wim-pliŋ) rippling
Wind-river Mountains part of the Rockies in Wyoming
Winthrop, John Governor of Massachusetts Colony (1588-1649)
wire fence still is not where no fences have been built
wis ('wis) think
withal (wi-'thȯl) besides; also

with devotion translated carried away by religious enthusiasm; for Elijah, *see* II Kings XI
with im pu ni ty (im-ˈpyü-nə-tē) without punishment
wold (ˈwōld) plain; pasture
wolfish starved
wont (ˈwȯnt) accustomed
wordy in words (as opposed to the snowball)
world has gone a-slumming people are on the side of the poor
world kings governments whose power is controlled by one man
worldling one unused to simple life
worthies great men
wreathed horn the sea-god, Triton, blew a trumpet, made from a spiral sea-shell, to raise or calm the sea
wrest (ˈrest) to obtain by force
writhed (ˈrØthd) twisted
wrought (ˈrȯd) made; worked; wrought me her shadowy self to hold, cast a shadow for me to mirror; wrought its ghost, cast its shadow

X

Xer xes (ˈzərk-sēz) king of Persia (486-465 B. C.)

Y

Ya ka bow ski (yä-kä-ˈbaủ-ski)
yellow Tiber the sands in the riverbed made the water appear yellow
yeoman (ˈyō-mən) farmer
Yp si lan ti's Mai note Greeks (ip-sə-ˈlan-tēz; ˈmi-nōt) revolutionary cavalry recruited by Ypsilanti, Greek patriot from Maina, to fight against Turkey
Yu kon (ˈyü-kän) valley of the Yukon, in Alaska
Yus souf (ˈyə-səf)

Z

zeal enthusiasm
zeph yr (ˈze-fər) gentle breeze